Praise for

Just like she always does, Jody Hedlund weaves an exquisite romance in this sweeping historical romance. *Finally His Bride* invites the reader into a world rich with detail, where you can smell and taste what her characters do. I loved her swoon-worthy hero and cheered on her heroine all the way to the last page.

— LACY WILLIAMS, USA TODAY
BESTSELLING AUTHOR

In *Finally His Bride*, Hedlund has once again proven her mastery of the Christian Historical Romance genre, delivering her trademark adventure, sizzling chemistry, and vivid detail. This story as richly textured as the gowns that grace her characters.

Readers seeking a poignant historical romance need look no further—*Finally His Bride* is a journey of the heart that will leave you breathless and yearning for more.

— MISTY M. BELLER, *USA TODAY* BESTSELLING AUTHOR OF THE BROTHERS OF SAPPHIRE RANCH SERIES

Returning to Jody Hedlund's Vancouver in Bride Ships: New Voyages was like wrapping myself in a beloved blanket that had been packed away at the start of cold weather. Long-awaited, much anticipated . . . this book was everything I hoped it would be and more.

— ALYSSA, GOODREADS

Jody Hedlund is a masterful story teller. She paints a beautiful picture of the Pacific Northwest, I swear I can smell the pine trees.

— STACI, GOODREADS

Oh the bliss of it. What perfect words from the novel to describe how wonderful the book was!

— FAITH, GOODREADS

As always, Hedlund writes spot-on romance! The story is swoony yet realistic. I have never regretted picking up one of Hedlund's novels; I highly recommend all of her books, and *Finally His Bride* is a great place to start! I'm looking forward to more in this series.

— SYLVIA, GOODREADS

Finally His Bride

BRIDE SHIPS: NEW VOYAGES ⚓ BOOK ONE

JODY HEDLUND

sunrise
PUBLISHING

Finally His Bride
Bride Ships: New Voyages, Book 1
Published by Sunrise Media Group LLC
Copyright © 2024 Jody Hedlund

Print ISBN: 978-1-953783-76-9
Large Print ISBN: 978-1-953783-79-0
EBook ISBN: 978-1-953783-78-3

Scripture quotations are taken from the King James Version of the Bible.

This is a work of historical reconstruction; the appearances of certain historical figures are accordingly inevitable. All other characters are products of the author's imagination. Any resemblance to actual events or locales or persons, living or dead, is entirely coincidental.

For more information about Jody Hedlund please access the author's website at www.jodyhedlund.com.

Published in the United States of America.
Cover Design by Hannah Linder
Cover images from Shutterstock

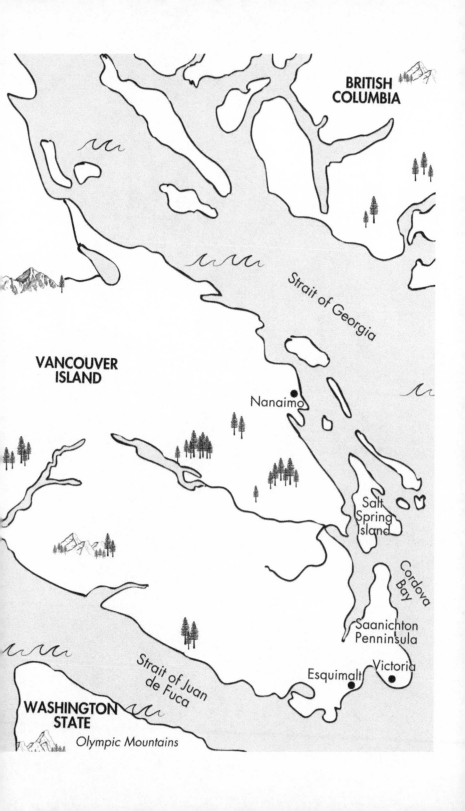

The LORD is my strength and my shield;
my heart trusted in him, and I am helped:
therefore my heart greatly rejoiceth;
and with my song will I praise him.
Psalm 28:7

One

"You have to go, Willow." Dad's voice was low and pleading. "We wouldn't ask this of you if there was any other way."

Willow Rhodes tried to draw a breath into her rapidly constricting airways. She sat with her head bent and elbows on her knees, but instead of the position helping her, she only seemed to gasp more.

Her mum rubbed her back. "It really is the best plan, poppet."

"The only plan," Dad mumbled, drumming his thumbs on the table.

On the bench across from him, Willow pushed down the rising panic. As the oldest of five daughters, she knew she had to be the one to save her family from their desperate situation, but this . . .? Go on a bride ship halfway around the world? She couldn't.

1

"I'll do it." Briar spoke up from the edge of the bed where she, Fern, and Clover were perched, watching the unfolding drama in their one-room flat, their pretty heart-shaped faces, dainty chins, and high cheekbones characteristic of all the Rhodes women. Briar shared brown eyes and darker auburn hair with Fern, taking after their dad. But Willow and Clover had the same blue eyes and reddish-blond hair as their mum . . . and so did Sage.

Smart, capable, and pretty Sage. Mum and Dad would never consider sending their most responsible daughter away. Besides, Sage would be married soon enough to David who worked in the catgut factory and hadn't been affected by the lack of cotton that had closed the mills.

Briar stood, her wooden clogs slapping against the thin floorboards, her faded skirt having been washed so many times it was as gray as the Manchester sky. "If Willow doesn't want to go, then I'll happily take her place."

"You're too young, luv." Dad ran his fingers through what was left of his thin hair. His shoulders were bony, and his clothes hung on his frame too loosely. Long gone was the robust, sun-tanned, muscular man who'd once spent his every waking moment farming.

"I'm almost seventeen." Briar stood as tall as she could, but even holding her head high, she was still shorter than Fern and Clover. "I heard Miss Rye isn't particular about the age."

"I'm particular." Dad slid back from the table, but before he could stand, he burst into a cough—a deep, hacking cough that had grown worse over the summer and didn't appear to be getting any better with the coming of the cooler autumn days.

No one would say the words *white lung disease*. But everyone knew that's what afflicted him after fifteen years of toiling in the cotton mill as a mule spinner, making sure the threads didn't get caught or tangled as they wound around the many spools. He'd inhaled the humid air full of cotton dust for so many years, his lungs were irreparably damaged.

Willow's own breathing problems were probably related to the mill too. She hadn't worked there as long as her dad, but laboring ten-hour days for the past four years had taken a toll. It was one more reason her parents wanted her to leave Manchester, so that when the mills finally reopened, she wouldn't be tempted to return and ruin her lungs even further.

With the start of war in America, no one knew when cotton imports from the southern states would resume. Most speculated that the conflict wouldn't last long, maybe would be over in a few months by the end of 1862 or early next year. Until then, without cotton, hundreds of thousands of mill workers in Manchester and Lancashire—Cottonopolis—were unemployed.

Willow's stomach grumbled, and she fisted her hand against it, trying to ease the ache. But the ache hadn't gone away over the past couple of months since they'd had no income and no way to purchase food. They'd had to rely upon the charity groups who'd heard about the widespread unemployment and had come to Manchester to assist. As well-meaning as the charities were—and she was grateful for them—the lines were long and the portions were never enough to truly satisfy.

"Think about it, poppet." Mum rubbed her back again and stared unseeingly out the lone high window of their ground-floor flat that showed only the narrow street that ran in front of their rowhouse. "You'll get out of the city, get the fresh air you need, and have plenty of food."

Her mum was probably envisioning the borough where she'd grown up, the wide-open fields of rural Lancashire that they'd called home before being forced off the land through the enclosure laws.

Mum's face, like Dad's, had grown pale and thin over the years of living in the dirty, overcrowded city where the coal smoke blasting from hundreds of factories cast a haze over the sky so that the sun was a rare sight.

Mum had tried to bring the sunshine into their home by painting their walls and furniture yellow. The chairs, the table, the sideboard, the chest of drawers, and even the trunk at the end of the bed were all yellow. She'd painted every glass jar and bottle she could find yellow and had filled them with wildflowers she'd picked and dried whenever they ventured out of the city on holiday.

Willow's gaze touched on each bright spot in the home. The yellow had faded regardless of her mum's efforts to wash and repaint and keep the color bright. Even pale, the yellow amidst the drabness of everything else had always reminded Willow of how hard her parents had worked to love her and her sisters and give them a good life in spite of the hardships.

Was it her turn to do something good for them . . . no matter how difficult it would be? And it would be difficult. New tasks always took her longer than usual to understand. It had been the same with reading at the Ragged School. She'd mixed up letters and words and had to reread the passage a couple of times before she comprehended it.

Dad finished coughing and cleared his throat. "Miss Rye says that as a domestic in the colony, you'll have a free place to stay. In no time, you'll have enough to cover the passage for your sisters. Yeah?"

"And you and Mum."

With drawn brows, Dad shared a glance with Mum.

"Send both Willow and me," Briar insisted. "We'll be able to save for everyone."

Dad shook his head, his eyes growing sad. "Miss Rye filled up the last of the spots."

"Then let me go since Willow isn't sure—"

"No, Briar." Willow stood. "If anyone is leaving home, it'll be me."

Her dad's pallid face was turning splotchy red, likely in an effort to keep from hacking again. "I'd be the one to go ahead if I could."

Even in the dimness of the evening, Willow had no trouble viewing her dear family. They meant everything to her. And if her going would help them, how could she reject the plan? "Where is the ship heading?"

"Vancouver Island." Her dad spoke with forced enthusiasm. "I'm told it's a twin sister to merry old England, that everyone who lives there feels right at home."

"Right at home? Where?" The door opened, and Caleb stepped inside. With the brim of his flat cap pulled low over his short dark hair, his face was shadowed, giving his scruffy facial hair a darker than usual tint. He carried his wool coat slung over his broad shoulders, revealing his suspenders and shirt stretched taut over his muscular frame.

"Caleb." Dad's face lost some of the haggardness that seemed ever present. "Help me convince Willow that she needs to leave."

Caleb halted abruptly, as if Dad's words had surprised him. Then he finished closing the door and at the same time removed his hat. His murky, dark brown eyes searched the room until landing upon her. With one sweeping look, he took her in.

She didn't need to pretend with Caleb that she was okay. Even if she did, he'd see right through her acting. He always had. As her best friend for the past decade, he knew everything about her. Sometimes she felt as if he knew her even better than she knew herself.

One of his brows rose in a silent question, one that asked if she was okay.

The tightness in her lungs eased just a little, and she nodded. Now that he was here, everything would be all right. Caleb would make it all right. That's just the way he was.

"When Dad was out looking for employment today, he met Miss Rye." Willow lowered herself back to her chair, her legs suddenly weak. She wasn't sure if it was from hunger or worry or both.

Caleb's intense gaze scrutinized her as he waited as patiently as always for her to finish speaking.

Her dad nodded at her to continue, to go ahead and be the one to tell Caleb the news.

She drew in another breath, this one deeper into her lungs. "Apparently Miss Rye is organizing a transport for a select group of mill workers to sail to Vancouver Island where they'll be employed in domestic service."

Caleb's jaw flexed, bringing out the scar on his chin. A vein in his temple pulsed, highlighting the scar above his left eye. And his mouth flattened, revealing the tiny thin scar above his lip.

Because of his scars and his brawny build, Caleb held an intimidating air. He was tough and sullen and gruff to most people. But with her and her family, he was loyal and kind almost to a fault.

What did he think of the news? "Dad and Mum want me

to go so that I can save up money for everyone else to emigrate."

Caleb remained silent, stoic. Only his jaw ticced again. Was he opposed? Would he figure out how she could stay?

She couldn't tell what he was thinking. She'd tried countless times over the years. But he kept his emotions locked away and rarely revealed them.

Dad stifled a cough then gave Caleb a pleading look. "Caleb and me, we talked about trying to find a way for Willow to emigrate to America or Canada just last week. Yeah?"

"You did?" Willow directed her question at Caleb.

He didn't respond, but that was answer enough.

"Why?" She couldn't keep the hurt from her tone.

Before Caleb could answer, her dad spoke. "Now I've found a way for her to go on Miss Rye's bride ship, the *Robert Lowe*."

"Bride ship?" Caleb's voice held contempt.

"Yes," Dad replied. "Miss Rye sent women on the *Tynemouth* several months ago, women from the London area. Now she's organized a second group from among the unemployed mill workers of Manchester."

"Why not just provide transport for the women?" Caleb asked. "Why call them bride ships?"

All eyes shifted to Dad. Of course, most people knew about the bride ships that had been sent out to other English colonies over the years, but why was Miss Rye sending them now? And why to Vancouver Island? Willow was as curious to know the answer as Caleb.

Dad gave a shrug as though to say it didn't really matter. "There are many more men in the colony than women. So the men there have asked for marriageable women to be sent."

Caleb's forehead creased with a growing frown.

"Miss Rye assured me the women aren't required to get married, only that they'll have plenty of opportunities to make good matches."

Caleb's scowl remained in place.

Dad held Caleb's gaze. "There aren't many good men left here in Manchester for my Willow. You said so yourself, yeah?"

Dad was right. Willow hadn't met a man in Manchester that caught her fancy. Besides, the conditions in the city had been bleak even before all the unemployment. Housing was limited, the violence and vices on the streets were increasing, and disease often ran rampant. It wasn't the ideal place for raising babies and young children.

Obviously, Sage and David were planning to get married and live in Manchester. So it wasn't impossible to find happiness in the slums. It just hadn't happened for her.

Caleb was shaking his head. "Willow can't go marry a stranger."

"I don't intend to marry a stranger." In fact, if she hoped to save enough for her entire family to be able to emigrate, then she'd have to work for quite a while. "But if I'm lucky, maybe I'll find someone eventually."

"Lucky?" Caleb scoffed. "Luck has nothing to do with love."

"And who made you the expert in love?" She could feel her strength returning as it always did whenever she was with Caleb.

"I know a bit more than you, that's for certain."

"What? You think because you've been with half the girls in Manchester, that suddenly you know everything about relationships?"

Caleb clamped his mouth into a stubborn line, one that said he refused to argue with her again about his being a rake. He'd told her many times that he'd given up his womanizing ways, but she still heard rumors from time to time that made her wonder.

Mum squeezed Willow's shoulder. "If you'd just marry Caleb—"

"Mum, please." Willow's exasperation rose swiftly as it did every time anyone suggested that she and Caleb get married. "We've been over this a hundred times."

Her dad was looking between her and Caleb, his brows raised, as though giving them one last chance to admit they'd been pining after each other.

Caleb gave a curt shake of his head.

But before he could protest, she said the familiar words. "We're friends. And that's all we'll ever be."

"Friends can get married," her mum retorted. "In fact, friendship makes a wonderful basis for a marriage."

"That might work for some people. But Caleb and I agree that our friendship is too important for us to risk ruining it."

There was also the tiny fact that Caleb had made it clear long ago that he didn't have any intention of ever getting married, and she wanted to respect his wishes, especially because she knew how deeply he'd been affected by the way he'd seen his dad treat his mum.

Her mum brushed back a loose strand of Willow's hair. "You don't have to ruin your friendship—"

"Caleb's like my brother. And I'm like a sister to him. It would be weird and awkward." *She* was weird and awkward when it came to relationships, not at all polished and confident like Sage.

Silence settled around the flat that was growing darker by

the minute. And since they had no money for fuel, they wouldn't waste the precious little amount of coal and kerosene they had left. They were saving it for the colder and bleaker days to come.

Caleb scraped his hands through his hair, his biceps bulging. He expelled a short huff then directed his brooding gaze to Dad. "When does this bride ship leave?"

"The group is taking the train to London tomorrow."

"Tomorrow?" Willow spoke the question at the same time as Caleb and with just as much surprise.

Her dad nodded. "Tomorrow morning. Early."

"That's so soon." Willow's airways began to constrict again.

"Miss Rye has the three dozen women she needs."

Three dozen women? Willow felt like she was starting to drown. "I can't possibly be ready to go by tomorrow."

"Why not?" Mum continued to smooth Willow's hair.

She could list a hundred reasons. "For one, I need time to say goodbye to everyone." She took in her three youngest sisters, Briar having sat back down on the bed next to Fern and Clover. Their beautiful faces and eyes reflected their dismay at the unfolding plan.

"No sense dragging out the goodbyes," Dad said through a cough.

She wanted to rattle off more excuses or at least discuss other solutions to their dilemma. But as she drew in a breath, her lungs decided to stop cooperating, and she could only manage a wheeze.

Caleb stalked across the room and was at her side, helping her to her feet before anyone else realized that she was having a breathing episode. His grip on her upper arm was firm and decisive, giving her no choice but to let him guide her to the door. As he led her out and up the short flight of steps, she struggled with each inhale.

She didn't want to admit it to anyone, but the worst part about leaving would be losing Caleb. After so many years of having him in her life and being best friends, how could she possibly live anywhere without him?

Two

C aleb Edwards gentled his hold on Willow's arm as she bent over.

The narrow street was shadowed by the rows of homes connected to one another, rising on both sides at least three stories high. The bricks were blackened from the coal dust in the air, and the small windows were grimy. But the Rhodes's home on Greengate was a world apart from the labyrinth of deadly streets of Angel Meadow where he lived in an airless cellar with his older sister and her family.

Willow labored for another breath, and he placed a steadying hand on her back.

The air was tainted with the scent of the alleys with their urine-soaked privies and rotting garbage heaps. The nearby River Irk, dark except for its pools of green slime, only added to the stench. Even so, the Rhodeses were lucky to be in one of the better slum neighborhoods.

But for how much longer? With Mr. Rhodes and both Willow and Sage not having an income, they were behind on their rent. Some landlords were showing mercy to their tenants during the difficult days. But others didn't care, and already the homeless were swelling into the wretchedness of Angel Meadow, into the crowded hovels that were hardly fit for animals, much less entire families.

The Rhodes's landlord seemed to be one who lacked compassion and had suggested applying for the housing relief that some charities were offering. Mr. Rhodes was rightfully worried about what would become of his family and had mentioned emigration. But Caleb hadn't thought Mr. Rhodes would consider anything as crazy as sending Willow away to one of the colonies, especially on a blasted bride ship.

Every muscle inside Caleb tightened in protest of such a plan. He wanted Willow to be safe and taken care of, but he didn't want her moving to a distant land where he'd never see her again, especially because she'd end up married in no time. She was naïve and would easily be swept off her feet by a smooth-talking fellow who liked her for her beauty and was unable to see beyond that to her tender spirit which needed nurturing every day.

She wheezed again.

"Hey now." He bent beside her. "It's gonna be all right. I promise." He knew he shouldn't be promising her anything. But he had to try to make her happy. That was what he lived for.

She nodded then raised her head. "I have to leave tomorrow, don't I?" She swept aside the loose strands of her silky hair, hair that was gold with a tint of rose. Her big, beautiful eyes framed by long lashes met his. Even though the evening was fading, the blue of her eyes was still bright and stunning. As always, just one look from her took his breath away, and the words of a new poem began formulating in his mind.

I'm a wanderer in this life,
Lost and full of strife.
But one look from you,
Eases the ache in all I do.

Did she have to leave?

For a second, he scrambled to find another solution, anything except her sailing away from England. But he didn't have to think long to know that it was the best option not only for Willow but her entire family. That's why so many people were moving to the colonies as well as America, because those places promised a better life for the working class when England only promised more misery.

Willow would never take up her mum's suggestion to wed him. But if by some odd chance she changed her mind, could he really consider marriage to her? He'd always told himself he'd never, ever take a wife.

But marry Willow? If it would save her, he might make an exception.

He could admit that somewhere in his secret dreams, he'd considered the possibility before, maybe even multiple times. But with how broken and shattered his past was, he always came back to the fact that a woman as beautiful and kind as Willow deserved a better man than him.

Even if he'd been a better man, he wouldn't be able to provide for her right now. After he'd lost his job at the Brunswick Mill where he'd worked with Mr. Rhodes, he'd been fortunate enough to find odd jobs, mostly at warehouses unloading and loading goods from the trains and barges that shuttled between Manchester and Liverpool.

He was making a pittance now compared to the twelve shillings a week he'd earned as a spinner, but it was enough that he could give some to Claire for letting him live with her. It was also enough to buy a little extra food for Willow and her family. But he didn't have a steady enough income to take care of a wife.

He pulled his wool coat down from his shoulder and fished in the pocket. "I have something for you."

Her lips curled into one of her devastating smiles. "You're trying to distract me, aren't you?"

Of course he was. She knew him too well. He unwrapped the brown paper from around the delicacy, and her breathing began to even out just as he'd hoped.

She drew close, holding his arm and leaning against him as she waited for him to reveal his gift. Her warmth, soft curves, the tickle of her hair, and even her exhalations—he was conscious of everything about her, even the tiniest details down to the way she worked at her bottom lip whenever she waited for him. And that *working* always drove him crazy with the need to kiss her.

But he never had, and he never would—no matter how much he might want to. Willow had made it very clear over the years—like she just had with her mum—that she saw him as a friend and nothing more.

Over recent years, she'd even started referring to him as her brother. Every time she did, he wanted to punch something and shout at her that he wasn't her brother.

But what would that accomplish? He'd only confuse her and make things strained between them. So he'd become proficient at keeping his feelings to himself, masking them, ensuring no one saw them—although at times he wondered if Mr. and Mrs. Rhodes suspected his infatuation with Willow.

She insisted that she didn't care if people thought their friendship was strange.

Maybe what they shared *was* strange. But he wouldn't trade it for anything. She was his whole world, and he couldn't imagine his life without her in it.

He finished peeling away the paper to reveal a crispy baked shell with a creamy raspberry tart filling it.

Her eyes rounded, and she drew in a breath, one of delight. "Oh my."

With pleasure rippling through him, he held it out to her.

"Caleb." She whispered his name reverently, just the way he loved. She reached for it, hesitated, then pulled her hands back. "I can't."

"Don't worry. It didn't cost much." He wasn't about to tell her that the cook from the pub he'd been at earlier in the day had given it to him for next to nothing because of his fame from his days of bare-knuckle boxing in Angel Meadow. Willow had loathed his fighting with a fiery passion and had done everything she could to convince him not to box. When he'd finally quit, he'd promised her he'd never do it again. But that didn't mean he could avoid all previous ties to the dark world of fighting.

She stared at the tart, her expressive eyes telling him that she was already imagining the taste. "I should divide it up among my family."

"I bought it for you." He gentled his tone and held the tart up to her mouth, giving her no choice but to take a bite.

As she closed her mouth around the flaky crust and soft middle, her lashes fell over her now rosy cheeks.

His gut tightened. Why did he do this to himself? Put himself into this proximity with her where all he could think about was how much he wanted her? He was torturing himself every time. And truth be told, it was only getting worse.

16

She released a soft groan as she chewed.

Heat fanned to life inside him.

Her tongue flicked out and captured a stray crumb at the corner of her lips.

Heaven help him. He could only stare at her mouth, the heat spreading inside him like a runaway fire.

Her lashes fluttered up as she opened for another bite. He forced himself to focus on the tart and only the tart. He had to if he had any hope of being able to treat her as a friend and nothing more.

The sugary confection was smaller than the palm of her hand and by the fourth bite, he was able to feed her the last of it.

Once again, she closed her eyes, and this time moaned even louder.

Saints have mercy upon his poor soul. He took a step back and scrubbed a hand over his face, trying to block her out. But all he could think about was the need to lick the rest of the tart off her lips.

He stuffed his hands into his trouser pockets to keep from reaching for her, and he peered down at his scuffed leather boots.

How could he live this way the rest of his life? Desiring her but always holding himself back? Eventually, he would drive himself insane, wouldn't he?

Maybe this plan for her to leave was for the best. As difficult as the parting of ways would be, it would finally force him to end his obsession with her. Yes, because that was the truth—he was entirely and totally and completely obsessed with her.

She made another soft, pleasurable sound in her throat as she finished the delicacy.

He nearly groaned himself. Instead, he turned his attention down the street. Only a few men loitered outside, smoking their cheap cigars, and a group of boys played a game of marbles on the stoop of another rowhouse.

She was quiet for several heartbeats, likely licking her lips and fingers and getting every last morsel. Finally, he could feel her presence draw up behind him. He braced himself for her touch, and it came a moment later—her hand lightly upon his back. Sometimes she held his arm, other times his back. He suspected she did it unconsciously, didn't realize she had made a habit of it over the years.

Most of the time, her touch comforted him. But sometimes he couldn't keep from wanting more than just comfort.

"Thank you, Caleb." Her voice held gratitude—and a little reverence again.

"Anything for you." And he meant it. But still, it wasn't fair that he was the one who felt all the attraction and that she didn't feel any. With as well as he could read her, he would have seen her attraction if she'd had even the slightest ounce.

"So will you tell me what you think I should do?" She didn't move her hand from his back.

He had the sudden urge to shake off her hold—and not just physically. Maybe it was time for him to let her go so that he could move on with his life. Even if he didn't intend to get married, he could distract himself with other women.

He wouldn't deny that women flirted with him everywhere he went and that he could have his pick. But Willow was wrong about him sleeping with those women. When he'd given up his boxing, he'd also given up the women. None of them tempted him anymore, not when he couldn't imagine himself with anyone but her.

But that was the problem—he had to stop imagining himself with her.

"Tell me the truth about my dad's plan, Caleb." She spoke quietly and earnestly.

He sighed, his shoulders heaving. "The truth?"

"Yes, only the truth."

He swallowed the need to tell her to stay, to be with him, to never leave him. Instead he spoke the words that would set them both free. "You have to go."

"Really?" The one word was filled with pain.

He closed his eyes, forcing himself not to contradict himself even though he desperately wanted to. "Yes, your family needs you to do this."

Her hand fell away from his back, sorrow and helplessness and frustration rolling off her and filling the space between them. He could hardly restrain himself from spinning around, reaching for her, and pulling her into an embrace.

He'd only ever hugged her once. The summer his father had died. And the hug had changed everything, had awakened his body to what he'd already begun to notice, that she was no longer a girl, that she was turning into a woman, a very desirable woman. He'd tried to resist seeing her that way for months afterward, but she'd been irresistible, and she still was . . . which was why he had to walk away. Now. Before he did something stupid.

"I need to be on my way." His tone came out brusque.

"Okay."

"You'll do great, Willow." He spoke his parting words as calmly as possible. Then without waiting for her reply, he began to stride away.

"You'll come say goodbye tomorrow morning at the

station before I leave, won't you?" Her call followed after him.

Seeing her again and saying goodbye would kill him. But if she wanted him to be there at the train station, he'd have to do it, wouldn't he? There was no way he could ever deny her anything she wanted.

"Please?" Her voice held a note of desperation that matched the turmoil inside him.

"I'll be there."

"All right. See you then."

He kept walking, feeling her eyes upon him with every step he took. He tried to keep his bearing nonchalant. Only after turning the corner and ambling half the next block did he glance over his shoulder.

Amidst laundry hanging out to dry and the heaps of refuse, she was nowhere in sight.

He let himself double over, heaving and shaking. Nausea rolled around his gut, and he wanted to vomit. What was he doing walking away from the woman he loved more than life?

"Blast." His heart sped, and his breathing grew shallow. He'd never known what Willow's respiratory attacks felt like, but now . . . he could empathize. The sensation in his chest was an odd one, uncomfortable, even a little scary.

It would go away. Eventually.

But what would never go away, not even if he lived to be a hundred?

His need to be with Willow.

He was only fooling himself to think that he'd ever be able to forget about her.

He could never walk away from her. And he could never let her walk out of his life either.

Straightening, he expelled a tight breath. He wouldn't let her go, at least not without him. Yes, that was what he'd do. He'd leave with her. He'd travel to Vancouver Island too. There wasn't anything holding him to Manchester, not even Claire.

When he'd been discussing emigration with Mr. Rhodes last week, they'd learned that passage in steerage was fairly low and probably wouldn't be much more than ten to fifteen pounds. Apparently some ships were only charging five pounds.

Even when he'd been working at the mill, saving that amount would have been difficult.

But with less than twenty-four—maybe only twelve—hours until Willow departed, it would be impossible to come up with enough for the fare.

He could always join the body snatchers who crept into cemeteries at night and dug up bones to sell to the glue factories. But as gruesome as the work would be, and as much as he would detest desecrating the dead, it still wouldn't give him the money he'd need.

There wasn't anything else at the late hour. Or was there still one option?

He rubbed his hands together and ran his thumb across the scars that lined his knuckles. Could he make enough boxing in one night to pay for his journey?

It would be difficult. He'd have to face some of the best fighters in Manchester if he wanted the gambling pool to be high. And he'd have to fight most of the night.

He fisted both of his hands, the aches of broken bones and bruises coming back to haunt him. After his last fight, he'd suffered a fracture to his skull and cheek and nose. He'd been lucky he hadn't died, especially because there were plenty of bare-knuckle fighters who didn't survive the brutality.

But he'd survived many times in the past, and he could do it once more. He was still just as strong, if not stronger after the past month of such heavy lifting.

Willow would be livid once she learned that he'd put himself into mortal danger again. But he could face her wrath. He could face her frustration. He could even face her hating him forever. As long as he was able to be near her, that's all he needed.

Dragging in a breath of resolve, he started jogging down the street, turning first one corner then another. The slums were mostly deserted at the ever-darkening hour when gangs began to roam. Of course, most of those gangs avoided conflict with him. His fighting reputation was still legendary among the beer houses and back alleys.

With each step closer that he drew to Angel Meadow, his muscles tightened in resolve. He was fighting tonight.

And he would win.

The alleyways became narrower, the streets filthier, and the stench overpowering. But he'd lived in this hell on earth all his twenty years of life, and if not for Willow and her family showing him kindness, the true meaning of family, and God's love, he would have turned out like his brother and father—degenerates with no souls.

When he turned onto Ring Road, the lights of dozens of pubs and the raucous noises from within took him back to his foolish days of thinking he could become rich and famous from his boxing. He'd learned the hard way that no matter how well he fought, he'd never be more than a pawn among the gang leaders.

He passed the trapdoors that led to the illegal distilleries that brewed Irish poteen, a hard whiskey that made the drinking in the slums easier and more affordable—not that the men needed the hard liquor to flow faster.

At the next building, with the sign of a donkey with wings jutting out above the door, Caleb paused, took a deep breath, then pushed his way past the men crowded in the doorway.

The shouting and calls reverberated against the walls, drowning out the violent punches of the two men at the center of the large pub.

Through the dimly lit room with a haze of cigar smoke clouding the air, Caleb squinted at the spectators until he found a sharply dressed man standing at the front and center outside the ring, a man with a brawny build, dark hair, and the strong facial features that were so much like his own.

Caleb shoved his way through the crowd, which started to grow silent with each step he took. At the sight of him, the two men in the ring backed away from each other, sweat and blood mingling on their faces.

The spectators parted, clearing a path, excited whispers now filling the air.

Caleb didn't stop until he stood in front of his brother, the owner of the Flying Donkey.

Cole folded his arms across his chest, a smirk playing at the corners of his lips.

Caleb couldn't fault his brother for the mirth, not after Caleb's last words had been that he'd rather rot in hell than step foot in the establishment again.

"Well, well, well." Cole sized Caleb up, probably judging his worth by his ability to fight. "What is my long-lost little brother doing here?"

Caleb knew he didn't have to say anything, that his

expression conveyed why he was there. But Cole wouldn't let him return to the ring so easily, even though Caleb always brought him a fortune.

Caleb's fists tightened. Was he doing the right thing? Should he really box? He'd been trying hard to live an upright and godly life far from the vices of his past.

But if he didn't fight, he'd have to watch Willow leave. And he wouldn't be able to do that.

Pushing down the last of his reluctance, he crossed his arms, letting his bulging biceps show. "I'm here to box."

At his words, a cheer rose from the crowd. The sound pumped Caleb's blood, like it always had before. But his need to be with Willow pumped it even more.

He had to win tonight. There was no other choice.

Three

Where was Caleb?

Willow stood on the single platform of Manchester's London Road Station and peered out over the masses of people milling around the train depot under the haze of the gray morning sky.

Caleb was always easy to spot with his broad shoulders, thick upper arms, and swarthy chest. The way he held himself with an aloof, almost arrogant manner, made him stand out too.

But he wasn't anywhere. And Miss Rye was already at the door of their train compartment starting the boarding process. She was a petite woman with sharply angled features and a tight chignon tucked away in a simple bonnet. She wore finely tailored garments befitting her upper-class station. But like her hat, her skirt and bodice were plain and devoid of any fancy trimmings.

Miss Rye clearly didn't let her small size stop her from her work. She'd been moving in and out among the women and their families for the past hour, talking to each and reassuring them that they would be taken care of and well chaperoned for the duration of the journey.

Willow recognized a couple of women from the Brunswick Mill where she and Sage had worked. As one of the largest mills, it was seven stories high and had close to three hundred carding machines. Even so, it was one mill among over two thousand in Lancashire, which meant most of the women on the train platform were complete strangers to her and to each other.

How had Miss Rye determined who could join the group of emigrants? Perhaps she'd chosen those who appeared to be healthy and strong and able to work hard. They were all young, not many older than Willow's nineteen years.

But with so many women going, would there be enough jobs for them all? Wouldn't the women from the previous bride ship take all the available opportunities and leave their group without work? If they weren't able to find employment when they arrived, then what would happen to them?

Miss Rye had reassured them all this morning that Vancouver Island and British Columbia on the mainland were both thriving colonies and growing fast, and the demand for domestic servants far outweighed the supply.

Regardless, Willow hadn't been able to shake the feeling that she was making a terrible mistake. Even though she'd grown up helping with her family's cleaning and laundry, what if her new mistress asked her to do things she didn't understand? What if she failed? And what if instead of this move benefitting her family, she ended up ripped apart from them forever? And from Caleb?

Willow swept her gaze over the crowds again, hoping the raised platform would aid her efforts to find her friend. But as far as she could tell, he wasn't anywhere.

Her mum, dad, and sisters still stood along the edge of the depot right where she'd left them, and she waved again at them. She'd already hugged them each half a dozen times during their teary farewell before joining the other women on the platform.

Now she just needed to see Caleb one last time too . . .

A nearby train smokestack blasted a whistle, bellowing black fumes into the air. Was that their train? Was it time to go?

The knot in her stomach cinched tighter. Why wasn't he here? He'd told her that he'd come to say goodbye.

She clutched the cotton sack containing all her worldly possessions, including the gown that she wore to church, her extra stockings, a nightdress, as well as a few other personal items. And the small box containing the many mementoes Caleb had given her over the years—dried flowers, stones of interesting shapes, colorful bird feathers, a bright piece of blue glass the hue of her eyes, and a myriad of other interesting items he'd known she would like.

The swell of women inched forward several steps, but she couldn't make herself move.

Maybe she shouldn't go.

The thought had plagued her all throughout the long night as she'd tossed restlessly on her pallet. Surely there would be other opportunities for emigration in the future, perhaps for her entire family and Caleb all at once, instead of just her.

"You all right, miss?" One of the other mill women had stopped and was watching Willow, her eyes radiating kindness. Wisps of brown hair showed beneath the scarf covering her head, framing a pretty face with the hint of dimples in each cheek. The shawl wrapped over her thin shoulders was worn and plain. Even so, it was embellished with a ribbon and neat embroidery stitches, almost as if the woman had needed to add the beauty to her garments the same way Willow's mother had needed to add the yellow paint to their home.

Willow offered the woman as much of a smile as she could muster. "I need to say goodbye to a friend."

Another of the mill women lingered behind. "Tell us what she looks like, and we can help find her." The second woman was already casting her gaze over the crowd, her features etched with concern. She was devoid of a headscarf, revealing pale blond hair that was plaited into a long braid. Although attired in the same plain, worn clothing as the rest of them, somehow her delicate, thin features contained an elegance that made her look like she ought to be a wealthy noblewoman or even a princess.

"My name's Juliet, by the way," the woman said as she drew her frayed cloak closed.

Even the young woman's name was beautiful and elegant, as if she'd been born to lead a different life and had somehow ended up as a poor mill woman instead.

"And my name is Daisy." The brown-haired woman with the embellished shawl flashed a smile, one that indeed showed off dimples.

"I'm Willow." She was so used to the comments about her unique name, that she offered her usual explanation. "My mother named my sisters and me after all the things she loved about the countryside where she grew up."

"That's incredibly sweet." Daisy's smile was so genuine and beautiful that Willow had to swallow her irritation. "Since both our names are taken from nature, I guess that means we're meant to be friends."

"Maybe we are."

Although Willow hadn't ever had many friends besides Caleb, she wouldn't have him anymore. And she wouldn't have her sisters either. She'd be alone. On her own. She wouldn't even have Sage.

Willow's gaze snagged on Sage with her parents and other sisters, her headscarf hardly concealing her vibrance, so that she stood out like a rose growing in a dirty, gray alley. At eighteen and just a year younger than Willow, Sage held herself with the maturity and confidence of someone much older. She had her arm around Mum, likely comforting her.

After Sage had returned home last evening, she'd supported the plans for Willow to go away, agreeing that at the very least, Willow could send her earnings back to the family to help them survive. She'd also implied that without Willow, they'd have one less person to feed.

Later, after everyone else had been asleep and the two of them had been lying on their pallets beside each other in the dark, they'd whispered about the future and their plans, knowing it would likely be their last night together, maybe ever.

Finally, before drifting to sleep, Sage had said, "You've tried to end your friendship with Caleb in the past and you never could. Maybe now is your opportunity."

What Sage didn't know was that Willow had only tried to end her friendship with Caleb because he'd walked away from her first. He'd done it two times, each for three days. And yes, she had kept track, because those days had felt like an eternity.

On both occasions, she'd thought she'd lost him, had agonized over it, and had gotten angry enough that she'd told Sage she didn't want to be friends with Caleb any longer.

Just when Willow had despaired that she might not see

him again, he'd resumed their friendship as though nothing had happened. When she'd asked him where he'd been, he'd shrugged and told her not to worry about it.

But she had worried about it, had wondered if she'd done something or if he got tired of her neediness.

Maybe Sage was right that she could use this voyage as the opportunity to become more independent. At the very least, she would be traveling with these women for the next few months, and she didn't want to start the journey by alienating them, especially when they were making an effort to be helpful.

"So what does she look like?" Juliet persisted, still scanning the crowd below the platform.

"He." Willow stood on her tiptoes, as if that could somehow help her see beyond the enormous brick building that housed the depot along with the business offices. "He's of average height for a man, stocky, very muscular. And his hair is dark brown . . .similar to the color of those starlings." As she spoke, the starlings lifted off the roof of the depot and flapped away, disappearing into the sooty clouds.

Daisy was peering intently over the crowd, her expression innocent. "Is this fellow your beau?"

Willow wanted to release a snort or even a scoffing sound. But she forced herself to behave politely. "He's just a friend. My best friend, actually."

"A man as a best friend?" Juliet's question rose with disbelief.

"He's been my best friend for over ten years."

Juliet released a scoffing sound. "I've never known a man who was satisfied with only friendship from a woman."

"Then it's amazing"—Daisy's eyes rounded with seriousness—"and a blessing that Willow found such a man."

Before Willow could think of a response to the two, her gaze snagged on the stocky shoulders and flat cap of a man elbowing his way through the edge of the crowd near the depot. Her pulse gave a sudden spurt of relief. He was here. He'd come to say goodbye. Thank God above. She wasn't sure she would have had the strength to leave without seeing him one last time.

"There." She nodded in his direction. "He's finally here."

He was hurrying, but even with his haste, he carried himself with a self-assurance and toughness that intimidated most people. Although today, his steps seemed a little uneven. Was he limping?

She frowned.

"Where is he?" Daisy was scanning the wrong area of the depot.

But Juliet was following Caleb with narrowed eyes, as though perhaps she'd seen him before and was trying to place him.

Willow raised her arm. "Caleb! Here!"

His head snapped up and swiveled her direction, giving her a glimpse of his face.

She gasped at the sight of the black-and-blue bruises under both eyes, the long red gash along his cheekbone, the swelling in his nose, and his busted bottom lip.

Juliet didn't react, as if she'd seen her fair share of battered faces in her life. "Looks like he got into some trouble, took a good thrashing."

"Goodness gracious." Daisy was now searching the other side of the depot. "That's terrible."

Thrashing? Caleb? Impossible. Caleb was too strong and scrappy to let anyone beat him up. The only time Caleb had ever gotten hurt was in the boxing ring. But he'd given up his fighting.

Across the train yard that still separated them, she caught Caleb's gaze. The apology in his eyes told her everything. He'd fought again.

Anxiety rushed in to replace her confusion, and she scanned the length of him as best she could through the press of bodies around him.

He seemed okay. He was alive. He wasn't badly injured. He only seemed to have the usual bruises. Maybe a limp.

"Oh, Caleb, why?" She didn't want to part ways with his battered body her last image of him. And she certainly didn't want to go away whilst worrying about how he was faring.

Juliet gave a low whistle. "Holy Moses. Even with all those bruises, he's still a handsome fellow."

A twinge pricked at Willow, the same she felt whenever any woman commented on Caleb's looks. She'd long ago decided the twinge was annoyance. Yes, the compliments annoyed her, although she couldn't rightly say why. She supposed she didn't like to be reminded that her best friend was an attractive male. And she didn't like thinking about him being with other women. It wasn't jealousy. It was possessiveness of her friend.

"Those eyes." Daisy's lips curled into a smile. "They're swoon-worthy."

Caleb was bounding up the stairway and was almost upon them.

"Ladies," came Miss Rye's call from the train car. "Please make your way toward me. It's time to board."

Daisy took a hesitant step toward the rapidly shrinking line of women left to get on the train but then stopped as Caleb reached the platform.

Up close, he looked even more battered.

"Caleb Edwards." Willow scowled and began to cross toward him.

He halted, his shoulders deflating, as if he'd been expecting her wrath.

Well, he should expect it. He'd broken the promise he'd given her after the last time when he'd almost died. "I can't believe you fought again." She didn't care that her voice was loud and angry.

He held out a hand to keep her ire at bay, but at the sight of his bloody knuckles, he quickly hid the hand behind his back.

But it was too late. She stumbled to a stop, and tears filled her eyes. He was more battered than she'd realized. How many men had he fought?

He was watching her face, likely saw her tears. "Willow, let me explain."

She blinked back the tears then fisted her hands on her hips. "What's there to explain? You broke your promise."

His gaze flicked behind her to the other women, as though to say he would rather face her fury without an audience.

She glanced over her shoulder to see Daisy and Juliet watching the interaction with undisguised interest. "Will you tell Miss Rye that I'll be right there?"

Daisy nodded and began to back away, but Juliet didn't budge, not until Daisy clasped her cloak and tugged her. "We'll go ahead and save you a seat."

"Thank you." Somehow Willow managed the words before she spun around and glared at Caleb again.

He waited several more long seconds as Daisy and Juliet made their way toward the train car.

Willow, in turn, studied his bruises and cuts and swollen splotches, her frustration only mounting.

When he finally dropped his gaze to her, she blew out a breath. "Well?"

He lowered a bag to his side, then reached into his coat pocket and pulled out a wad of money. "I earned this."

She couldn't see exactly how much it was, but it looked like a lot. "Why, Caleb?"

"Because I'm going with you to Vancouver Island."

The clamor of all her frustration silenced. "What?"

"I want to go with you." His dark eyes held hers.

For several seconds, she could only stand before him rendered utterly speechless.

"I have enough to cover the train and steerage on the ship."

"You really want to move halfway around the world?"

He shrugged. "I've heard that jobs are plentiful and wages fair. Together we'll be able to save up for your family faster than if you tried by yourself."

For the first time since her dad had brought up the possibility of joining the bride ship, she felt a small swell of hope. She hadn't wanted to emigrate, hadn't wanted to part from her family, hadn't wanted to leave Caleb.

But last evening, outside the flat, when he'd told her she had to go and then had walked away without a glance back, sobs had crowded into her throat—disappointed, almost devastated sobs.

She'd expected Caleb to show a little more indecision, to ask her to stay, to possibly even display some sadness about her leaving. She'd never expected that he'd all but order her to go as if he didn't care whether he ever saw her again.

But maybe he did care after all. "So does this mean you'd miss me if I left?"

"Of course I'd miss you." He stuffed the wad of banknotes back in his pocket. "And I'd worry about you, how you'd get on without me to keep you out of trouble."

"I'd get on just fine." She lifted her chin, trying to prove to him—and to herself—that she was strong enough for the move without him, except that she wasn't sure if she really was capable. "But I'd miss you too."

He slung his bag over his shoulder. Was he already packed? Was he planning to leave with her today? Now, at this very moment?

More relief pulsed through her.

"Can you forgive me for breaking my promise?" he asked softly.

She took in his battered face again. "Yes. But that doesn't mean I'll stop being mad at you for getting so beat up again."

"I promise I won't fight anymore."

"You better keep your promise this time."

"Miss Rhodes?" Miss Rye's call beckoned to her.

Willow took a step away from Caleb and nodded at the diminutive woman who was waving her forward.

She couldn't delay the departure any longer. Honestly, she no longer had a reason to. Caleb was coming with her, was joining her in this new adventure, would be with her throughout all the unknown.

Well, maybe not quite . . .

"I won't be able to see you much during the voyage," she rushed to explain. "Miss Rye says we women will have separate quarters from the rest of the passengers on both the train and ship, that we're not to fraternize."

"It's alright." Caleb was already scanning the length of the train, likely trying to decide where he'd find a seat. "I'll be close by, keeping my eye on you."

For the first time all day, a genuine smile lifted her lips. "I'll be keeping my eye on you too."

"Miss Rhodes." Miss Rye's voice was more urgent. "We mustn't dally."

Willow sent one last wave to her family who'd noticed Caleb with her.

Her dad had begun to shoulder his way through the crowd, as though he'd intended to climb to the platform.

"Caleb is going to Vancouver Island too," she called to him.

He halted. The worry lines creasing the corners of his eyes melted away. "Good." He shared a look with Caleb, one she didn't quite understand, but that she suspected was his way of asking Caleb to take care of her.

Caleb nodded.

Then her dad lifted his hand in farewell.

This time when she waved her goodbye in return, her smile was real.

Now that Caleb was coming along, she could admit she was ready to go, maybe even a little excited to start a new adventure.

Four

Caleb clutched the bench of the tender as a wave tossed the boat high and the wind blew a spray of droplets over him. With each pull of the oars by the oarsmen, the *Robert Lowe* loomed nearer, its three masts growing larger and its long bowsprit with a figurehead of a sailor taking shape.

He scanned the passengers who'd already gone aboard and were standing at the rail. Where was Willow? His body was tense with the need to see her and assure himself that she was doing well.

The women had arrived by train in London yesterday and had been taken to a boarding house near the station. Early this morning, they'd left by wagons for Gravesend. Then their petite leader had organized them in a tender, wished them well, and sent them aboard the *Robert Lowe*.

The port on the south bank of the River Thames, east of London, was the loading and unloading point of seafaring vessels. Ships of all shapes and sizes were anchored in the waterway. Some were large, old ships masted with numerous sails that flapped in the cool breeze. Others were the more modern steamboats that chugged along, their tall smokestacks pumping out black smoke from steam-powered engines.

From what Caleb had gathered from the other passengers who'd awaited transport on the wharf with him earlier, the *Robert Lowe* was one of those older, full-rigged wooden ships with iron frames that had been outfitted with engines and a propeller so that she was powered by a combination of both sails and steam. Apparently, the vessel used the sails whenever the wind cooperated, but had coal-fueled engines to keep her moving the rest of the time.

Everyone seemed confident the *Robert Lowe* was sturdy and could withstand the long voyage to the Pacific Northwest. Caleb prayed they were right. Even if they were wrong, it was too late to change courses now that the mill women were aboard.

Wherever Willow was going, he intended to follow.

Another misting spray rose over the edge of the tender which sat heavily in the river with several dozen passengers—mostly men like him who'd been trading stories about the gold to be found in British Columbia.

Caleb had learned a lot from listening to them, namely that a few years ago gold had been discovered in the mountains on the mainland of British Columbia. Men had been pouring into the canyons and river valleys ever since, hoping to get a share of the newfound wealth.

Caleb had pondered the possibility of hunting for gold himself when he got there. But in spite of the men's claims that the gold was still readily available for anyone willing to look for it, Caleb guessed that after three—almost four—years, the easy gold was long gone, and only those who could mine deeper into the earth would be able to find what was left.

No, he intended to take a job wherever Willow found employment. He didn't care where it was as long as he was near her.

Again he surveyed the women leaning against the railing. With scarves covering their heads, he couldn't spot her beautiful blond-red hair, and he was still too far away to distinguish the faces.

He hadn't spoken with her since the train depot yesterday morning, and already he missed her and wanted to at least ask her how she was faring.

Even though she'd warned him that the women wouldn't be able to mingle with other passengers, he wouldn't let that stop him from seeing her, even if only briefly or from a distance. Nothing could keep him from her.

He lifted a hand to his bruised cheek and traced the largest of the gashes. The pain in his side told him he'd suffered a few cracked ribs. And the ache in his thigh was where he'd been kneed.

The night of fighting at the Flying Donkey had been rough. He'd lost track of how many times he'd fought. But it had been most of the night. By dawn, after winning every round, no one else had dared to go against him, even though he'd been bloodied and bruised and exhausted.

Finally Cole had clamped Caleb on the shoulders and told him he had to go to London and Liverpool and Birmingham to bare-knuckle fight. Just like in the past, Cole had been full of promises to make him the best fighter in the United Kingdom, earning enough money that he'd never want for anything ever again.

Caleb had told his brother no thanks and said all he wanted was his share of the profits.

Of course, in response, Cole had brought out his thugs,

the ones who guarded the winnings. And he'd hedged on giving Caleb the full amount, telling him he could have it in installments over the next month.

Caleb had expected his brother to manipulate him since he'd done it in the past. Caleb had been left with little choice but to knock out the first thug with a smartly placed punch, and then hold Cole at knifepoint until the second thug had handed over half the earnings from the fights.

Maybe at one time, Caleb wouldn't have blinked an eye at Cole's abuse. After all, he'd grown up with the lying, cheating, and swindling, not only from Cole but also from their father.

But Caleb had learned what love was from the Rhodes family, along with loyalty and kindness and truthfulness and integrity. And once he'd seen the difference in their families, he'd vowed that he would never be like his brother and father.

As it was, he'd almost missed the train yesterday morning because of all that had happened with Cole. After Caleb escaped from the Flying Donkey, Cole had sent his men out after him. Even now, Caleb glanced to the shore, expecting to see one of the thugs climbing into another tender, following him, ready to drag him back to Manchester.

But none of Cole's men were lurking about—at least that he could see. Hopefully, the *Robert Lowe* would be on her way to the Atlantic before his brother discovered where he'd gone. Then he'd be away from his family and their influence forever.

Caleb dragged in a deep breath of air.

Even though the River Thames was polluted and stank of waste, the busyness of the port, the size of the river, the magnificence of the sails all called him to pull out the small journal and pencil that he kept in his coat pocket. He wanted to take notes on everything. Words were formulating in his mind.

Where did the journey lead?
Where would it end?
What untold adventures lay around the bend?

Though the lines begged for pen and paper, he'd have plenty of opportunity during the weeks to come to capture everything. From what he'd overheard, the voyage would take at least three months, maybe longer.

It wouldn't be easy. They might face rough seas. There was the possibility of seasickness or other illness. They could experience food or fuel shortages.

But through it all, he'd be watching over Willow and making sure she was safe. As long as he knew she was okay, he could endure anything.

As the tender crossed the last of the distance to the *Robert Lowe*, he realized that up closer, the vessel was smaller than it had first appeared. And as he climbed up the hull along with the other passengers and stepped onto the deck, he took in the coal bins lashed to the deck, the heavy coils of rigging, the blackened funnels that were devoid of smoke, the sailors loitering nearby in their unbuttoned pea coats gawking at the women at the railing. The mill women.

Willow had to be among them.

He scanned them, a strange desperation forming in the pit of his stomach. He needed to see her today, wasn't leaving without knowing she was there.

Finally, he caught sight of her pretty face filled with earnestness, as she wound her way toward him.

"Caleb." Her voice held welcome and maybe even a note of relief. "You made it."

"Were you worried I wouldn't come?" He tried for a teasing tone, but he'd never been very good at bantering, and his question came out too serious.

She halted in front of him and reached out to clasp his arm as though to reassure herself he really was there. The wind had wrested her hair from her scarf headcover and now whipped strands around her face. Her normally pale cheeks had some color. Already she looked healthier. "If you hadn't shown up in the next hour, I was planning to jump into the river and swim ashore to find you."

"Liar," said the blond-haired woman who'd been with Willow yesterday at the train station. She was standing next to Willow and smiling. "You wouldn't have waited an hour. Ten minutes more was all the longer Daisy and me would've been able to hold you back."

The other woman—presumably Daisy—bumped Willow's shoulder companionably. "I kept reassuring Willow that any man—friend—who would subject himself to such brutality"—she glanced at Caleb's face and grimaced—"wouldn't abandon her."

"And I told Willow that *the* Caleb Edwards"—the blond-haired woman eyed him with curiosity, obviously having figured out his identity—"the boxing champion of Angel Meadow would have fought his way aboard to be with her."

Willow swatted at both women the same way she did her sisters when they were teasing her too much.

Had these new friends already figured out how much he cared about Willow?

Caleb worked at making the muscles in his face remain stoic and unaffected by their comments. He'd kept Willow from discovering the depths of his feelings for years, and he wouldn't let anyone expose him in mere seconds.

For several moments, Willow and her friends told him about their quarters in third class, with bunkbeds attached to the walls, the clean blankets on each, the floral porcelain washbasin and pitcher on a stand, and the small mirror attached to the wall.

All the while Willow shared so animatedly, he felt his heart rate slowing and his breathing evening. She was fine. She was more than fine. She was excited about the coming trip. He could see it in her eyes and gestures and in the laughter she exchanged with the other women.

She was happy.

That's all he needed to know to sleep well in steerage, down in the bowels of the ship. He wouldn't have a bed or blanket or washbasin. But he'd do what he always did in his sister's home—he'd find a spare spot on the floor whenever he'd needed a place to get out of the cold.

"No need to go to Vancouver Island to find a husband," called one of the sailors perched atop a barrel, grinning broadly and flexing his arm as he coiled a rope. "We'll marry you right here and now."

The sailors were attired in loose-fitting slops made from old sailcloth, dark blue jackets, and neckerchiefs. Their faces were a weathered sun-brown, and most had long hair pulled back with leather thongs.

Of course, the sailors had an air of dashing and danger that created an allure so that some of the mill women giggled.

"You won't find better men than us," another sailor called as he lifted his low-crowned, flat-topped hat of tarred canvas and bowed. "Not in the colonies, not anywhere."

Willow and Daisy and the third woman—who he'd

learned went by Juliet—had ceased their chattering and were now watching the sailors along with everyone else.

Was this what was in store for these mill women everywhere they went once men learned they were part of the bride-ship group? Why did they need to call it *bride ship* anyway? Couldn't the women simply be referred to as emigrants like the rest of the passengers?

Even if the men in Great Britain's colonies really did need wives, Caleb didn't want Willow to be a part of that.

Over the years, Willow had attracted the attention of eager young fellows. It was only natural that she would with how beautiful and lively she was. She didn't know that he'd made a point of discouraging fellows from coming around her, warning them away, even threatening a few.

But he couldn't scare off everyone forever, could he? Since she'd already made up her mind that he could never be the one for her, eventually he'd have to let her court a man so that she could settle down and get married. Was that time finally coming?

"Ladies!" a gentleman in a simple suit and clerical collar called as he finished climbing out of one of the hatches that led to the decks below. "I'm Reverend Reese, your chaperone for the trip. May I have your attention, please." As the fellow straightened, he steadied his top hat, which was perched upon a head of silvery hair.

The sailors hurriedly pretended to be busy with the rigging, one of them climbing up the main mast. But the reverend glared at them anyway, as if to say they weren't fooling him. Then he turned his severe gaze upon Caleb. "Young man, I must ask you to take your leave of the bride ship women. They are to remain separate from everyone else for the duration of this trip."

Caleb widened his stance and crossed his arms like he did any time someone confronted him. He had a problem submitting to authority. He could admit it. But it was especially difficult for him when anyone told him what to do regarding Willow.

She squeezed his arm for a brief moment before releasing him. "I'll be just fine, Caleb."

He hesitated, but then he backed up, not wanting to bring trouble upon Willow.

At least she wasn't sailing away without him. He'd have to be content with that fact. If only he could be satisfied.

With Willow, he had the feeling he'd never be fully satisfied until she was fully his.

Five

"Do you see him?" Willow scanned Victoria's waterfront that was lined with what appeared to be several hundred men, possibly more.

She stood at the railing of the steamer with Daisy on one side and Juliet on the other. The choppy waves of James Bay lapped against the *HMS Grappler* chugging through the harbor. Thankfully, the low gray clouds overhead were no longer spitting rain.

"Fiddle-faddle," Daisy replied, wrestling with the cold January wind to tie her brown hair back into a knot. "I can't see him. Can you, Juliet?"

"You're both ridiculous." Juliet slapped a hand on her headscarf before a gust could send it flying into the water. "There's no way we'll be able to spot Caleb in that rowdy crowd."

"We might." Daisy continued to search intently, seeming

to take in each face.

Heedless of the breeze tugging at her own hair, Willow surveyed the men jostling for positions along the water's edge, then those perched on the boats along the shore, several having climbed onto the masts. Fellows farther back were standing upon fences to see over the crowd. Others loitered on the roofs of buildings close to the bay.

Men were everywhere. Word that the single women were coming must have spread when the other passengers—including Caleb—had been ferried from their ship in Esquimalt Harbor to Victoria earlier in the day.

The men would surely be disappointed to see only three dozen women—even less now that the two women who'd become sick during the voyage had been taken separately to the hospital. All of them had been silent and somber as they'd watched the two being rowed away.

After the past one hundred and fourteen days at sea together, they'd gotten to know and care about each other, especially because Reverend Reese and his wife had followed through on their strict regulations and hadn't allowed them to mingle with any of the other passengers on the ship, and they'd only had each other.

Oh sure, she'd seen Caleb every day and had conversed with him in whispers when he'd managed to sneak into their quarters when the reverend was busy. But their time together had never been long. And she missed him—missed sharing with him all that she was feeling, missed their deep discussions, missed listening to him read his poems, missed just sitting together and not having to talk.

She'd tried not to complain to her friends too often about how much she missed Caleb since at least she had someone from home, and they had no one. Even so, she hadn't been able to conceal just how important Caleb was to her.

Now, she couldn't hide how excited she was to be able to spend time with him again. Not that she felt she needed to hide it. She'd grown close to Juliet and Daisy during the long voyage with so little to do. Juliet had taught them board and card games that she'd learned from her grandfather, and Daisy had taught them a little bit about sewing. Mostly they'd talked and walked their small portion of the deck.

Of course, they'd had plenty of time to share about their pasts. Daisy had left behind her mum who was a fine seamstress but had never had enough work to support them, which was why Daisy had worked in the mills. Over the years in her spare time, Daisy had learned to sew too and loved it more than anything. Someday, maybe even in Victoria, she hoped to have a seamstress business of her own.

Juliet hadn't opened up quite as readily. But eventually, she'd shared that she'd been raised by her grandfather until he'd passed away. After that, she'd had a rough go of it and had eventually lived in an orphanage before getting work at the mill. She'd been so busy trying to survive, she'd had little time for men.

Juliet released a wistful sigh. "If I had a man like Caleb, I wouldn't be here looking for a husband." The young woman was the most street-savvy of their group and tougher than she appeared. The stories she'd shared about her days of being homeless were heart-breaking and reminded Willow of some of Caleb's tales.

An impish grin turned up Daisy's lips. "I agree. Caleb meets the qualifications on my list."

After a recently failed relationship, Daisy had spent the weeks during their voyage carefully crafting a list of the qualities she was looking for in a husband so that she could be better prepared when she arrived in the colony and wouldn't make the same mistakes again.

Willow wasn't surprised her two friends had become smitten with Caleb. Most women were. Not only had he caught Juliet's and Daisy's attention, but Willow had overheard some of the other mill women talking about him. And they ogled him every time he came near their cordoned-off area of the deck.

As always, such behavior annoyed Willow. But after getting to know Juliet and Daisy and learning just how kind and caring both women were, she'd stopped letting their remarks bother her. In fact, she honestly couldn't think of two nicer women for Caleb. "Caleb doesn't want to get married. But if he ever changes his mind, I'll be your matchmaker with him."

Daisy beamed. "That's so sweet of you to be willing to serve as a matchmaker for us."

"Sweet?" Juliet snorted. "No, Willow's in denial."

Willow dragged her attention away from the shoreline and the crowds of men and narrowed her eyes on Juliet. "In denial? What does that mean?"

Juliet's pretty smile turned smug. "You know what it means."

"Clearly I don't."

"It means that your Caleb doesn't have eyes for anyone else but you."

"He's not *my* Caleb."

"Oh he's all yours." Juliet spoke with such assurance that Willow's ready retort got caught in her throat. "That man is madly in love with you."

Madly in love? No. Absolutely not. Of course, now if she

protested, she'd only make Juliet think she really was in denial. But if she said nothing, Juliet would assume she was right. "I've known Caleb for years. I think I know him better than you."

"You're blind and only seeing what you want to."

"What do you see that I don't?"

"Obviously everything."

Willow rolled her eyes. "Name one thing."

"The way he looks at you."

"He looks at me like he cares about me. As a friend."

Juliet's eyes took on a sassy gleam. "He looks at you like he wants to pick you up and throw you into his bed."

At Juliet's brazenness, Willow cupped a hand over her mouth to hold in a gasp.

"Goodness gracious, Juliet!" Daisy glanced around as though to see if anyone else was listening to their scandalous conversation. But thankfully the other women were too focused on the men lining the shore.

Juliet just shrugged one of her elegant shoulders. "It's true."

Willow could only shake her head. Even after having gotten used to Juliet's unpredictable statements and behavior, sometimes the pretty woman still surprised her.

"I also see that he can't live without you," Juliet continued, as brash as always. "He has to see you and talk to you. Every. Single. Day."

"And I have to see and talk to him—"

"Because you're madly in love with him too."

"No, because he's an important part of my life. As a friend." That was all. There had been a period of time during that awkward stage between being a girl and a woman when she'd felt attracted to him. But letting that attraction flare had nearly ruined their friendship.

The first time she'd almost lost him was after he'd gotten the news of his father's death in prison when she'd been fifteen and he'd been sixteen.

Caleb had seemed upset, even a little sad. So she'd wrapped her arms around him in a hug. He'd embraced her back, had even pulled her tighter. She'd only meant to comfort him, but after a moment, he'd wrenched out of her arms and walked away. She could admit, she'd liked the hug, liked the feel of him. But clearly he hadn't felt the same, and he'd avoided her for three days after that.

The second time had been a few months after the hug. One hot summer evening when they'd been resting on the roof of her tenement, she'd reached for his hand and told him she liked him. He'd held her hand awkwardly for only a few seconds, then he'd pulled back from her, stood, and walked away for another three days.

After that, she'd realized she had to stamp out any attraction to him if she wanted to keep him in her life.

So she'd spent years extinguishing even the tiniest of sparks that flared inside her. After working so hard at controlling herself, she no longer had even the slightest attraction to him. It was long gone, and she intended to keep it that way.

The undeniable truth was that Caleb only ever saw her as a friend and nothing more. He'd never hinted at wanting a different kind of relationship, not even in the least. Now, she didn't want a different relationship either. She was happy with what they had and didn't want anything to change.

"You have to understand." Willow tried to gather her thoughts together. "Caleb's my brother."

Juliet released an unladylike scoff.

"He is," Willow said quickly before Juliet could contradict her. "He's the only brother I've ever had."

Daisy slipped her arm around Willow and leveled a stern look at Juliet. "Willow came all this way like us to find the love of her life. She wouldn't have done so if she wanted to marry Caleb."

Mostly she'd come so that she could help her family escape the destitution in Manchester. She wasn't opposed to finding love. She just wasn't sure how adequate she'd be as a wife. She'd likely end up disappointing any man who decided to marry her.

She hugged Daisy back, thankful for the young woman's support nonetheless. She was thankful for Juliet too, for her honesty and willingness to speak what she thought . . . even when she wasn't always right.

Juliet turned her attention away from the Victoria shoreline and gazed again at the majestic scenery that surrounded them.

They'd been oohing and aahing over the landscape since the moment the ship had left the Pacific Ocean and started down the Strait of Juan de Fuca, the narrow body of water that separated Vancouver Island from the territory of Washington in the United States. The jagged, towering peaks of the Olympic Mountain Range had been more incredible than anything else they'd seen on their voyage, even more beautiful than the Falkland Islands and Cape Horn at the southernmost part of South America.

Even whilst they'd been anchored and detained on the *Robert Lowe* in Esquimalt Harbor the past couple of days, they hadn't been able to stop admiring the wilderness—the endless dark green of the pine and fir trees, the untouched and untainted beauty, the vibrancy of the colors, and the endlessness of it all.

They'd seen all manner of wildlife including otters, sea lions, salmon, orcas, and waterfowl they hadn't been able to name. They'd caught glimpses of elk, deer, fox, and even a black bear that had been fishing along the shore.

At times, Willow had to pinch herself to make sure she wasn't dreaming. It was all so different from the overcrowded, dirty Manchester, that she almost couldn't believe a place this pure and spacious could exist. She'd begun to understand just why living in the city had been so difficult for her mum after having grown up on a farm.

Willow breathed in a deep lungful, something she hadn't been able to do in Manchester, not with how polluted it was. Here, even with smoke from the *HMS Grappler* billowing into the air, the blue overhead had been clearer than any sky she'd ever witnessed, even on the few occasions that her family had taken short trips to the countryside.

The city of Victoria was different than what she'd expected too. Gone were the endless factories and tenements. Instead, piers, wharfs, and warehouses lined the bay. The town spread up a gently sloping hill. A few brick buildings and houses stood out, but mostly the capital city was a sprawling mixture of wooden framed buildings that lined wide streets. At the pinnacle among the pines that hadn't been cleared away, a white church steeple rose above the other structures surrounding it.

"I'm sorry, Willow." Juliet slipped her arm around Willow too, so that the three of them stood linked together. "If you want to be just friends with Caleb, then I'll respect that."

"Thank you." Willow squeezed her friend, grateful all over again that God had brought these two young women into her life. Juliet and Daisy had helped fill the emptiness and loneliness that had come from leaving home.

Yes, she still worried about her family every day, and she hoped they were managing to survive without too much hardship. But after three months of being gone, she didn't feel the ache of missing everyone quite as keenly anymore.

Now that she was about to disembark and step onto solid ground for the first time since leaving England, she could only pray that she would find the work she needed and be able to save money quickly.

Hopefully Caleb would find work right away too. And hopefully she'd still be able to see him often.

He has to see you and talk to you. Every. Single. Day.

Juliet's words whispered through Willow's head. Were they true? Certainly the statement about Caleb looking at her like he wanted to take her to his bed wasn't correct.

It was ludicrous, actually.

But it was true. Caleb did see her every day. Except for those two times when he'd walked away and cut her off, he'd never missed a day of seeing and talking with her, not even during the past three months when it had been nearly impossible to be together.

Regardless, that didn't mean that Caleb couldn't live without her. He was a strong man and would make his own way whether she was with him or not.

Juliet might think Caleb's devotion meant more than friendship. But it didn't.

He was truly the best friend any person could ever ask for. That's all.

She wasn't sure what the future would hold once she was in Victoria. But she did know that whatever it was, she wanted Caleb to be by her side every step of the way.

Six

C aleb stiffened his arms and forced himself to keep his fists in his pockets so that he didn't start swinging at the men in front of him.

The onlookers had already been swarming the waterfront when the *Emily Harris* had arrived earlier with the paying passengers from the *Robert Lowe*. The men had cheered and shouted in a frenzy of excitement—believing the single women were coming.

By the time Caleb had set foot on the wharf, the men had realized the women weren't yet arriving and so had turned their attention away from the passengers and focused instead on a fistfight between two fellows.

Caleb had paused to take in the familiar scene—the bloody noses and lips, the torn clothing, the bruises and cuts. He'd fingered the scar on his cheek, all that remained from his night of fighting at the Flying Donkey. He always healed, but he also always had more scars. Scars that would never go away.

He'd intended to move on from the waterfront to find lodging. He still had a few shillings of his earnings from that last fight to tide him over until he found work. But he hadn't been able to tear himself away, not with so many men there and not with the possibility of Willow having to face them all.

Now as the first of the women stepped onto the pier, the men crowded closer and were cheering again.

"Marry me!" some of them were shouting.

"I love you!" called another young fellow nearby, laughing and shoving with his companions.

"You're beautiful," bellowed a shaggy fellow who looked like he hadn't shaven in months. "Yes, you!"

"Never saw such fine women in all my days."

The comments rose around Caleb, irritating him more with every passing second. The women didn't need to hear all the heckling as they came ashore. He didn't want Willow subjected to it.

Worst of all, he didn't want the men seeing her. Once they did, they'd want her, and they would probably stop at nothing to get her.

And Willow was his. His and only his.

He knew such a thought was completely irrational. It was almost as if he'd turned into a chest-thumping barbarian ready to barrel through the crowds yelling, "Mine, mine, mine."

If only he hadn't heard the story about the *Tynemouth*, the previous bride ship that had arrived in the autumn. But as he'd been standing milling about, several men had been going on about how a miner had stepped into the line of women making their way up the shore. Apparently he'd singled out one of the pretty young women, dropped on one knee before her, and offered her two thousand dollars if she'd marry him. If the story could be believed, the woman had accepted the proposal and had married the miner only a few days later.

Surely nothing like that would happen again.

Even so, Caleb had edged his way through the men so that he was standing alongside the planks that had been laid down in the sodden, muddy grass. It was a makeshift boardwalk that led up the shore to several government buildings, including the Marine Barracks where the women would be housed until they found employment or marriage—whichever came first.

Employment would come first for Willow. Caleb wouldn't let her get coerced into a quick marriage. Even though he didn't deserve her, he'd marry her before he let any strange man get ahold of her.

As more and more of the women stepped onto land, the relief and excitement in their faces matched what he'd felt when he'd landed. After so many days stuck on the crowded ship without once being able to go ashore, he'd been tempted to drop to his knees and kiss the ground like some of his fellow steerage passengers had.

The steerage had been dark and dank and noisy. During those few times when they'd run into rough water or storms, it had become nearly unbearable with the stench of vomit from all those who'd become seasick. He'd weathered those days well enough and had done his best to help with the suffering wherever he could, both in steerage and in the cabins.

Thankfully, Willow hadn't gotten too seasick. She'd had a little nausea from time to time, and she'd had trouble with her breathing a few times, but the ailment hadn't seemed as bad or occurred as often.

Even the food had been tolerable—hard biscuits, salted fish and pork, and dried potatoes. At least they hadn't had to worry about where their next meal would come from like they had in Manchester.

Through the long days, he'd written a lot of poetry. The endless ocean, the constant crash of the waves, the salty sea breeze, the flapping sails against the cloudless blue skies . . . it had all been so new and raw and beautiful.

As usual, he'd drawn inspiration from the faces around him—the joy of the woman who persevered through her travail to hold her newborn, the haggardness in the expressions of the coal trimmers, the leathery face of an old sailor.

Caleb's one bright spot of every day had been those precious minutes when he'd been able to see Willow. They'd whispered hurriedly in the dark, her asking him about his day and then sharing about hers.

Now that they were in the colony, he'd make sure there was no more whispering in the dark. He intended to spend as much time with her as he wanted and as often as he wanted.

At the sight of her stepping onto the pier, all his rambling thoughts came to a halt. He hungrily took her in like he always did, first making sure she was unharmed and healthy, and then letting himself feast upon her beauty.

Her body was still too thin from the lack of nutrition over the past months, but her face had lost all pallor and was a healthy, rosy color from the days sitting on the ship's deck in the sun. Her hair had lightened too, so that the pale red had almost faded into all gold. Her features radiated with new strength—her pretty lips set firmly, her fine brows knit with concern, her blue eyes determined.

The two women who'd befriended Willow hurried after her, worry creasing their faces as the men continued to bombard them from all sides with their declarations of love and offers of matrimony.

A group of distinguished-looking men and women waited at the end of the pier—an Immigration Committee including the mayor's wife and several other important women of the community.

They shook the hands of Captain Congalton of the *Robert Lowe* and the Reverend Reese and his wife. Then the mill women took turns curtsying to their superiors before being directed down the long plank walkway.

The women hurried along the boards, some smiling at the men that lined the path, others flushing with embarrassment. Willow simply held her chin high and walked as though she didn't see or hear anyone.

She'd always been tough, never letting much weaken her resolve—not the long hours at the mill, not the frustration of losing her job, not the constant hunger, and not even this adventure into the unknown. She was unshakeable and strong, and he liked that about her.

As she drew near, he wanted to call out to her. But he also didn't want to draw unnecessary attention her way. So far, none of the men had jumped into the line of women and proposed marriage. Other than a slew of obnoxious comments, the men had behaved properly toward the women, and he wanted to keep it that way.

When she was but half a dozen paces away, he had a sudden and overwhelming desire to reach for her. His heart hammered with the need to claim her, to show every man present that she wasn't available.

But that wasn't the truth. She didn't belong to him and never would in that way. As much as he hated to think about it, maybe here in the colony she'd find a husband, one who could appreciate her and care about her the way she needed.

In the next instant, her gaze collided with his, almost as if she'd felt his turmoil and it had drawn her. As she walked past, she held his eyes in an unbreakable bond, one that seemed to encourage him that together they'd make it through the uncertainty ahead and that he didn't need to worry about her.

He didn't move, didn't say anything, and didn't reveal any emotion. But inside, his heart was thumping at double the pace. Heaven help him, he loved her more than he ought to love anyone. But he couldn't stop himself. He'd tried often enough to know.

She moved beyond him all too quickly, and their connection came to an end. Several of the fellows around him teased him good-naturedly, obviously having noticed Willow's attention upon him.

He didn't respond. Instead, he moved out of the line and tried to elbow his way through the crowd so that he could see her again.

But even with his hard jabs clearing the way, he couldn't keep up, and she disappeared from sight.

Soon enough, she'd be inside the Marine Barracks and away from the men. And hopefully she'd be safe there. He wasn't sure what the security situation was like—he hoped it was good enough that none of the gawking, love-struck men could bother Willow or any of the other women. Even if it was good, nothing could stop him from sneaking inside the government complex to visit her. Maybe tonight after darkness fell.

As he slung his bag of possessions over his shoulder and started away from the waterfront, he let himself finally breathe normally.

They'd made it.

Surely they'd faced the worst, and now things could only get better.

Seven

⌒◦⌒

W illow climbed out the window onto the sloping roof of the Marine Barracks. Caleb's short note earlier in the evening had instructed her to meet him there after all the women had gone to sleep.

With the darkness in the bedroom behind her, she'd finally crept from the lower bunk bed where she'd been resting and had quietly opened the window, trying not to wake anyone.

Now as she glanced around the roof, the January breeze nipped at her, and she drew her blanket around her body more securely, her nightgown and stockings worn thin from years of use. The blackness of the night was broken by a few stars overhead, giving her only the faintest of light to locate Caleb.

"Caleb?" she whispered.

A second later, soft scuffling sounded behind her. She turned to find Caleb on the section of roof above her. He was lying on his stomach with an arm outstretched toward her. "Up here."

She took his hand and let him hoist her up.

Once she was lying beside him, she wrapped the blanket around her again and rolled to her side so that she was facing him. Her mind flashed with all the memories of being on the roof with him back home, especially the many summer nights when it had been too hot to sleep inside. They'd lain on their backs, talking side by side, until they'd fallen asleep.

She wouldn't be falling asleep with him tonight on the roof. Not with the chill of the night curling around her toes and ankles and creeping underneath the blanket. She doubted she'd last but a few minutes.

"How are you?" She tried to see his face in the darkness, but it was too shadowed. "Did you find a place to live? A job? Do you have enough to eat? How do you like Victoria so far—"

"Whoa, slow down." He released a low chuckle that warmed her insides.

She reached out a hand and grasped his arm, needing to reassure herself that he was really there. "Well?"

"I'm fine, Willow. I have a bed in a room above one of the pubs. And I had enough to pay for a filling meal."

"Oh good, I've been worried." After seeing so many men along the shore, she hadn't been able to stop wondering if Caleb would find a place to live.

"I don't have a job yet." He was resting his head on one of his arms and facing her too.

"Hopefully you'll find something soon."

"Tomorrow." He said it with such confidence, she knew he would. He always seemed to get whatever he set his mind to. Even in Manchester, he'd landed odd jobs when no one else could.

"Do you think you'll like Victoria?" She didn't want him

to regret following her to the colony. She wanted him to be happy, wanted him to thrive.

"I never realized it would be so beautiful here." His voice contained a note of awe. "It's what I imagined paradise might be like."

"I agree." She breathed out a contented sigh, envisioning the endless green of the pine trees and the clean and clear water. She'd never seen even a spot of green growth in Manchester—not even a lone tree. And the water? The rivers? The canals? She couldn't imagine a time when they'd ever been as clean and clear as the water surrounding Vancouver Island and the many smaller islands they'd passed.

"I'm sure you must have written a poem today about Victoria."

"I did."

"Read it to me." Her sentence ended on a shudder, the cold shifting in again.

He began to shrug out of his coat.

Of course he'd noticed her chill. He always noticed everything. "No, Caleb." She pressed her hand more firmly against his arm. "You keep your coat."

He continued to wiggle out of the garment then draped it over her.

"Ca-leb," she gently chided even as she let his lingering warmth in the fabric envelop her.

"I'm fine." He returned to lying on his side.

"Read me one of today's poems." She loved his way of capturing what he saw, the conciseness of his words, the vividness of his descriptions, and the depth of his emotion that filled his poetry.

"It's too cold tonight. You have to go back inside in a minute."

The icy breeze touched her nose and cheeks, and she knew he was right. Even so, she wanted to linger for a while with him. After the past weeks with such rushed conversations, she wanted to talk for hours without any pressure to stop.

"What about you?" he asked. "Are you okay after having to walk the gauntlet?"

"Gauntlet?"

"All those fellows waiting on the shore wanting to marry you?"

"They didn't want to marry me."

"Every single man there was looking for a wife."

The men *had* been eager. There was no doubt about that. When she'd finally stumbled into the Marine Barracks with all the other mill women, they'd laughed together about the enthusiasm of the men and some of the antics they'd witnessed. The humor and joking had been the only way to process what they'd experienced.

"Did you meet anyone that you want to marry?" Caleb's voice held a note of teasing.

She playfully shoved at his arm but then didn't move her hand away. "You know I didn't. I can't get married yet. I have to work for a while and save up money."

"Well, when you're ready, you won't have a shortage of choices."

"Clearly not."

"So no one caught your interest?"

Was that a note of worry in his voice? Didn't he want her to get married? "Do you really think I'm so shallow that I'd find the man I want to marry on my first day here?"

In all the discussions they'd had over the years, they'd rarely talked about love and marriage. On the few occasions he'd brought it up, it had been to tell her about how bad his parents' marriage had been and how he never wanted to get married. But tonight, she supposed it was only natural the topic would surface after all that had transpired on shore earlier.

"Then you don't believe in love at first sight?" he asked.

"Of course not."

He expelled a long breath. Was it one of relief?

She wished she could scrutinize his face and try to discover how he was feeling. Juliet had seemed to have no trouble seeing things about Caleb. Why couldn't she?

"When will you find out where you'll be working?" he asked softly.

She pushed up to one elbow on her side. "A woman by the name of Mrs. Moresby on the Immigration Committee listed off all the domestic jobs that are available, and so I picked one this afternoon and will start tomorrow."

He propped himself up too, their faces only inches apart. "That was fast."

"But that's a good thing, isn't it? The sooner I start working, the sooner I can start sending the money home."

"We'll both send money to your dad, and they'll all be able to come soon."

She loved that he was so generous. She couldn't think of anyone else who'd make such a sacrifice.

Caleb was the best person she'd ever met. Just one more reason why she couldn't dwell on any of the things Juliet had mentioned earlier today. It would make things awkward between her and Caleb.

The problem was, Willow had dwelt on them most of the day—even though she'd tried not to.

She shifted back from him just a little, needing some space, although she wasn't sure why.

He didn't budge. "Who will you be working for?"

"The Mann family. I don't know much about them, other than that they live on a farm just north of Victoria."

"So you won't be in town?"

"It's not far. Only a few miles."

"How many is a *few*?"

"Mrs. Moresby didn't rightly know. But when she mentioned there was a domestic post in a farmhouse manor, I just had to take it, Caleb. It's on a farm. How could I not?"

He grew silent, a sign that he was thinking, or brooding, or both.

"It's close enough to Victoria that we'll still get to see each other." At least she hoped so.

Had she picked too rashly? Should she have waited until she knew more? After all, even a job in the city limits of Victoria would feel like country living compared to Manchester. "Do you want me to find a different position? In the morning I can ask and see what's left here in town."

He shrugged, his muscles rising and falling against her hand on his arm. "If you want to be on the farm, I'll get a job there too."

She did want to be on the farm. She'd heard her mum's stories so often that she wanted to experience it for herself. And maybe someday she'd learn enough that she could have a little farm of her own. With all the unsettled land in the colony that she'd only just glimpsed, surely there was enough left for anyone willing to work for it, maybe even enough for her parents to also have a farm.

She didn't really know what was realistic. But during the voyage on the *Robert Lowe*, everyone had been talking about the colony and sharing what they knew. It hadn't been much. Most of the women, like her, didn't read well and didn't have access to the news and what was going on in other parts of the British empire.

But from the little she'd heard, land in the colonies was cheap and available. Natural resources like wood and coal were easy to access. And jobs and food were plentiful.

"Tell me what you want me to do." She squeezed Caleb's arm. Thankfully, he never seemed to mind that she often held his arm. The connection didn't reveal much, but it was one way that she could sometimes sense his moods. "I'll do whatever you think is best."

"I'll go with you tomorrow and find work on the farm."

"What if they don't need the help?"

"I'll convince them they do."

She smiled. "You probably will."

His muscles in his arm relaxed. "Then it's settled."

"It's settled."

He was silent for a beat. "I've heard domestic work is demanding."

She'd talked about that with the women on the ship too. None of them had ever done domestic work, but some had siblings or relatives who'd gained employment as servants in wealthy homes. And those women had shared stories about the hardships, long hours, and many rules.

"I'll be able to handle the work." At least that's what she'd been telling herself. "Don't you think?"

"You can do anything you set your mind to." His voice rang with sincerity.

Even so, she couldn't keep the doubts from rushing back in. Would she be able to understand everything expected of her? Would the other servants take the time to explain tasks?

She shivered again, unable to keep her teeth from chattering.

He sat up. "Time for you to go in."

"But I've missed you, and I'm not ready to go back."

He began to tug her up. "It's too cold out here."

Reluctantly, she let him help her climb down to the window. As she peered up at him, she finally got a fuller glimpse of his face and all the strong lines and rough edges. "I don't know what I'd do without you as my friend," she whispered.

"I'll always be here," he whispered in return.

She squeezed his arm one last time, then ducked to the window. As she did so, she heard him expel a taut, almost exasperated breath.

Was he frustrated with her about something?

She stretched up to the spot of roof above her, but he was already moving away, climbing over the top toward the rear of the Marine Barracks. If she called out to him now, she'd likely alert the guard who was on duty at the gate of the government complex.

She returned to the window and began to inch it up. Maybe that sigh didn't mean anything. Maybe she'd only imagined his exasperation. Or what if he'd sensed something different about her tonight? What if he'd picked up on her inner turmoil over all that Juliet had said?

She released a frustrated sigh of her own. She had to be careful to maintain their relationship the way they'd always had it. There was no sense at all in thinking about Juliet's insinuations. It would only stir up trouble. And that's the last thing she wanted.

Eight

He didn't like Mrs. Mann. Then again, he didn't like too many people, so his opinion didn't count for much.

Caleb leaned against a hitching post across from the entrance of the Marine Barracks, arms and ankles crossed, watching the gentlewoman in the barouche interacting with her Chinese coachman perched on his elevated seat. She was belittling and nagging him with every move he made.

No doubt, the woman would do the same to Willow. And Caleb wasn't sure how he'd be able to stand back and watch such treatment. The truth was, he probably wouldn't be able to put up with it and would eventually say or do something.

Willow hadn't made her appearance yet, and Mrs. Mann had complained loudly about having to wait. The guard at the gate had gotten an earful and had gone a second time to the Marine Barracks to call for Willow.

She was probably saying goodbye to the other women. And it was early. The church bells hadn't yet rung the nine o'clock hour.

The bright sunshine of the previous day was nowhere to be seen, and a thick layer of clouds blanketed the sky, spitting a mist of rain. The hood of the barouche was up, sheltering Mrs. Mann who was as finely dressed as any gentlewoman in Manchester. Her youthfulness was still evident in her features, and Caleb guessed she was a young mother with a few children.

He'd thought about the prospect of working on the farm more throughout the night as he'd stared at the low ceiling of the lodging house from his uncomfortably small wooden-framed bed. He'd never been on a farm, didn't know the first thing about how they were run. But he suspected that laborers were needed for all sorts of tasks—everything from planting the crops to taking care of livestock. Surely he could learn quickly and prove himself to be an asset.

At the clang of the gate, he straightened to see Willow thanking the guard and stepping through carrying her flimsy sack with her few belongings. She glanced around, taking in first the waiting barouche with Mrs. Mann then finding him across the street.

He gave a curt shake of his head, hoping she'd understand that it was best if Mrs. Mann didn't know about their friendship and chance her refusing to hire him because she was worried about something developing between him and Willow.

Willow quickly shifted her attention back to Mrs. Mann, forced a smile, and approached the carriage. She curtsied and introduced herself, and then Mrs. Mann began to ask her questions about her skills.

"I'm sorry, ma'am," Willow said from beside the barouche as the rain began to fall more steadily. "I've only worked in a mill and never in a household. But I promise I'll do my best."

"Let's hope so." Mrs. Mann eyed her one last time then motioned at her impatiently. "Well, you'll have to do. Now come on and get in. We can't have you getting soaked, or you'll get me wet, too, and that will make for a long ride back to the farm."

As Willow climbed up and took the spot beside Mrs. Mann, Caleb used that as his opening to approach the carriage. "Ma'am." He tipped the brim of his hat up and let her get a look at his face which most women considered appealing, although he wasn't sure why. He could only pray that whatever appeal he had would work to his advantage today.

Mrs. Mann started to speak to her coachman, but then she halted and let her gaze settle over Caleb, taking him in from his dark hair down to his scuffed boots.

As her attention returned to his face, she cocked her head. "Yes? What can I do for you?" There was interest in her eyes and voice.

Hopefully that meant he could direct the conversation in his favor. "I'm newly arrived and looking for work." He lifted an arm and pretended to resituate his hat, but all the while, he flexed his muscles, causing his shirt and coat to strain against the seams.

Her gaze shifted to his arms, and her eyes widened in appreciation.

Willow, watching the interaction, turned her head away, but not before Caleb caught the hint of a smile.

"You mentioned farm," he continued as the rain splattered against his cap, "and I figured you could use a strong man who can do hard labor."

"I'm sure I could—we could—I mean the farm could."

Mrs. Mann fanned her face with one of her gloved hands. "But unfortunately, I'm not in charge of hiring the farmhands. We have a bailiff who undertakes all things related to the farm."

Caleb touched the brim of his hat, faking indifference. He'd always found that indifference was more acceptable than desperation. "If you think paying him a visit would be worth my time, I could do that today."

"Oh, why yes. I do believe I heard Mr. Pidwell mention his need for another laborer"—Mrs. Mann's gaze trailed over his arms again—"such as yourself. I could let him know to expect you."

"That would be very kind, ma'am." Caleb took a step back, again not wanting to appear too eager. "I'll be sure to talk to him this morning, if you'd be so kind as to give me directions."

"My husband owns White Swan Farm on the peninsula north of Victoria on Cordova Bay. It's one of the largest farms on the island. You won't miss it."

"Thank you, ma'am." He tipped his hat again.

"There is a road of sorts, more of an overland trail, leading north onto the peninsula. But the quickest way to reach the farm is by boat."

"I'll likely make the trek by foot—"

"If you walk, it'll take at least two hours."

"I don't mind."

She studied his face again, and he made sure to keep his expression polite. She'd all but assured him of a job. He'd be willing to walk the distance as long as he could be near Willow.

She finally nodded toward the harbor. "If you meet us at

Broderick's Wharf in a quarter of an hour, you may ride with us to the White Swan. Lum could most certainly use the help with the rowing." She shot a glare at the coachman who bobbed his head to acknowledge her statement.

The fellow had a weathered, lined look to his face that meant he wasn't youthful anymore. But though slight of stature, he seemed strong enough to handle the rowing alone.

"I'll be there." Caleb hoisted his bag over his shoulder. He was ready to go.

As the barouche rolled away, he caught Willow's gaze and could see the humor in her expression once more. He kept his own face stoic, but inside he was smiling too. He'd gotten what he'd wanted. He'd be able to work near her and see her every day.

Now if only he could figure out a way to get her to love him, and not just as a friend.

When she'd made her declaration of friendship last night on the roof again, for at least the millionth time, he hadn't been able to hold back his frustration. The sigh had come out, and he was pretty sure she'd heard it.

How much longer could he hide his feelings for her? Sooner or later, he was going to crack under the pressure of trying to conceal everything. What would happen then? Would he end up losing her?

Maybe the risk was worth it. Maybe he needed to stop being a coward and simply let her know how he really felt.

He watched the carriage turn a corner and start down a gently sloping road toward the waterfront. When she was well out of sight, he let his shoulders slump. As much as he wanted to gather the courage to express himself, he couldn't.

He'd long ago accepted the fact that he was too broken and battered to be worthy of a wife, especially of her. She always saw the best in him, but he knew all the parts of himself that were shattered and could never be completely fixed.

His father's fists had crushed him one too many times when he'd been young. While the beatings had taught him to use his own fists in self-defense, the abuse had also taught him that the world was a hard place where he wasn't wanted or needed.

After one brutal pounding that had left him with a broken arm and a busted hand, he'd decided he'd had enough. He'd only been ten, but he'd run off and had never gone back. For months, he struggled to survive on his own, scrounging for food and searching for a place to lay his head at night.

He'd been near to freezing and starving, holed up in a rubbish heap in an alley when a gang of older boys had picked a fight with him. Of course, he'd already been a strong and quick fighter even at the young age, and he'd been able to defend himself from all but one of the boys who'd pulled out a knife.

Willow had been passing by, and at the sight of the knife, she'd taken off running. He'd noticed her around from time to time and knew she belonged to what appeared to be a nice family. He'd been relieved when she left him, hadn't wanted to subject an innocent girl like her to his plight.

He hadn't expected her dad to come barreling out of his flat several moments later with Willow on his trail. At the sight of Mr. Rhodes wielding a long metal pipe and swinging it hard, his tormentors had released him and scampered away.

Caleb had stood up and tried to run off too. But he'd been bleeding hard from the cuts in his neck and one on his face, in too much pain to do anything but limp.

Mr. Rhodes, with Willow by his side, had gently stopped

him and asked him to come inside their home and let his wife tend to his wounds.

Caleb had only shaken his head and declared that he was fine. But when Willow's eyes had filled with tears and she'd pleaded with him to let them help, he hadn't been able to resist. He still couldn't resist anything she asked of him.

Mr. Rhodes had been a kind influence and upright example ever since taking him in that first time—and had helped him find honest employment at the mill. Mr. Rhodes had also helped him make peace with God and had started him down a path of right living.

But deep inside, Caleb could feel his past warring with the present, a war he wasn't sure he'd ever be able to stop or win. He had too many vices that hadn't gone away even though he'd tried to change. He was a liar and a sneak and wasn't above breaking the law when it suited him.

He'd vowed he'd never be the kind of brute his father was. But a part of him feared he'd end up like his father whether he wanted to or not. And he wouldn't be able to live with himself if he hurt Willow in any way.

The truth was, he was better off remaining only friends with Willow. Their friendship was incredible, unlike anything he'd ever imagined he'd have with anyone. In fact, he'd never known that such a friendship was even possible—it probably wasn't possible with anyone else, because no one but Willow had ever been able to break through his reserves. Not only could she slip past any barrier he put up, but she could confront him, be honest about everything, and even boss him around, and he loved all those things about her.

He loved everything about Willow. He always had and always would. But the fact remained—she deserved a better man than him as a husband.

He straightened his spine, set his shoulders in a hard line, then started down the road toward the wharf. Friendship was all he would get with her, and he couldn't forget it.

Nine

The rugged rocky coastline, the thick endless forests, the calm green-blue waterway. Willow couldn't get enough of the view from her spot at the center of the dinghy behind Mrs. Mann who huddled beneath her parasol, trying to stay warm and dry. Lum rowed in the front, and Caleb sat in the stern maneuvering his oars as if he'd been rowing for decades instead of thirty minutes.

Everywhere Willow looked the beauty was never ending, filling her with such wonder that she could only sit quietly and take it all in. The continued drizzle couldn't dampen her awe. Not even Mrs. Mann's unending complaints could take away from the experience.

To the far east was the mainland and the colony of British Columbia. There, the pine-covered hills rolled out, culminating in a mountain range with Mount Baker rising above everything, covered in thick blankets of snow. She'd learned that the distant mountain was where gold had been discovered and where many of the men in Victoria went during the summer months when the trails were navigable and the weather warmer.

For now, many of those miners were wintering in Victoria with its milder temperatures and were awaiting spring which would allow them to resume their gold-mining efforts.

Apparently they were also awaiting wives.

She'd garnered attention again today just in the short ride down to the wharf and during the time it had taken to get into the rowboat. More than a dozen men had approached her, and one had even proposed marriage.

As soon as Caleb had arrived, the men had stopped bothering her. Probably because Caleb had glared and growled at them to back off. Eventually, he'd have to stop being overprotective. But for now, she had enough changes to worry about and didn't need the pressure of suitors.

"There it is. The White Swan." Mrs. Mann pointed to the open area of low sandy beach ahead with two long piers jutting out into deeper water. A steamboat was stretched out along one of the piers, and two men were loading crates onto the lower deck of the boat.

Mrs. Mann had described Saanichton Peninsula as a fertile area where a number of farms were located. And she'd boasted that her husband's farm was one of the oldest and biggest, that he'd settled it six years ago and had expanded it more with every passing year. She'd rattled off the crops grown on their land, but Willow had only paid attention at the mention of the variety of animals on the farm, including cows, sheep, pigs, and chickens.

At the news of the animals, Willow wished she could talk to the farm bailiff and ask if she could work with the livestock instead of in the house. But she guessed Mrs. Mann wouldn't be happy with such a suggestion, especially because other than Lum, Mrs. Mann only had a governess for her two young daughters and no other help. Willow had been tempted to say that her mum had raised five daughters by herself and had done just fine, but she didn't want to risk being fired on her first day.

Beyond the shore, an embankment rose into a grassy knoll with stately cedar and oak and other types of trees Willow couldn't begin to name, barren of their leaves during the winter months. At the hilltop stood a spacious multi-storied house with a twin-gabled roof. A broad stone chimney claimed one side of the house and a stove pipe ran up the other side. Painted a fresh white, the house had large windows and a wide covered front porch overlooking the beach.

The house wasn't as grand as the old manor homes in England. But it was bigger than anything Willow had ever visited. She'd only ever stepped foot into the mill owner's house one time in Manchester with her dad. Whilst it had been a spacious townhouse with lovely furnishings, it couldn't compare with the Manns' home. Willow could only imagine how picturesque the view was from the front of the house, especially at sunrise.

An ache pulsed in Willow's chest. Oh, how her mum would love this place, would probably think it was a piece of heaven on earth and never want to leave.

"Do you have white swans, ma'am?" Willow searched along the shore. She'd never seen a swan before.

"Of course we do." Mrs. Mann perched upon her bench stiffly, her lovely skirt damp and the hem dirty. "But they usually like to make their homes in the marshes and lakes farther inland, which is fine with me since they're such unfriendly creatures."

"Unfriendly?"

"The male is very possessive and can get aggressive when anyone comes near his mate or his children."

Willow's thoughts flashed back to Caleb's glares and growls just a short while ago when they'd been getting ready to depart from Victoria in the boat. He'd acted like a possessive and aggressive male swan, hadn't he? But she wasn't his mate, and she couldn't even let her mind wander in that direction.

She still blamed Juliet's comment on the steamer yesterday for her runaway thoughts of Caleb. Even so, the goodbyes with Juliet and Daisy had been hard this morning before leaving the Marine Barracks. Daisy had hugged Willow multiple times, offering a brave smile but blinking back tears. Juliet had been dry-eyed but had continued to give her *important* pieces of advice until Willow had finally torn herself away.

Both Juliet and Daisy had taken domestic positions for families living in town and would be starting soon too. They'd all agreed that they would try to meet in Victoria on Sundays on their half day off a week.

Willow would miss her new friends, although she suspected that both Juliet and Daisy would soon find husbands. Before long, the two would be married, settled in homes, and having babies.

Of course, Daisy claimed she wasn't in a rush to get married, that she wanted to earn passage for her mum to come to Vancouver Island the same way Willow was saving for her family. Regardless, Daisy was too sweet and attractive to remain single for long. The same was true of Juliet. Even if the young woman battled insecurities from her past, she was utterly lovely and had men practically fighting over her.

"Direct the boat alongside the pier." Mrs. Mann gave the

command to both Lum and Caleb, treating Caleb as if he was one of her servants already.

Willow hadn't dared look at Caleb during the short voyage to White Swan Farm. She didn't want to chance catching his eye, seeing his humor, and then smiling or snorting. She couldn't afford to behave in such a manner—not in front of Mrs. Mann.

As the boat reached the pier, Lum hopped out and began to secure the vessel. One of the steamboat workers, a short, stout man, who'd been loading the crates onto the waiting vessel, hobbled down the pier toward them. One leg seemed to be shorter than the other, giving him an uneven gait. He wore a greatcoat that fell to his ankles, and it hung open to reveal a yellow waistcoat and green trousers. His cap covered thinning brown hair, but it didn't conceal his round, clean-shaven face, or his squinting eyes watching their boat with curiosity.

"Hello, Mrs. Mann." He waved short, stubby fingers at the gentlewoman.

"Good day, Isaac." She rose and sidled to the edge of the boat.

"Let me help you, ma'am." Isaac picked up his pace, his limp growing more pronounced. He reached her just as she stepped one foot onto the pier.

"Isaac, I need you to go into town for me later." She took the offer of his hand and allowed him to assist her. "I've forgotten to retrieve the new gloves I ordered."

"Okay, ma'am." Although he was a hefty fellow, his every move was gentle, almost as if he was touching a porcelain doll that he was afraid he might drop.

When he'd made certain Mrs. Mann was firmly situated on the pier, he turned back to the boat and held out his hand to Willow. "Hello, new lady. I'd like to help you out of the boat, if I may." He spoke slowly and with such gravity, that for a moment Willow couldn't move, could only stare at the man hovering above her.

"Willow, meet Isaac Sayles." Mrs. Mann spoke the name matter-of-factly as her steps clomped away from the boat down the pier. "And Isaac, this is my new maid, Willow."

Isaac's arm remained outstretched. "Hello, new maid Willow. You're very nice to come work for Mrs. Mann. She's awfully busy and could use the help." His voice had a childlike quality that belied his age.

On the bench in the boat behind her, Caleb hadn't moved or spoken either. She cast him a quick glance to find him resting his arms against both oars, his shoulders relaxed, his dark eyes taking in the shoreline. The glaring and growling from the wharf in Victoria were absent.

Obviously, Caleb didn't see Isaac as a threat to her.

She placed a hand into Isaac's and let him help her onto the pier. His touch was as tender with her as it had been with Mrs. Mann.

When he finished, he offered a smile, one that crinkled his eyes even more. "You'll sure like it here at White Swan."

"I already do." She smiled in return, guessing that a childlike man such as Isaac didn't have any enemies and made friends everywhere he went.

"That's my boat." He tipped his head at the steamboat with the name *Boat* painted in red block letters along the hull. The steamer was only a fraction of the size of the *Grappler* that she and the rest of the women had ridden on yesterday. Whilst the vessel appeared to be well maintained, it was patched and rusty in places, had likely weathered many years of use. "I'm the pilot, and Jonas is my captain."

The other man, in the process of lifting a final crate from the pier, paused and nodded at Willow. Thin and wiry with ebony skin and dark curly hair showing beneath a bowler, he regarded her with as much curiosity as she was regarding him.

She'd never met a person of another color before leaving Manchester. One time her dad had gone to an abolitionist meeting put on by the Quakers, and a former American slave woman had spoken there about the trials she'd experienced. Her dad had come home and shared about the horrors of slavery, particularly on the plantations that provided the cotton for the Lancashire mills.

Since arriving in the colony, however, Willow had seen more diversity in a couple of days than she had her entire life—not only with Black people but with the Chinese and also the natives who'd apparently lived in the Pacific Northwest long before the European settlers arrived.

"Pleased to meet you, miss." Jonas touched the brim of his hat.

"I'm pleased to meet you too." If she had to guess the ages of Isaac and Jonas, she'd place Isaac as the older of the two, maybe thirty or forty years of age. Jonas had a more youthful look and was probably closer in age to Caleb.

"Come along now, Willow." Under her parasol, Mrs. Mann was already off the pier and was crossing a portion of sandy beach toward a series of stones leveled into the hillside to form a stairway that led to the house. "We have much to do to train you in your duties."

"Good day," Willow said to Jonas and Isaac—both watching her with wide eyes—before she hefted her bag over her shoulder and started down the pier.

She'd heard the rumors that men outnumbered women ten to one which meant she would have to get used to standing out and garnering attention, at least until more women moved to the colony.

As she stepped onto the beach, her boots crunched on broken clam shells among the smooth rocks and wet sand. The dampness in the air brought with it the distinct scent of brine and seagrass and fish—scents she'd learned well during the long past weeks of traveling across oceans. But here, there was also the rich odor of pine and soil.

She took in a deep breath, a sense of satisfaction stealing through her at the future that lay before her. She'd been given the opportunity for a new life here in the colony, a life that could be better than anything she'd known in Manchester.

And Caleb was here at the farm with her in this beautiful paradise where the sea and the sky and the land hadn't yet been tainted by progress and its pollution.

As she climbed the first stone step, she paused and smiled over her shoulder at him. She wasn't sure how she'd known he was watching her. But he was. He was still resting on his bench in the boat, his gaze trailing her.

He didn't smile in return. But somehow, she knew he felt the same way about this place and the future. She had no doubt that he'd be hired to work on the farm. They'd still be together. And they'd get to relish the beauty of this new place side by side.

What more could she ask for?

Ten

The list of tasks was endless.

Willow pressed a dripping hand to her chest to ease the tightness. But her ability to breathe was only getting harder as her first morning progressed.

Even though she'd technically started working yesterday after arriving at White Swan, it hadn't been a full day, and Mrs. Mann spent some of the day orienting Willow to the new job.

Part of that had included issuing a uniform—a black skirt with a matching black bodice and a spotless white apron that slipped over her shoulders and fell almost to the hem of her skirt. The white collar was stiff and itchy, as were the white cuffs added to the sleeves, but Mrs. Mann had insisted that they were part of the uniform, along with the lacy cap that needed to cover as much of her hair as possible.

Mrs. Mann had also given her a pair of black lace-up shoes that were too tight. But they were still the sturdiest and thickest shoes she'd ever worn.

After the uniform distribution, Mrs. Mann had taken

Willow on a tour of the house, rattling off the duties Willow needed to complete in each of the rooms. But the spaciousness, the elaborate decorations, and the elegant furniture had overwhelmed Willow so that she hadn't been able to concentrate on Mrs. Mann's instructions. Even if Willow had been able to focus, she wouldn't have known what the Japanese desk was that needed dusting every morning or the Oriental rug that needed beating every afternoon.

Honestly, everything had been as confusing—perhaps even more so—than Willow had expected. And she hadn't wanted to ask too many questions and frustrate Mrs. Mann. On more than one occasion, she'd wished Caleb had been with her throughout the day. Then later he would have patiently explained everything to her again in a way that made it easier for her to remember.

But Caleb, after being hired on yesterday, had been set right to work, and like her, he didn't have a spare moment in his day.

"Finish quickly." Lum's thickly accented voice penetrated Willow's haze. "The mistress needs you."

The bell from the front parlor had clanged two times in the last few minutes. But Willow had wanted to finish washing the last of the dishes, had hoped to do so quickly and then respond to Mrs. Mann who was hosting a visitor, the wife of the gentleman who had come calling upon Mr. Mann.

Willow thrust her hand back into the greasy water, now lukewarm, and scrubbed at the blackened remains of fish that were stuck to the bottom of the pan.

Lum stood at the center worktable of the kitchen and was rolling out dough and forming it into rolls. As the only house servant the Manns had been able to keep, Lum had been doing everything—the cooking, cleaning, laundering, chauffeuring, gardening, and more.

Even though Lum seemed to be a capable middle-aged man, such responsibilities were too much for one person, and Willow was glad that she could relieve him of some of the household duties.

It's just that she had no inkling of what she was doing half of the time. And with each new undertaking, she felt like she was trying to understand and speak a foreign language.

As she lifted the pot from the standing sink, she began to tip the water out into the drain that carried the dirty water outside the kitchen into the backyard.

"No." Lum's sharp tone stopped her short. "Dump outside or you will clog sink."

Already the bottom of the sink was covered with the remains from the other pots, pans, and dishes she'd washed, and the water was backing up into the sink. "I'm afraid I may have already clogged it."

Lum's forehead creased with a frown as he tossed down the rolling pin. With angry slapping steps, he rounded his table and crossed to her.

She hefted the pot higher, but in the process, water sloshed over the side and splashed on the floor . . . just as Lum reached the sink.

His foot slid in the greasy mixture, and he flailed his arms in an attempt to catch his balance. But in doing so, he bumped the pot and loosened her hold.

In the next instant, the pot dropped from her hands, hit the floor, and sent the rest of the dirty water everywhere.

The momentum of Lum's hit and the cascade of water caused her to slip. She tried to grab on to the edge of the sink, but instead, her fingers closed around Lum's apron. Before she knew what was happening, she was flat on her back, and Lum was lying motionless beside her, staring up at the ceiling.

She tried to drag in a breath but only managed to wheeze. If only Caleb could see her now. He'd know what to do to calm her and restore her breathing.

Last night after she'd finally retired to her room, she'd been waiting for him, hoping he'd find her. But he hadn't tapped at her window until after she'd extinguished her lone candle and been almost asleep. Even though it had been late, he'd climbed through, and they'd whispered together on her bed for a long while, talking about White Swan Farm, the Manns, and the other people who worked there.

He'd been surprised that the Manns had a large herd of dairy cows and that White Swan was the main producer of milk and butter for not only Victoria but also for Nanaimo, a bustling coal mining town to the north on Vancouver Island. Apparently, Mr. Mann also boasted of being educated as a judge, but he wasn't practicing the profession.

Among the dozen or more copper bells hanging on the far kitchen wall, the one marked with a small sign that read "Parlor" rang for the third time. It clanged louder and longer, signaling Mrs. Mann's growing irritation.

"Stupid girl," Lum mumbled.

"I'm sorry, Lum." She scrambled to sit up, the back of her uniform now as wet as the front. Lum, too, was covered in dirty dishwater.

She reached for the towel hanging from the sink and dangled it out to Lum, only to have it drip steadily down upon his apron. Apparently, like everything else, the linen was soaked too.

He batted it away and pushed himself up. "Go see what the mistress wants."

Willow's lungs squeezed again, but she managed to rise to her feet.

With the bell still clanging in an unending demand, Willow crossed the kitchen to the back servants' stairway, a steep and narrow passageway that went to all the floors of the house, including the top dormer where she'd been given a small room.

Mrs. Mann had made it clear yesterday that the servants were never allowed to enter or exit through the main doors of the home, nor were they allowed to use the family's staircase. In fact, Willow wasn't supposed to wander about the home at her leisure, was only permitted to clean a room if the family wasn't present.

She climbed to the first floor and entered the butler's pantry where all the glassware, flatware, and silver were stored in floor-to-ceiling shelving units.

She prayed that she wouldn't get lost in the maze of rooms that led from one to another with very few connecting hallways. She crossed through the dining room with its long, polished table and matching chairs. She'd already helped Lum clear away food and dishes and tidy the room after the family finished eating, and now it stood in readiness for the evening meal.

The dining room branched into what was called the morning room, which also served as a small family parlor. It was just as lavishly decorated as every other room with stained glass windows, red velvet wallpaper, an assortment of red and gold settees and chairs, and even a plaster bust of a historical figure.

On the other side of the morning room, a dark paneled hallway with gilded mirrors lining both walls separated the parlor and Mr. Mann's large billiard room—or his *saloon*, as

Mrs. Mann contemptuously called it. A grand staircase circled up to the next floor that held the spacious bedrooms, one for Mr. Mann and a series of chambers for Mrs. Mann, including her own private sitting room. The nursery and other rooms for the children were at the back of the house, along with an adjacent chamber for the governess.

During the tour of the house yesterday, Mrs. Mann had introduced Willow to the governess, Miss Bentley, who had come on the *Tynemouth* last autumn. Reserved and genteel, the young woman had been fashionably attired, likely from among the wealthy middle class, and Mrs. Mann had spoken with her as though she were a part of the family and not a servant.

Of course, Mrs. Mann had done nothing but talk down to Willow from the moment they'd met outside the Marine Barracks. Although Willow had expected it—especially after the stories the other women had shared during their ship voyage—she had hoped for an amiable situation with a kind mistress.

So far, Mrs. Mann wasn't showing herself to be either amiable or kind.

Willow paused outside the parlor door, bent at the waist, and attempted to draw in a breath. But at the impatient huff from within, Willow straightened and entered the parlor.

Mrs. Mann was in the process of rising from her chair, her expression taut with consternation, likely for having been kept waiting. As her gaze swept over Willow, a startled gasp slipped from her lips.

Willow glanced down too late to discover her state of attire was worse than she'd realized. Her once-white apron was now a dirty gray and was covered in flecks of blackened food. One of her cuffs had come loose and dangled from her sleeve.

She reached up a hand to discover her cap was askew and half of her hair had fallen out and was now hanging in disarray.

"Oh my." Willow shifted the cap back into place only to have it slide down and this time come undone completely. As it fell, she tried to grab it, but her loose cuff got in the way, and she only managed to pull that off too.

Mrs. Mann glanced to her guest, a middle-aged woman who sat frozen to her chair. "I apologize, Mrs. Lazenby. Willow is new to our household and has never been in service before. She clearly has a great deal to learn about appropriate decorum."

"Clearly," Mrs. Lazenby responded.

Mrs. Mann was already crossing to Willow, her mouth set in a tight line and her nose flaring. Grabbing Willow's arm, she began to steer Willow toward the door. "This is completely uncalled for, Willow." Mrs. Mann's voice held a sharp edge. "I'll be docking a day's wages for this behavior."

A day's wages? For an accident? "That's not fair—"

Mrs. Mann pinched hard, cutting off Willow's complaint. "I'll not be coddling you, or you'll never improve."

Before Willow could defend herself, Mrs. Mann shoved her back into the hallway and wrinkled her nose. "Not only are you filthy but you stink. Go change quickly and then return for my instructions on how to serve tea, that is if you're actually able to follow my instructions. So far, you've proven yourself to be nothing but an incompetent nincompoop."

Incompetent nincompoop. Stupid. Willow stumbled down the hallway, needing to get away from Mrs. Mann, from Lum, and from all the memories swirling together and reminding her of how useless she was.

When she reached the servants' stairway, instead of

heading up to her room for her extra uniform, she pushed out the back door and raced across the yard, wanting to find Caleb, needing his reassurance that everything would work out.

She halted in the farmyard, the sky the same gray as yesterday but without the rain. A large fenced-in garden spread out across the back of the house, the soil now barren, a few weeds and stalks blowing in the wind.

Beyond the garden, the large barns and other outbuildings were farther inland, well away from the house so that only the faint hint of manure lingered in the air. Large areas of fenced-in rolling pastures surrounded the barns, and dozens of black-and-white dairy cows were grazing contentedly among tall grass.

Cleared farm fields spread out past the fenced-in grassland, the soil dark with yesterday's rain and awaiting the spring planting. The fields were hedged by thick forests that led to the hills and mountains.

Every time she stepped outside the back door and took in the view, she couldn't keep from pausing to breathe in the fresh air and admire the endless wilderness. If only she could have a place like this of her own, a place she could share with her dad and mum and sisters. She wanted them to experience all of this, especially her mum. She could only imagine her mum's reaction. The dear woman would probably fall to her knees weeping, overcome by the beauty.

"Oh mum." Tears pricked Willow's eyes, homesickness swelling sharply inside. She wanted to run to Caleb for comfort for that too.

Her steps veered in the direction of the barns to seek him out, but she made herself plop down in the grass. She let herself fall back, stretched her arms over her head, and drew in a deeper lungful.

Without her family or her new friends for support, Caleb was all she had left. But if she wasn't careful, he'd eventually get tired of her neediness. Maybe he'd realize she was too much of a burden. And then what if he decided to leave her or end their friendship?

She couldn't let that happen. She had to stop relying on him so much.

But even as she chastised herself to let go of him, she dug her fingers into the damp grass as if that could somehow help her cling to him for just a little bit longer.

Eleven

I f Willow didn't come soon, he was tromping into the house and dragging her out.

From the shadows of the barn, Caleb watched the kitchen door across the spacious yard between the house and the vegetable gardens.

His pulse was pounding harder with each passing moment that she didn't make an appearance. With the fall of evening and with the start of the supper hour, she would have a few minutes of freedom from her duties. And she needed that freedom. After the past three weeks of constant work from well before dawn until well after dusk, she was exhausted.

He could admit he was exhausted too, that his long hours were no different. At least with his chores in the barns and with the livestock, he didn't have someone constantly telling him what to do and nagging him about all the things he'd done wrong.

Not that Mr. Pidwell was easy to work for. The burly man with a mass of gray hair had immigrated from Scotland where he'd run a large farm—collecting rents from tenants, keeping records, buying and selling produce, planning crop rotations, overseeing the livestock, and more. Mr. Pidwell boasted about how much his workers had accomplished back in the *old days*, and he expected just as much from his current laborers, including Caleb.

So far, Caleb hadn't been able to complain about the pay. It wasn't as much as he'd hoped to make, and it wouldn't allow him or Willow to save as quickly as they'd wanted. But it was better than what they'd been making in the mills.

Except that work was unending, especially for Willow.

The back kitchen door of the main house opened a crack, and a moment later Willow slipped outside. She wore the uniform Mrs. Mann had given her—a black dress with a white apron over the top. The white head covering was required, too, and every strand of Willow's blond-red hair was tucked out of sight.

She quietly closed the door and began to stride toward the livestock barn—just as his note had directed.

The structure was spacious and warm, and it contained all the animals except the cows, which were housed in a separate neighboring barn, all four dozen of them.

On his first day, Mr. Pidwell had assigned Caleb twelve cows to milk just like the other fellows. But as the newest farmhand, he'd been given the most stubborn of the lot. Combined with the fact that he'd never touched a cow before much less milked one, Caleb had struggled to manage milking. The other fellows could empty an udder in fifteen minutes, sometimes less. Even so, the process for milking twelve cows took a couple of hours for the best of milkers.

For him? He'd finally started completing the task in three hours—three hours every morning and three each evening.

Two other men were in charge of the butter-making, which, along with the milk, was one of the main productions of the farm.

When the cows were finally put out to pasture, there was still work to do like mucking stalls, filling water troughs, tending the other livestock, fixing fences, sharpening tools, and a dozen other jobs.

Today, they'd spent hours in a northern part of the farm cutting down trees. With spring planting only weeks away, Mr. Pidwell was anxious to get more of the land cleared, especially because Mr. Mann wanted to start growing hops so that he could invest in his own brewery.

Caleb had only seen Mr. Mann a handful of times. With his long sideburns and slicked back hair, the gentleman was a dandy and spent most of his time entertaining visitors to White Swan. Apparently he had a billiard room in the house where he hosted his callers and gambled until the early hours of the morning.

The other farmhands gossiped about how Mr. Mann could grow threatening, even violent, when he'd been drinking too much.

Caleb hadn't liked the news and had warned Willow to stay away from the man, especially at night. Even though Willow had assured him that Mr. Mann and his guests never bothered her, Caleb still worried, couldn't help himself, not after growing up in a violent home and knowing how volatile things could get.

As Willow neared the barn door, Caleb stepped out of the shadows and showed himself.

At the sight of him, her eyes lit, and she hurried her pace. In spite of the dark circles and the paleness that had returned to her face, she was as beautiful as always. Unfortunately, the other farmhands had noticed her, too, and wouldn't stop talking about her and taking bets on who would win her first.

Even that afternoon, when they'd been clearing trees, the talk had circled back to Willow and how pretty she was. The fellows had started comparing who had garnered the most of her attention.

Caleb had wanted to scoff at their excitement over getting a raised brow from her or even a smile. He'd had the urge to obliterate their hopes by boasting that he was sneaking into her room every night after dark, sitting on her bed, and sharing about their days until they couldn't hold back their yawns.

But he'd restrained himself, knowing the fellows would assume a whole lot more than talking was taking place. Not only that, but they would think Willow was a loose woman and might take liberties with her that would only enrage him.

For now, he'd resigned himself to keeping his friendship with Willow a secret, contenting himself with the knowledge that he was the only man she cared about.

She stepped inside the barn, the lantern by the door casting a warm glow over her and bringing her to life so that he wanted to pull her against him and just hold her.

She flapped his hastily scrawled note in his face, the one he'd written instructing her to meet him in the barn during the supper hour. "What's so important that you couldn't wait until tonight?"

"Follow me." He started down one of the side aisles that led to an area at the back of the barn where most of the hens roosted.

"What is it?" She trailed after him, and though she tried to make herself sound exasperated, her voice held a note of excitement.

"You'll see."

"Another foal?"

He'd called her into the barn earlier in the week to show her the foal that had been born. He'd known she would love seeing the creature, and she had. She'd adored it.

Even though the work was demanding for both of them, at least there was so much beauty, not only with the animals and the farm, but with the surrounding countryside. Every time he was able to explore more of the farm, like he had today during their tree-chopping expedition, he was all the more grateful he'd come to the colony.

The forested hills, the distant mountain peaks, the perfectly blue water, the scattering of islands covered in thick growth—he would never tire of looking at the land. And he hoped he'd have the rest of his days to live in the colony, that eventually he'd have his own place in the wilderness.

"Tell me." Her hand pressed into his lower back.

"Close your eyes."

She did as he instructed, used to his surprises. As he took both of her hands and guided her forward, she nibbled at her bottom lip, trying to bite back a smile. But as usual, the sight of her nibbling only made him want to stare at her lips.

He swallowed the desire that so easily surfaced, and he focused instead on the fenced-in area ahead and the lanterns hanging above it to provide much needed warmth.

As he drew her to a halt at the makeshift pen he'd created earlier, he wanted to keep on holding her hands, but he'd never lingered in touching her, and he couldn't start now.

"Okay." He released her and took a step away. "You can open your eyes."

Her long lashes fluttered up, revealing the bright blue he

loved. She looked at him and then glanced around before finally dropping her sights to the pen.

"Oh my." Delight spread across her features and rounded her eyes as she took in the fluffy bundles of pale yellow—some walking around and pecking at the ground and others resting.

"Chicks. A day old."

"Only one day?" She lowered herself until she was kneeling next to the pen.

He crouched beside her. "Most hatched last night."

As she watched them, she seemed to be holding her breath. "They're adorable."

He lowered a hand and stroked one of the chicks.

She reached into the pen but hesitated.

"Go ahead. They won't hurt you."

"And I won't hurt them?"

"They're tough little creatures."

She gently stroked one with a single finger then laughed with pleasure.

Her laugh, as always, went straight to his heart, warming his insides and spreading through his blood. He needed to give her more of these kinds of moments—simple yet enjoyable—that made the rest of the long hard days more bearable. Surely he could figure out more ways to bring her joy. After all, they'd come to the colony with the hope of a better life, not one where they worked all the time.

Of course, they'd had a half day off on Sunday to attend church, and they'd ridden by boat with some of the other workers into Victoria. Willow had spent most of the time with her friends, and they'd returned to White Swan all too soon.

Within moments, she was stroking all the chicks and even

picking up the ones that would let her. Her smile was the happiest since she'd said goodbye to her family.

At the call of his name in the yard outside the barn, he froze.

She grew suddenly still and silent too, watching him intently.

"Mr. Pidwell," he whispered. "Probably wondering why I stopped my milking."

"You should go." She pushed herself up.

He wasn't ready for their time to end yet, wanted to give her a few more minutes with the baby chicks. She deserved it and so did he.

"Caleb?" The call came again, this time closer to the barn.

He surveyed the dark corners, his gaze locking in on a fresh pile of hay that had been dumped into the haymow from the loft above.

"Let's hide." He stood and took a step toward the pile.

She grabbed his arm and stopped him. "You can't be serious."

"Very serious." He slipped his hand over hers and tugged her with him.

"I don't want you to get in trouble."

"I won't."

"You might."

He shrugged, and as he reached the hay, he dragged her down with him into the middle of the pile.

She released a soft laugh, one that told him she was enjoying this moment too.

He burrowed further and then began to pile hay on top of them. She helped, and within seconds they were thoroughly covered. He suspected that if Mr. Pidwell looked closely enough at the pile of hay, he might see a spot of color or the outline of one of their bodies.

But Caleb doubted Mr. Pidwell would pay attention to the hay in the corner, not with the chicks distracting him.

Beside him, Willow settled back. "You're too much sometimes," she whispered. "You do know that, don't you?"

"You love it." He bumped her shoulder lightly.

"Maybe. But if you get fired, I'll be very angry at you." She laid a hand on his arm, and at her familiar touch, he released the tension in his chest and let himself relax beside her. The hay was tickling his face, but he didn't mind, as long as he got a few extra moments with her.

"If I lose my job, I'll go get some free land on Salt Spring Island near Jonas." Caleb had helped carry the crates of milk and butter down to Isaac Sayles's steamboat every day. He'd learned that although Isaac's mind worked a bit slower than most people's, the man more than made up for the deficit with his kindness.

Jonas was a good man too, patient with Isaac in a way Caleb never could be. Jonas, as it turned out, was also a walking newspaper. He knew everything there was to know about Vancouver Island, probably because he spent his days steaming up and down the island's eastern coastline. No doubt he heard plenty of gossip and news as he picked up produce from the farms and then delivered it to stores and markets.

Just yesterday, Jonas had informed him about the farm on Salt Spring Island that he and his brother lived on but hadn't paid for yet. The governor was allowing people to claim land and settle on the island through a pre-emption system with the understanding that eventually they would need to pay the going rate for the land.

"It's not exactly free," Willow whispered back, having listened to him go on about Salt Spring Island last night when they'd talked in her room.

"It's freer than anything we could ever have in England."

"True enough."

"Your mum and dad could have their own farm there."

Her hand on his arm tightened. "Wouldn't that be wonderful, Caleb? Just think about it."

"I have been." Ever since Jonas had told him about the pre-emption, he hadn't been able to stop thinking about it.

She leaned her head against his arm, likely to give him another squeeze. But at Mr. Pidwell calling his name, this time inside the barn, she grew motionless, her body practically pressed to his side.

Of course every inch of him was aware of every inch of her—the brush of her head near his cheek, her arm against his, even her thigh flush to his. She was warm and soft and smelled faintly like lemon cleaning oil.

He could hear Mr. Pidwell opening and closing stall doors and calling his name. But with Willow so near, nothing else mattered. This was what he wanted every day, to be near her. But he could admit he wanted more. He wanted to touch her—skim his hands over her arms, run his fingers through her hair, glide his thumbs across her lips.

In fact, with every passing moment, his muscles were growing tenser with his need—a need he'd denied for years, a need that was getting harder to resist, a need that demanded action.

Before he could stop himself, he slid his hand over hers where she was gripping his arm, and he gently squeezed her fingers.

She immediately squeezed back, probably thinking he was reassuring her and was attempting to do the same in response.

Except that wasn't what he was doing. She should know by now that he wasn't afraid of Mr. Pidwell or getting caught. He didn't care about those kinds of things.

The truth was, he was touching her because he wanted to and was tired of restraining himself.

He skated his fingers across the back of her hand, then shifted to her wrist. He trailed one finger slowly along the swell of her vein.

She drew in a soft breath and held herself absolutely still. Was she doing so because of his touch? Did he have the power to affect her more than he'd realized?

Maybe it was time he found out.

He slipped his finger under her cuff then made a circle over her skin—skin that was velvety . . . and addictive.

She didn't move, didn't breathe, and didn't offer any protest. That had to mean something, didn't it?

Now that he'd been bold enough to explore her wrist, he wanted to let his fingers blaze a trail in other places. Preferably up her arm. But what if he pushed up her cuff and sleeve and caressed her forearm only to have her pull away?

For now, he'd have to be content with just her hand.

Without giving himself all the reasons why he should refrain as he usually did, he shifted his fingers down to hers. This time he glided all of his fingers along all of hers, slipping them through hers, and in the process, pushing hers apart.

She sucked in another breath, this one shorter.

The burst of heat in his gut was only one thing—desire. And it made him braver so that he delved deeper, almost intertwining his fingers with hers.

She didn't resist him. Instead, she seemed to be waiting, as if she wasn't sure what to expect next.

What should he do? Did he need to pull away, jest with her, and ease the tension?

He shifted his hand backward, let each of his fingers lightly graze hers again.

But he couldn't make himself pull away altogether. He was too far invested in the moment to stop now. Need was pulsing through him, each spurt harder than the last.

He trailed his thumb up the back of her hand, tracing first one tendon and then another.

Her hand trembled just slightly. What did the tremble mean? If only he could see her expression. But under the hay and in the dark, it was impossible to tell if he was frightening her or not.

She shifted just slightly. For a second, he was certain she was putting some distance between them. But in the next instant, she seemed closer, her warm breath near his cheek.

His heartbeat raced faster.

Yes, she'd definitely changed positions so that her chest was pressed more fully against his arm.

Saints have mercy upon his poor soul. He'd tried not to allow himself to dwell on her womanly figure, tried not to think about her curves, tried not to fantasize about her body, but in this moment, all he could think about was her soft flesh molding to him.

He forced his thoughts away from her body fitting with his and turned his attention to her mouth near his cheek. Near enough that if he turned, he could brush her lips with his. Her full, rounded, and perfect lips. That plump bottom lip that she often nibbled.

He bit back a rising groan. Kissing her would be too

much, would cross every boundary he'd set into place. And there would be no going back from a kiss.

Another exhalation caressed his face, tantalizing him more than was endurable for any one human.

Heaven help him.

He couldn't kiss her, and yet a part of him knew it was inevitable.

Twelve

What was happening between her and Caleb?

Willow could hardly focus on anything but his fingers gently touching hers. One might even say that he was doing more than touching. One could even conclude that he was caressing her hand. Intentionally. Not even accidentally.

Maybe he was doing so absentmindedly as they waited for Mr. Pidwell to stop searching the barn. Maybe he was just trying to reassure her—no, distract her—so that she'd remain quiet.

Or maybe he'd gone without womanly contact for so long that he was having a difficult time refraining, and since she was here and available, he was simply acting like a man with needs.

Whatever the case, his calloused fingers were wreaking havoc with her insides. And somehow, she'd ended up sitting close enough to him that she was practically in his lap.

He didn't seem to mind the proximity. At the very least, he hadn't scooted away or pushed her back. He was still holding her hand. Or was he?

Just because his fingers were slipping through hers languidly didn't mean he was holding her hand. And just because each touch of his fingers had a strange power to spark her every nerve and set them on fire didn't mean he was on fire too.

She was more than on fire. Her insides were an inferno, and she had the unholy urge to flatten Caleb in the hay and lay down on top of him. The very idea sent even more heat mixed with embarrassment through her.

What was wrong with her tonight? And why was she thinking so wantonly? It was a good thing Caleb couldn't see inside her head.

She drew in a breath, needing to say something, to at the very least give him the chance to escape from her. But before she could speak, it was his turn to shift. Just his head. But it was enough that she could now feel his exhalations on her mouth. Were they growing more ragged by the second? And faster?

Her nose grazed his jaw and the layer of scruff there. Oh my. The rugged scrape, the hard clench, the manly shape. She let her nose brush him again. This was something she could do every day all day.

His fingers slipped through hers, this time pushing deeper, and grasping her more firmly.

"Caleb?" The voice came from a dozen paces away.

Startled, Willow pulled back. Through the hay, she could see the tall Scottish bailiff with his puffy gray head of hair stepping into the haymow. His attention went straight to the chicks. He watched them for a few seconds before sighing and ambling off.

Willow didn't dare move, not until the squeak of the barn

door opening and then closing signaled his departure. She couldn't wait a second longer in the hay beside Caleb. She had to get away from him, had already overstepped the boundaries between them by allowing her thoughts to get off track.

She scrambled forward, letting the hay fall away. She was on her feet in an instant, shaking the hay from her uniform.

Caleb didn't move. In fact, he relaxed into the hay, crossed his arms behind his head, and watched her through half-lidded eyes.

She could barely make out the darkness of his eyes, but the murkiness was enough to fan the heat that was still burning inside her.

Why was she letting him have this kind of effect on her? She had to put an end to this before she made a mistake that would push him away.

She straightened her lacy cap. "I have to get back to the house."

He didn't respond except to watch her as she brushed the remaining specks of hay from her apron and bodice. His silence was nothing new. But there was something different in his mood, something she couldn't name. Or was she merely imagining things based on her own strange feelings?

Maybe it would be for the best if she addressed what had just happened between them. She didn't want to ruin what they had. She would assure him that she'd simply gotten caught up in the moment. And so had he. Any sparks that had flared between them were only fleeting.

Besides, what if he hadn't felt anything? What if she'd only imagined that he was reacting? What if his gentle touches had been given as a friend and nothing more?

She crossed to the chicks, bent, and brushed one of their fluffy backs. "Thank you for showing me the chicks." She somehow managed to keep her voice from wobbling.

With his legs stretched out and crossed at the ankles and his broad chest straining against his shirt, she couldn't keep from taking a second look at him, her gaze roving over him until reaching his chiseled face with all its sharp angles and scars. The almost arrogant lift of his mouth made him all the more handsome.

Why did he have to be so good-looking?

"What's wrong?" he asked, flexing his arms as he did from time to time when he knew people were admiring him.

Well, she wasn't about to join the line of people who gawked at him for how he looked. He never had any trouble garnering admirers and didn't need her too.

Instead, she couldn't forget that they'd weathered many storms together because they were friends—best friends. It didn't matter that a little heat in her stomach had been fanned to life. That was bound to happen from time to time, wasn't it?

"Nothing is wrong with me." She tried to keep her tone cheerful. "How about you?"

"I'm fine." His tone didn't hint at any inner turmoil or confusion.

That didn't mean she couldn't pry just a little. "Are you happy with our friendship?" She hadn't ever mastered the art of being subtle.

He opened his mouth to answer, then closed it.

A whisper of worry shimmied up her backbone. He clearly had something to say and didn't want to hurt her. "Just tell me the truth, Caleb."

He sat up, the casualness of his pose gone, his body tight with seriousness. "Things will need to change eventually."

"Change? How?"

He dug his hand absently into the hay, silent for a few heartbeats before responding. "We aren't children anymore."

"I realize that."

"We can't act like it forever."

"So you're saying I'm acting like a child?"

"No, but we have to grow up and get on with our lives."

"Can't we do that and still remain friends?"

He released an almost frustrated sigh and dropped his head, as though weary.

"Are you tired of being friends with me, Caleb?" She couldn't keep a twinge of panic from her question—the panic that had been rising with each passing moment. She couldn't lose him. But a part of her—the deepest, most honest part— had always been afraid that one day she'd finally do something to push him away for good.

Was today that day? Had she gotten carried away with her attraction in the hay and in doing so made him question their friendship?

"Are you?" she asked again.

He lifted his face, and the indecision warring on his features reflected his answer.

She pressed a hand to her mouth to hold back a cry of despair, and swift tears heated the backs of her eyes.

"It's not like that, Willow." He climbed to his feet and started toward her.

"No." She held up a hand to stop him from coming nearer. "You don't want to be friends anymore."

"Of course I still want to be friends." He halted half a

dozen paces away and jabbed his fingers into his hair. "But at some point, I need more."

"What do you mean *more*?"

"More than just friendship." His dark eyes were almost black.

She studied him, trying to understand what he was saying, but her desperation was too keen and her need for him too strong. She loathed that about herself, wished she could just walk away from him. But during those two times in the past, when he'd grown distant and cold and she thought he was ending their friendship, she hadn't been able to stop being friends with him, even then.

So what did he want now? What did he mean by wanting more than friendship? She threw up her hands at the only thing she could think of. "Are you trying to tell me that you need a woman to warm your bed?"

"No!" He scrubbed a hand over his face, then lowered his voice. "No. That's not it."

She almost rolled her eyes at his denial.

"I'm wanting more than just casual relationships."

"Like what? You've always said you don't want a wife."

He studied her in return, as though he was looking for answers in her face. "Maybe I'm changing my mind."

"Are you?"

He hesitated.

"If you are, then I'll help you find someone . . . as long as you assure me that you won't stop being my friend."

"Blast it all, Willow." His tone was loaded with emotion she didn't understand, emotion she'd never heard there before.

She should have left the barn, shouldn't have pried into

what happened in the hay pile. "I'm sorry for even bringing this up."

"It's probably past time . . ." He drew in a breath as if gathering the courage to say more.

"I just don't want anything to change between us." The words came out hoarse with her earnestness. "Please." She didn't care that she was begging him or that she was nearly crying.

He stood silently, stiffly for several long moments. Finally his shoulders sagged. "Fine."

"Promise nothing will change?"

"I promise."

"Thank you." She tried to catch his eyes, wanted to assure herself that everything would return to normal between them.

But he just folded his arms and stared at the chicks.

"I better go." She twisted around to leave, but then paused. "You're not mad at me, are you?"

"No, of course not." His tone held an edge.

She waited another second, hoping he'd at least give her a nod, one that would assure her he was all right. But he didn't look up.

As she made her way through the barn, she had the sinking feeling that for all Caleb's reassurances, their friendship wouldn't be the same ever again.

Caleb perched on the one-legged stool beside Bully, his fingers working the teats in the rhythmic pulling and squeezing motion that he'd begun to perfect. The soft squishing into the pail filled the silence along with the crunching of ground corn as the cow stood contentedly eating while Caleb drained her udder of the last drops, the richest of the milk that made the cream.

Even though he was in a hurry to complete the nightly milking since the others had finished while he'd been with Willow, he knew he couldn't rush. Mr. Pidwell had warned him enough times that if the cow wasn't thoroughly milked out every time, she'd soon dry up.

Bully shifted and swished her tail, the coarse hair slapping at Caleb as if to remind him that she was still irritated he'd made her wait so long. Not only had the cows been disgruntled, but Mr. Pidwell had been too.

When Caleb had shouldered his way inside past Mr. Pidwell, the older man had followed after Caleb, scolding him in his thick Scottish brogue and warning him that he wouldn't tolerate any more obstinance.

Caleb had been so frustrated with himself and with Willow, that he'd almost spun around and walked away from Mr. Pidwell and White Swan Farm. He'd wanted to shout that he didn't need the work, didn't care about the farm, and didn't want Willow.

Only a thin thread of reasoning had held him in place— the fact that if he acted rashly tonight and quit, he'd end up regretting it in the morning. Because the truth was, as much as he might try to convince himself that he didn't want Willow, he did. And he'd never be able to walk away from her.

He heaved a sigh and let his head rest against Bully's flank, having grown accustomed to the strong scent of cow and hay and dung that permeated the humid barn air.

Bully paused in her chewing, released a soft snort, then snuffled in another mouthful of dried corn. While the other laborers claimed Bully had earned her name because of how mean she was—particularly to the other cows—Caleb had only ever sensed tenderness from the creature.

"I made a mess of things," he whispered, as if she could understand him.

The lantern hanging on a beam outside the stalls was hardly enough to see what he was doing. But thankfully, now that the milking was becoming more automatic, he didn't need as much light.

And tonight, he wanted to hide in the shadows, wasn't in the mood to talk to any of the other men. Not that he was ever in a mood to talk to them. But with how discouraged he felt after the discussion with Willow, he didn't want to see anyone. He might even bed down in the loft in the other livestock barn just so that he could be alone.

The others bunked in log cabins behind the barns, and he'd been given one of the beds. Compared to the roof tops, streets, and filthy patch of floor he'd slept on at his sister's home, the cabin was the best home he'd ever had, even if it did stink of dirty socks and sweat-stained shirts.

He also couldn't complain about the food. The Chinese cook provided the farmhands with three meals a day, and they ate in the bigger of the two cabins, the one outfitted with a table and chairs. Though the fare was simple, it was still better than anything he'd eaten in Manchester in a long time, if ever.

No, he couldn't leave his new job. Not yet. But he had to give himself a break from Willow.

How had a conversation ever gone so wrong?

He released a low groan, and his hands grew idle. All he'd wanted to do was tell Willow that he longed for more from her than friendship. He'd hoped his caressing in the hay would show her that he cared.

Since she hadn't seemed to get the message, he'd hoped she'd take his hints in their conversation afterward that he cared about her.

But he'd botched it all. Somehow he'd made her believe that what he was feeling was lust, that he was craving a woman in his bed. To make matters worse, he'd been trying to explain that he wanted their relationship to change, but in the process, he'd done a terrible job assuring Willow that he still wanted to be friends with her.

He'd never stop valuing their friendship. And if that's all she'd ever be willing to give him, he'd take it. But he thought he'd sensed some interest when they'd been hiding in the hay, and he'd allowed himself to think that she might be able to see him as more than just a friend eventually.

Bully released another snort, and Caleb began tugging again, the spray of milk weaker and not as musical.

"She panicked," he whispered to the cow. "I could see it in her face and hear it in her voice."

As it was, if he didn't take a break from her, he was liable to pick right up where he left off and find more ways to touch her and initiate contact. And that would only frighten her and send her running from him again.

What had he been thinking anyway? He'd never seriously considered taking a wife before. When she'd asked, he'd told her that he'd changed his mind. But why?

Why was he letting his resolve weaken?

He sat up straighter. "That's what I need to do, Bully. I need to make sure my resolve is back in place before I see her again."

He'd remained strong for so many years, resisted his urges, kept himself under tight control. Just because he'd had an intimate moment in the hay with her didn't mean he was ready to throw aside all caution and consider taking a wife.

He didn't want to get married.

Even as he forced the words through his head, the echo of what he'd told Willow resounded loudly. What if he really was changing his mind? Was that so wrong of him?

Thirteen

ᑲᕐᑲᒧ

Four days. Caleb had avoided her for four days.

Willow's hand shook as she scooped up cinders from the ash pan. She tried to hold the shovel steady as she dumped the residue into the pail beside her, but even under the best of circumstances, she hadn't mastered the task of cleaning out the stove, much less today when she was an emotional wreck over Caleb's absence.

Some of the ashes fell onto the white marble hearth of Mrs. Mann's bedroom.

With a sideways glance toward the sitting room, Willow prayed Mrs. Mann wouldn't be able to see her from her spot at her desk where she was writing letters.

Bracing the shovel across the pail, Willow used the hem of her uniform to hurriedly wipe the ashes, but her efforts only caused dark streaks. The last rays of the setting sun slanted through the long windows and past the draperies as if to highlight her ineptness.

With a huff, Willow sat back on her heels, her attention drawn to the window and the hills to the west, where the sunset was turning the tops of the pine trees to silver and the dry meadow grass to gold. As beautiful and inspiring as the scenery was, she wasn't admiring the landscape tonight. She couldn't. Not when her heart was breaking. Not when she was looking for Caleb. Just as she had been every time she was near a window.

Hadn't she learned her lesson years ago not to pressure him? Why had she tried it again?

She rubbed at the ash streaks again, the stain only darkening, as if her efforts were only spreading the ashes instead of removing them. Even as she did so, fresh tears spilled over onto her cheeks. She'd tried not to cry, tried to tell herself that this separation from him would help her be stronger.

But nothing helped. She missed him so much that she ached.

"Oh Caleb." She paused and swiped at her cheeks, not caring that she was probably adding ashes to her face now too. "I'm sorry. I promise I won't ever question our friendship again. And I promise I'll be the perfect friend."

But even if he came to her room tonight and they tried to pick up their friendship where they'd left off, she wasn't sure she could ever forget their conversation and the fact that he'd admitted he was tired of their friendship.

In the future, every time they were together, she'd think about that and wonder if he really wanted to be with her or whether he was wishing he was with a different woman—one he could marry.

She hadn't realized he was ready for marriage. After his impassioned declarations that he never wanted to get married because he was too afraid of becoming like his father, she hadn't expected him to ever change his mind.

But perhaps after having more life experiences and maturing, he was realizing he didn't have to reject marriage because of his past and because of his parents, and he could instead continue down the path of being different from his family.

Whatever the case was, he was right. They weren't children anymore. And if he was ready to have a wife, she didn't want to stand in his way.

She picked up the shovel and slid it back into the coal stove. It was one of her many evening duties, one that Mrs. Mann reminded her to do so that the bed chamber was warm in time for the nightly bath.

Willow lifted the shovel out again and then carefully swiveled the heap toward the pail.

Caleb had said he wanted more than friendship and more than casual relationships. But he hadn't wanted more from *her*, had he?

The question had nagged her often over the past few days. Surely he'd been talking in generalities about all women, had been craving a woman the way he had in the past.

But what if he'd been alluding to her? After the way he'd touched her hand . . .

In an instant, she was back under the hay beside him, the hard length of his body against hers, his hand covering the one she'd laid upon his arm, and his fingers sliding through hers, caressing in a way that went way beyond the bounds of friendship.

In fact, just the thought of his fingers mingling with hers sent a flutter of warmth into her stomach, a flutter that made her hand tremble with a strange need.

More ashes tumbled from the shovel, and this time landed

upon the plush Oriental rug that filled the center of the bed chamber.

"Willow?" came Mrs. Mann's sharp call.

Willow stared for a moment at the mess of darkened soot that contrasted the pale pinks and creams of the rug. Then she began frantically trying to remove the ashes, but as before, only spread them further.

The tap of footsteps across Mrs. Mann's sitting room drew closer, and Willow worked faster.

At the swish of Mrs. Mann's skirt as she stepped into the room, Willow shifted her body so that she was blocking the mess. But Mrs. Mann crossed the room until she was standing directly above Willow.

"Oh for heaven's sake. Stop." Mrs. Mann's tone was filled with her usual irritation. "You're just making matters worse."

Willow stood and inwardly agreed. "I'm sorry, ma'am. I'll get it clean. I promise."

Already attired in her evening gown, Mrs. Mann looked lovely in the yellow silk taffeta, the skirt made of wide pleats and worn over crinoline to give it a bell shape. Willow had helped her change into the dress a short while ago and had also coiled her hair into the tight chignon she always wore, with a headpiece of dried baby's breath.

At least Willow was getting better at assisting Mrs. Mann with her garments and hair.

If only she could finally learn all there was to know about the thousand and one other tasks she was asked to do every day.

Mrs. Mann released an impatient huff. "You'll need to roll it up, haul it outside, and give it a beating."

"I will, ma'am." Willow gave the curtsy Mrs. Mann expected. "I'll do it first thing in the morning."

"You'll do it this instant." Mrs. Mann swiveled and started toward the doorway that led to the nursery where the governess was likely doing everything perfectly and never having any trouble with her duties in taking care of the children who were so well-behaved that Willow rarely heard them.

Willow scanned the rug. "It's too big for me to clean alone, ma'am. I'll wait for Lum's help tomorrow."

"You must do it tonight." Mrs. Mann didn't bother to turn as she breezed from the room. "If you don't learn from your mistakes, you'll never stop being so clumsy." A moment later Mrs. Mann greeted her children in a singsong voice.

Willow stood motionless, the ache in her chest only growing.

Did she have anyone who really cared about her? She no longer had her family. Caleb was mad at her. Her friends were busy with their new jobs in Victoria. And here she was, lonely and tired and a failure as a domestic.

For long minutes she could only stare out the window, the bleakness of her life spreading out before her, especially the bleakness of a life without Caleb in it.

As the voices began to draw near, Willow bent and started to roll the rug. She had no choice but to drag the carpet outside, hang it, and beat it as Mrs. Mann had instructed.

Willow had learned her first few days that she had no rights, that she was expected to do whatever was demanded of her. For as much as she wanted to complain, every time she was tempted, she thought of her family, then closed her mouth. She was doing this for them. And she couldn't forget it.

Huffing and heaving, she managed to roll the rug, drag it

down the stairs, and tow it through the hallway toward the servants' entrance.

A rapping upon the front door halted her. She dropped the rug, wiped the perspiration from her brow, and then hurried to answer before Mrs. Mann scolded her for delaying.

As she swung the door open, the smiling, round face of Isaac Sayles met her. She'd greeted him earlier in the day—as she did most days—when he came up to the house after docking his steamer at the pier.

Still attired in a tight brown coat over a white waist coat with stripes of bright blue and breeches of equally bright red, he beamed at her with squinting eyes. "Hello, new maid Willow. I have a pretty new hat for Mrs. Mann." He held up the circular box as if Willow needed proof.

She didn't like that Mrs. Mann was constantly using Isaac as her delivery boy, having him run errands for her either in Nanaimo or Victoria, whichever was his destination for the day. Mrs. Mann almost always asked him to return later even if she could wait until he arrived the next day.

Willow also didn't like that Mrs. Mann never compensated Isaac for his efforts. She and Caleb had discussed the matter at length during their late-night conversations, and they'd both agreed that Mrs. Mann was taking advantage of Isaac's slow mind as well as his generous spirit. She and Caleb had tried to figure out ways they could stop her from using Isaac, but they hadn't come up with a solution yet.

And maybe they never would . . . not if Caleb didn't talk to her again.

Tears sprang to her eyes.

Isaac's ready smile vanished, and his forehead creased. "Why are you so sad, new maid Willow?"

She blinked rapidly, but at the concern radiating from his expression and his eyes, several tears slipped out.

"Oh no!" He carefully lowered the hatbox to the porch then dug in his coat pocket. "I don't want you to be sad. Tell me what I can do so that you aren't sad."

Although she'd gotten to know this kind man over the past month at White Swan, she didn't know him well enough yet to unburden her heart and reveal that Caleb was mad at her. And it wasn't the right time or place to do so either.

He fumbled around in his pocket before pulling out a handkerchief. "Here." He stretched out and wiped the tears from her cheeks.

His gentleness and concern only seemed to unleash more tears. Several more trickled out.

"Oh no!" he called again, tears shining in his eyes.

He clearly wasn't used to facing emotional women, and she had to stop crying before he burst into tears himself.

"I'm fine, Isaac." She forced a smile through trembling lips. "I'm sad because I miss my home and my family." It was part of the truth, the part she could reveal.

Isaac dabbed at another tear on her cheek. "Write and tell them to come here. They'll love this place as much as we all do."

"I have no doubt they will love it. But I have to save money first and then send it back to them for their passage. And that might take a while." She was afraid it would take forever with the low wages Mrs. Mann was paying her.

Isaac reached into his pocket again and drew out several banknotes. "I'll help."

She couldn't tell exactly how much money he was offering, but it wouldn't be enough—not even close. Besides, she couldn't take anything from Isaac and use him the way that Mrs. Mann was.

Behind her she could hear Mr. Mann exit from his billiard room into the hallway, still conversing with his gentleman caller. What would they think if they saw Isaac offering her money?

She closed his fingers around the money. "Thank you. You're a kind man, but I can't take any money from you. That wouldn't be right. Besides, I'll need much more than that."

With brows furrowing, he stuffed the banknotes back into his pocket. As he tucked the money away, his fingers wiggled around, then his face lit up and his eyes crinkled with a smile. "I know just what to do."

"You don't have to do anything, Isaac."

He withdrew a larger than average brass key and held it out to her. The heart-shaped bow was intricately engraved with a lion's head. Its expression was fierce, and its teeth bared, as though perhaps it was standing guard over something. "Take this." He spoke solemnly, caressing the key with his short fingers.

Mr. Mann and his friend had grown quiet and were watching her interaction with Isaac, making no effort to hide their eavesdropping.

She shook her head. "I couldn't—"

"It's for the treasure my brother buried."

"Treasure?"

"Yes. He found gold up in the mountains, and to keep it safe, he buried it."

She'd heard the tales of gold that had been discovered on the mainland. But she never knew whether to believe the stories. Most seemed far-fetched. Isaac's probably was too.

"Take the key." Isaac thrust it into her hand. "And next time I'm home in Nanaimo, I'll get the map for you."

She pushed the key back into his hand and then took a step away from him. A treasure of gold sounded like something out of a storybook. Even if there really was a chest buried some place, she'd never take it from Isaac.

Isaac's eyes radiated with earnestness. "I'm sure you'll find the treasure in no time. Then you'll have enough so that your family can come live here with you."

"You're so thoughtful, Isaac." She truly did appreciate his kindness in wanting to help her. He had generous intentions even if he believed a hidden treasure would solve all her problems. "But I can't—"

"Please, new maid Willow." Isaac's childlike voice was sincere.

She had to find a way to tell him no without hurting his feelings. "I don't think your brother would want you to give me his gold."

"Not to worry. My brother died."

"Oh." Was the death recent? Should she offer Isaac condolences?

"Good evening, Isaac." Mr. Mann stepped forward into the wide doorway beside her.

She almost breathed a sigh of relief at his intervention and offered him what she hoped was a smile of gratitude.

He smiled at her, as if to say he'd finish taking care of the matter. In his dark evening suit and with his thinning blond hair slicked back and sideburns neatly trimmed, he was the picture of a perfect gentleman. Willow rarely interacted with him, but whenever she did, he had impeccable manners and was always respectful toward her. If Caleb's warnings about

Mr. Mann's violent nature were true, she hadn't seen evidence of it.

"Hello, Mr. Mann." Isaac was still holding out the key. "I'm trying to help new maid Willow so that she's not sad anymore."

"That's thoughtful of you, Isaac." Mr. Mann eyed the key.

Isaac tucked it into his pocket, his rounded face flashing with guilt. "My brother warned me not to let anyone see the key."

"It's all right, Isaac." Mr. Mann clamped him on the shoulder companionably. "You know you can trust me."

"That I can, sir." Isaac's smile was back in place, crinkling his eyes again.

"Mr. Tammedge and I were just about to sit down to supper." Mr. Mann waved Isaac inside. "Since you're here, why don't you join us?"

"That's awfully nice." Isaac glanced past him to the guest waiting in the hallway.

Mr. Mann nodded at Willow, and she knew he was giving her permission to escape now that Isaac was distracted.

She backed away and hurried down the hallway toward the rug she'd abandoned. As she reached it and picked it up, Mr. Mann had an arm draped across Isaac's shoulder and was leading him toward the dining room.

Even though Isaac was a full-grown man, he was too trusting and gullible. Maybe his brother had once taken care of him, and maybe his partner Jonas also kept him from trouble.

But Isaac needed more supervision. In fact, if someone didn't look after him better, he would end up with nothing, maybe even hurt.

Thankfully Mr. Mann had so kindly stepped in tonight. Yet, somehow, she sensed it wasn't enough and wanted to talk to Mr. Mann about it further and see if they could do more to protect Isaac.

More than anything or anyone, she wanted to talk to Caleb. She wished she didn't need him so much, but she couldn't deny that she did.

Fourteen

A nother night had passed without Caleb seeking her
out to talk.

On her way down the servant stairway, Willow finished
pinning her lacy cap into place and at the same time
swallowed the lump in her throat that threatened to make
her cry.

She couldn't cry again. She'd already embarrassed herself
by shedding tears in front of Isaac last evening, and that had
been enough. Today, whether Caleb liked it or not, she would
find him, and they would have a conversation. She couldn't
give up on their friendship without fighting for it, could she?

As she stepped into the pantry and crossed into the
dining room, she shivered. She set her candle down and
rubbed her arms. If only a shawl was part of her uniform,
especially before dawn when the chill of the night lingered
throughout the house. But of course, Mrs. Mann considered
that sloppy, had already reprimanded Willow one morning
for wearing a covering for extra warmth.

At a burst of laughter coming from the front of the

house, Willow stopped short. Voices, men's voices and more laughter.

She wasn't the only one awake at the pre-dawn hour. Mr. Mann must have stayed up all night gambling and drinking with his guests. It wouldn't be the first time. She was learning it was a regular routine of Mr. Mann's at least a couple of times a week.

Willow shook her head as she knelt in front of the dining room hearth. It was an odd way to live. But she supposed the wealthy could afford to do whatever they wanted, spending their nights carousing and their days in idleness.

Sometimes, resentment settled into the crevices inside Willow's chest, resentment that people like Mr. and Mrs. Mann had to do so little and yet had so much, especially when there were people—like her family—who did everything they could to get by and still had nothing.

"You're awfully good at this game, Mr. Mann," came a childlike voice that sounded like Isaac's.

As she reached into the woodbin for a handful of kindling, she paused and craned her body to listen again.

"You'll get better." Mr. Mann's response was slightly slurred but noticeably cheerful. "You just need to practice more."

"You're right," Isaac responded just as cheerfully. "More practice. That's what it took to learn to pilot my steamboat."

Mr. Tammedge guffawed. "Yes, that's exactly what it takes to win at cards."

Willow dropped the wood shavings and stood. A strange foreboding nudged her out of the dining room and through the breakfast room into the hallway. Low lantern light spilled into the hallway from the open doorway of the billiard room.

"In order to give you more practice," Mr. Mann said

through a puff—likely his cigar, "you can come back and play again tomorrow night when you bring me the map."

Willow's heartbeat stuttered. What map? Surely not the map to the treasure that Isaac had mentioned last night.

"I don't know, Mr. Mann. I might need to sleep. I'm awfully tired."

The men chuckled as if Isaac had jested with them.

Had they kept Isaac up all night gambling? That was insensitive. Isaac couldn't slumber the day away the same way they could. He had important work to do.

But even as indignation filled her, the bigger question demanded an answer. What had Isaac lost whilst he'd played cards with Mr. Mann and his friend?

She wasn't sure she wanted the answer, although she suspected she already knew.

"Practice or not, Isaac," Mr. Mann said, "I won the map and the key fairly. I have the key, but I'll expect you to stop by sometime today to deliver the map."

She was right. Isaac had gambled his treasure.

Willow pressed a hand to her chest as if that could somehow stop it from racing faster. Why had Isaac given up his treasure? If it wasn't really gold or wasn't worth much, then he probably hadn't cared that he was losing it. Yet from the earnestness with which he'd offered her the treasure to help her family immigrate, maybe it did amount to something.

Why had Mr. Mann allowed Isaac to gamble at all? Mr. Mann knew Isaac was slow and simple and easily influenced. He'd even invited Isaac to dinner to keep him safe . . .

Safe? She nearly scoffed out loud. Asking a man like Isaac to gamble wasn't caring or kind. Isaac wouldn't know what to do or how to play. He'd be all too easily persuaded to bet things he shouldn't . . . like a treasure.

What if Mr. Mann had invited Isaac inside with ulterior motives? What if the mention of the treasure had sparked his interest so that he'd used dinner to gain more information about it? Then he'd likely easily persuaded Isaac to stay and join him for cards.

She wanted to shake her head, wanted to deny that Mr. Mann could do such a thing. But he'd taken poor Isaac's key already and intended to also take the map just as soon as he could. If Mr. Mann really cared about Isaac, why would he take advantage of Isaac like that?

As footsteps thudded out of the billiard room, she took a rapid step into the shadows of the hallway and flattened herself against the wall. She peeked sideways to see Isaac limping through the entryway toward the front door, his steps slower than usual. Because he was tired, sad at the outcome of the night, or both?

A moment later, Isaac exited the house and the front door closed behind him. Standing in the hallway just outside the billiard room, Mr. Tammedge slapped Mr. Mann on the back. "Well, that was an interesting night."

"I'd heard rumors about Paul Sayles finding gold." Mr. Mann's voice dropped low. "But no one knew what he did with it, and we all speculated he took that knowledge with him to the grave."

Willow tried to calm her heart so that Mr. Mann wouldn't realize she was hiding nearby.

"Lucky for me," Mr. Mann continued, "Paul passed that information on to his brother."

"Lucky?" the other man said with a yawn. "You'll have to find the treasure first."

"I'll find it." Mr. Mann headed back into the billiard room. "As soon as the spring thaw clears the way, I'll set out."

Mr. Tammedge followed and closed the door behind him, leaving the front hallway dark.

Willow pushed out of the shadows. She fisted her hands on her hips and stared at the door. That treasure wasn't Mr. Mann's to find, not after he'd swindled Isaac out of it.

Paul had probably wanted Isaac to have the treasure so that he would be well taken care of and never lack for anything. Even if Isaac was able to provide for himself through his steamboat transports, the treasure would help him be even more secure and safe.

The fact was, Isaac needed the treasure more than Mr. Mann. And even if he didn't, Isaac had more right to it than anyone else.

With indignation stiffening her spine, Willow spun on her heels and raced through the house to the back door. She let herself out quietly then sped across the backyard and around the house to the stone steps that led to the beach and piers.

Although the darkness of the night still lingered, a half-moon hung low in the sky over the water. The light illuminated the steamer rocking gently in the calm waves. Isaac was already at his steamer and was bending to loosen the ropes on the pier.

She wanted to call out his name. But at the bright light still glowing from the window in the billiard room, she decided that for now, secrecy was the best path forward, at least until she could figure out what to do next.

She hurried down the steps and across the beach. When she arrived at the pier, she whisper-shouted, "Isaac."

In the process of climbing onto his steamer, Isaac startled.

He spun and wobbled precariously, grabbing onto the railing and clinging to it with both hands.

"I'm sorry," she whispered as she started down the pier.

"New maid Willow?" His voice echoed too loudly in the silence of the early morning.

As she reached him, she helped him find secure footing on the pier. Once he was facing her, she grasped both his arms. "You can't give Mr. Mann the treasure."

"I can't?" His face scrunched with confusion.

"No. He's stealing it from you."

"Stealing?"

Maybe *stealing* was a harsh word. But she had to make Isaac understand that he'd been tricked. "Yes, Mr. Mann knew you couldn't play cards and knew he could beat you. But he convinced you to play against him anyway, so that he could have your treasure."

Isaac stared past Willow back at the house. "He said he won it fairly—"

"He didn't. He lied and cheated to get it from you."

"Oh no." Isaac's eyes rounded.

"Don't give him the map, Isaac."

"But he told me to bring it."

"It doesn't belong to him. It belongs to you."

"But what if he gets mad at me?"

"Maybe take a break from him, from coming here. Let Jonas do the deliveries for a while for you."

"What if he comes looking for me at my place in Nanaimo?"

"Can you live somewhere else?"

Isaac looked first at his boat and then at the harbor. "My brother built a cabin up in the Fraser River Valley near Hope. It's still there."

"You could stay there for a little while until Mr. Mann has the chance to see the error of his ways and realize he can't steal from you." *If* he was the sort of man who would see his errors.

Isaac nodded. "I'll go there today."

She squeezed his arms and then took several steps back. "Don't tell anyone else about the treasure, okay?"

"That's what my brother said before he died. He grabbed me tight and said not to tell a single soul about the key or the map."

Obviously Isaac hadn't heeded his brother's advice. If he'd shared the news of the treasure so easily with her, how many others had he inadvertently told? One thing was certain, the more people who knew, the more danger Isaac was putting himself into.

"When the spring thaw comes," she said, "you can go look for the treasure yourself. Once you find it, no one can take it from you."

Isaac nodded, and then with a worried glance at the house, he boarded his steamer.

As Willow made her way back into the house and hurried to start her chores, her thoughts were jumbled. What if she'd given Isaac the wrong advice? What if by withholding the map, he'd be in greater danger?

Should she ask Caleb about it? He'd surely know what to do.

When the first lanterns sprang to life in the barns, she wanted to rush over and pull him aside. Even though she'd told herself she would talk to him today about their friendship, a strange new hesitation held her back. Something had changed between them. She couldn't say what it was, but she'd known it from the moment she'd left him lying in the hay.

Throughout the morning, Willow tried to make herself go talk to Caleb. But every time she neared the back door, she turned around and started another of her chores.

As she finished dusting the parlor and stepped into the hallway, she sighed with exasperation at her cowardice. She couldn't put off confronting Caleb any longer.

She paused, fisted her hands on her hips, and drew in a steadying breath. Her sights strayed to Mr. Mann's billiard room across the hallway. It was the one room Lum cleaned upon Mrs. Mann's insistence that no woman belonged in a den of such iniquity.

From the half-filled glasses, overflowing ashtrays, and cards scattered on the table, it was clear Lum hadn't been in the room yet. Coins and cuff links also littered the table. And a single large key.

Willow's heartbeat crashed to a halt. Isaac's key to the treasure. The one Mr. Mann had swindled off him.

She glanced down the hallway toward the rooms at the back of the house. Mrs. Mann's voice resounded from the breakfast room where she was going over the menu with Lum. Light footsteps and laughter came from overhead—the children with the governess. Mr. Mann was asleep in his chamber, and his gentleman friend had retired to one of the guest rooms.

No one was around . . . And the key belonged to Isaac. Mr. Mann didn't have a right to it, not even a small one.

Squaring her shoulders, Willow marched into the billiard room directly to the table. She grabbed the key, slipped it in her skirt pocket, and then walked out of the room.

Even if Isaac didn't come back for a few weeks, she'd find

a way to return it to him. Maybe if Jonas stopped by, he'd be willing to track Isaac down. Or maybe someone trustworthy going to Nanaimo could give it to Isaac when he came back from the cabin.

Whatever the case, she wouldn't let Mr. Mann keep it. He'd probably be confused when he awoke and discovered it was missing. She could only hope he'd been inebriated enough last night and would blame himself for misplacing it. At the very least, maybe he'd be too embarrassed by his swindling of Isaac to make a mention of the missing key to anyone else.

No matter what happened, someone had to protect Isaac, and she intended to be that person.

Fifteen

C aleb's chest ached. And the ache was only growing more painful with every passing day that he avoided Willow.

He plodded, head down, behind the other laborers as they hiked back to the barns from the far northern field where they'd been chopping trees. They weren't used to quitting when they were making good progress on clearing the new field, especially on a sunny afternoon with almost balmy temperatures.

But when one of the laborers who churned the butter had ridden out and spoken in grave but urgent tones with Mr. Pidwell, they'd lowered their axes and waited for news. They hadn't expected Mr. Pidwell to instruct them to return to the farm, not when they had at least five hours of daylight left before needing to return for the evening milking.

Over the past weeks, Caleb had learned a lot about how to cut away the underbrush and where to chop into the tree trunks so that the tree fell in the most advantageous direction.

He'd also learned about the different types of wood they

dragged back to the harbor to be sold. Some was more suitable for constructing buildings and others, like the hardwoods, would be made into furniture.

They were burning most of the slashings while the land was still damp enough to prevent the fires from spreading. Eventually, the stumps would be burned out too, but according to Mr. Pidwell, that process was more complicated and took longer.

Caleb didn't mind the hard labor. It hadn't taken him long to become the best and fastest worker, felling the most trees every day. He'd earned the men's respect, including Mr. Pidwell's, for his single-minded work ethic and his strength.

Regardless of the admiration, he remained a loner and liked it better that way, especially because over the past few days he'd been angry, mostly at himself for letting his attraction to Willow turn him into a groveling weakling.

As the barns came into sight, he tipped the brim of his cap lower. Even though he wasn't sure how he could last another day staying away from her, he didn't want to glimpse her if she happened to be outside the house. The sight of her would undo him and break through the resolve he was trying to rebuild—the resolve to be satisfied with only friendship.

He'd maintained the friendship for years. He could do it again, couldn't he? Or was he changing too much to ever go back? Because even though he'd been in the colony shy of one month, he *was* changing. He was seeing all that was possible here, opportunities that had never been available to him in Manchester. He'd heard the other men talking about what could be theirs if they persevered, the tales of immigrants like himself who'd built fortunes and had become successful.

He didn't need a fortune. But he did know he wouldn't

be content forever working as a laborer on someone else's farm when he could have his own.

Maybe this new land was not only making him dream about having a life that was different from his father's, but it was also making him dream about having a marriage that was different too—marriage to Willow. Could he eventually become the kind of man she deserved? If he worked hard enough?

The problem was, he'd have to convince her to see him as more than just a friend. And his attempt at it the other day had failed. Instead, he'd ended up promising her that nothing would change between them—a promise he'd already broken by avoiding her this week.

He hated when he had to break a promise to her.

He hated even more that he'd probably hurt and confused her by his absence. Every night when he'd forced himself to lie in his bed instead of going to her room, he'd been reminded of another time when he'd done the same thing.

It had been the summer after his father had died, after he'd hugged Willow and realized how womanly she was becoming. He'd tried to stay away from her but hadn't been able to do so for more than a few days.

He'd battled his desires all summer after that.

One evening, when they'd been together on her roof, he'd been lying close beside her, and they'd been talking—he couldn't even remember about what.

But he did remember he'd been struggling against the urge to roll over onto his side and pull her into another embrace. He'd wanted to feel all her curves again, and he'd been imagining them all in ways he shouldn't have been.

He'd grown silent and unresponsive. She'd probably noticed. And as usual, she'd tried to comfort him. Most of the time she held his arm or touched his back. But that time, she'd reached for his hand, cupped it in hers, and squeezed it tightly. Then she'd quietly reassured him that she liked him.

Of course, his mind had immediately started to make more of the moment. He'd been young and lustful. And he'd wanted her. The need had been strong, but so had his respect for her and her family.

Instead of doing something he knew he'd come to regret, he'd left her lying there and hadn't looked back. He'd spent the next three days fighting and womanizing and giving in to every urge that he had. That had been the start of a downward spiral for a couple of years.

But she hadn't given up on their friendship. She'd stuck with him through his confusion and rebellion. She'd been loyal and understanding, but she also hadn't been afraid to confront him about how he was living.

It hadn't been until a fight had left him badly battered that death had become real, and he'd known he had to stop for her sake. Even though at that point he hadn't cared whether he lived or died, he hadn't wanted to leave her. So when she'd asked him to give up fighting again for the hundredth time, he'd finally agreed.

He'd given up the women and the drinking too. And over the past two years, he hadn't been tempted by any of it. He'd only been tempted by his desire for her . . . and since arriving in the colony, the temptation had only grown harder to resist.

He blew out a breath, and nearly hit the backside of one of the laborers in front of him as the others came to an abrupt halt.

Ahead, Mr. Pidwell released a soft slew of curses, his Scottish brogue growing more pronounced whenever he was upset.

"Wait here," he said as he started toward Mr. Mann.

Caleb couldn't keep his head down, was too curious. He stepped past the others and drew up short at the sight of Willow and Lum standing stiffly side by side in the farmyard with Mr. Mann stalking back and forth in front of them.

The gentleman was more disheveled than Caleb had ever seen him. He was not only hatless with rumpled hair, but he was devoid of a waistcoat and coat, his shirt tails untucked, and his trousers held up by only one suspender.

Mrs. Mann, the governess, and the two young daughters stood in the shade of the home, clearly having been called to be present as well. But for what? Why was Mr. Mann so upset?

Caleb's gaze couldn't stay off Willow for long. She was like a magnet, drawing his attention, and he couldn't resist looking at her any more than the sun could resist shining on the earth.

In her uniform, she had her hair pulled back as Mrs. Mann required. The severity of the hairstyle only highlighted Willow's high cheekbones, wide eyes, and full lips. Though the afternoon temperatures were above freezing and the wind was mild, her cheeks were still a rosy pink.

Why was she flushed?

A warning went off inside Caleb. Something wasn't right, and that something had to do with Willow. He'd put a bet on it.

At Mr. Pidwell's approach, Mr. Mann paused in his pacing. The gentleman's gaze darted immediately to the men, skating over each one of them as if he was searching for something important.

"Line your men up, Mr. Pidwell." Mr. Mann began crossing toward them with long strides, revealing that not only were his spats unbuckled, but he wasn't wearing any socks. "An important item of mine has been stolen, and I intend to discover who took it."

Willow called out after him, "Since you gambled and won the key from Isaac, then perhaps you are the one who stole it from him."

Mr. Mann's stride didn't falter at Willow's impertinence. But Caleb's stomach bottomed out. He didn't understand what was going on, but Willow was definitely upset. And Mr. Mann was too. If Willow wasn't careful, Mr. Mann would turn on her, maybe even make her his scapegoat.

Mr. Pidwell nodded at them, as though encouraging them to line up and cooperate as best they could. Obviously none of them had been around to take anything that belonged to Mr. Mann, so the questioning would be a huge waste of time.

When Mr. Mann halted in front of them, his appearance was even worse up close. His eyes were bloodshot, his face in need of a shave, and his white shirt wrinkled and stained. "Someone went into my billiard room today and took a key that I won."

Caleb's gaze slid back to Willow as he tried to process everything. Had Isaac really gambled with Mr. Mann last night? If so, a simpleton like Isaac wouldn't have a chance against an experienced card player like Mr. Mann. Had that been intentional? So that Mr. Mann could take the key away from Isaac?

Willow had turned her gaze upon him too. Her eyes held a wariness—and hurt—that had never been there before.

Blasted. He hadn't wanted to hurt her. But what had he expected by staying away without an explanation? He could have, at the very least, let her know he wasn't mad at her, that he merely needed time to think.

I'm sorry. He tried to project the words with his eyes and his expression.

Instead of acknowledging his silent communication, she pursed her lips and focused her attention back on Mr. Mann.

"The key must be returned immediately to my possession." Mr. Mann had begun studying each laborer's face.

What did he expect to see? Guilt?

Caleb almost scoffed, but something in Willow's expression halted him, and a chill shimmied over his skin. She had the key.

He wasn't sure how he knew, only that he did. And clearly the key was for something important, or Mr. Mann wouldn't be going to such great lengths to reclaim it.

"How could any of my men sneak in and steal from you," Mr. Pidwell groused from beside Mr. Mann, "when they've been out clearing trees all day?"

"One of them could have slipped in after the milking."

Mr. Pidwell shook his head. "Don't know why you're blaming my men when it had to have been one of your house servants."

"I've questioned everyone in the house extensively, and I went through all of their belongings quite thoroughly."

"They could've hidden the item someplace else."

Mr. Mann straightened and turned a haughty gaze upon Mr. Pidwell. "Are you doubting my investigative abilities, Mr. Pidwell? You do know that I have trained to be a judge, do you not?"

Mr. Pidwell didn't reply in words, but his expression said that he didn't give a farthing about any training.

Neither did Caleb. But if the gentleman's arrogance and self-importance would keep his attention away from Willow, then that's all that mattered.

Willow shouldn't have gotten involved in this conflict between Isaac and Mr. Mann. But of course it wasn't in her nature to pass by someone who was being harmed. Wasn't that what had first drawn her to stop and rescue him that long ago day?

Mr. Mann's bloodshot eyes flitted from one man's face to the next. "If whoever took the key returns it to me today, I'll refrain from prosecution. I will obviously need to let you go from your position. But I won't hand you over to the Victoria police and press charges."

The trouble was, Willow was a terrible liar. She wouldn't be able to hide that she had the key for long. Caleb was surprised Mr. Mann hadn't seen right past Willow's sassy comments and figured out her guilt already.

Caleb's gut tightened. What would happen when Mr. Mann finally realized Willow had stolen his key? He wouldn't stop with just firing her. He'd probably punish her. And Caleb couldn't allow that to happen. He refused to let Willow get in trouble with this man for trying to help Isaac.

There was only one thing left to do. As Mr. Mann's gaze came to rest on him, he tried to fake being nervous— twitching, avoiding eye contact, fidgeting, and twisting his neck as though he were easing the tension there.

"Young man?" Mr. Mann's eyes narrowed upon him. "I have the feeling that perhaps you'd like to say something."

"No, sir." He let his voice squeak, then cleared his throat.

From the corner of his eye, he could see one of Willow's brows rise, the sign that she knew he was acting out of character.

Mr. Mann held himself regally, as though he really did consider himself a judge presiding over a courtroom. "Did you or did you not sneak into my house and take the key?"

Caleb purposefully hesitated a moment longer before nodding. "I was awake when Isaac was leaving the house this morning and getting on his boat. When he told me he'd lost his key while gambling with you, I could see his distress."

"I won the key fairly. My friend Mr. Tammedge is my witness." Mr. Mann gave a pointed look at the fellow who was leaning against the far side of the house. He appeared to be more properly groomed. Even so, his face contained a haggardness that came from too much hard liquor and not enough sleep.

Mr. Tammedge took a puff on his cigar. "It was, indeed, fair. No doubt about it."

The gaming had been far from fair. Anyone who knew Isaac would realize it. But until Caleb could appeal to an unbiased authority—preferably someone who knew about Isaac and his shortcomings—then he had to go along with Mr. Mann and his cohort.

"Isaac was upset," Caleb persisted. "So I snuck in, got the key, and gave it back to him."

"You gave back the key?" Mr. Mann's voice rose.

Caleb shrugged. "You can go through my belongings. I've got nothing to hide."

"Oh you can be sure we'll do a thorough search."

"I didn't think it would matter. It's just a key."

"It's not just a key." Mr. Mann fisted his hands, his body tightening with the need to take a swing.

Caleb had seen that look enough to know, and he fisted his own hands, ready to defend himself. He didn't want to fight Mr. Mann. Didn't want to hurt him. Didn't want the situation to get any worse.

But in the next instant, Mr. Mann lunged for him, delivering a hard jab to his stomach.

Caleb responded reflexively with an uppercut, aiming the heel of his palm into Mr. Mann's chin, followed by a second hit to his jaw. Both sent the man reeling backward but were light enough that they wouldn't cause any broken bones or blood.

"You're a worse imbecile than Isaac." Mr. Mann steadied himself, his eyes filling with a familiar venom that Caleb had seen all too often in the eyes of his opponents. "And you need to be taught a lesson not to meddle in business that isn't yours."

"I was helping a friend. There's nothing wrong with that."

"You stole from me. And there's everything wrong with that." Mr. Mann leapt again, but Caleb easily dodged him, and this time landed a punch to Mr. Mann's stomach that had him doubling over.

The gentleman didn't know the first thing about fighting. He also didn't know Caleb's capabilities. Or perhaps his elevated sense of importance made him believe he was a better fighter than he was.

Whatever the case, Mr. Mann released an angry yell, straightened, then came after Caleb again. He swung his arms and fists like a little child, the hits bouncing off Caleb, hardly making an impact.

Caleb swiveled out of the fray. A part of him knew he needed to walk away, that this man wasn't worth the altercation. But another part of him couldn't let the conflict go.

As Mr. Mann swung at Caleb's chin and connected, a smugness curved up the man's lips. Caleb had the sudden picture of his father's smug smile the time he'd thrown Caleb against the wall and slammed his head back, nearly knocking him unconscious.

The memory ignited his anger into a low rage. And in the next instant, he shoved Mr. Mann back enough that he could take the swings that would show the man who was stronger and deadlier.

He leveled the first hit to one of Mr. Mann's eyes and the next to his cheek. Then he aimed at the fellow's ribs and began to throw punches that would most certainly bruise the man, even if they weren't hard enough to break ribs.

Mr. Mann held up his arms over his head in a protective gesture and began to shout. "Get him off! Pull him away!"

"Hold on now, Caleb." Rough hands grabbed at him.

Caleb twisted in an effort to break free, the anger inside driving him to do more damage. But even as he took another swing, he caught sight of Willow striding across the grass, determination in her eyes and in each step. If she intervened, everyone would learn that they knew each other, and that would only make matters worse.

He let his arms drop as Mr. Pidwell and two other laborers wrestled him backward away from Mr. Mann. They didn't let go of his arms, and he didn't struggle against them.

Mr. Tammedge was already at Mr. Mann's side as was Mrs. Mann, her face wreathed with alarm as she took in the blood dribbling from Mr. Mann's nose and bottom lip.

Mr. Mann spit a glob of blood into the dried grass flattened beneath his feet. His eyes were wild as he gazed around at everyone. "You all saw what happened!" he shouted. "That man was trying to kill me."

Caleb stiffened at the accusation. He'd never killed a man in all his years of boxing. But he couldn't say the same of other bare-knuckle fighters.

Mr. Mann wiped at the blood dribbling from his nose, making a vibrant red streak across his sleeve. "Not only is your worker a thief, Mr. Pidwell. He's also murderous."

"Now, Mr. Mann." Mr. Pidwell's forehead furrowed above troubled eyes. "Caleb here is a good boy—"

"Lock him up." Mr. Mann took a handkerchief from his wife and dabbed at his busted lip. "We can't have a dangerous man like him on the farm. There's no telling what else he'll do."

"No! You can't lock him up." Willow had crossed and was standing only a few feet away. "That's not fair." She held herself stiffly, her hands fisted at her sides as though she wanted to start taking punches now too.

Even if she was hurt by his slighting her, she'd never be able to stand aside and let him get into trouble. She was too much of a rescuer to do that.

All eyes turned upon Willow. No doubt everyone was wondering why she was intervening on his behalf. Her interest in him would only cast suspicion on her and make matters worse.

He caught Willow's gaze, hoping to silently assure her that he'd be fine, that she shouldn't say anything more, that he could take care of himself.

Her narrowed look told him that she wouldn't let him take the blame for her.

"I'm sorry, Mr. Mann." Caleb had to say something to keep her from talking, and he'd grovel at the gentleman's feet if it would keep Willow safe. "I was a bare-knuckle boxing champion back home, and I get carried away sometimes."

Mr. Mann's brows rose, his eyes brimming with criticism—and an interest Caleb had often seen in his brother's eyes.

Caleb spoke again before Willow could. "How about if I pay off the worth of the key by winning you a few fights?"

Mr. Mann scoffed. "It'll take more than a few fights to pay me back."

"I'll earn you a fortune in one night on just the gambling alone."

Willow was shaking her head, but at least she'd pressed her lips together and was staying silent.

Mr. Mann exchanged a glance with Mr. Tammedge. With Mr. Mann's love of gambling, Caleb was taking a gamble himself that the gentleman would be tempted by his offer and maybe forget all about the key.

His fellow laborers were sizing him up with new interest. They'd watched him fight for only a minute or two, but it had been enough for them to believe his declaration about being a champion.

Mr. Mann whispered with Mr. Tammedge for a few moments before pulling back, holding the handkerchief against his nose gingerly. "How do we know that you can really win?"

From the corner of his eye, Caleb could see Willow shake her head, but he ignored her. "Find me someone worthwhile to fight, and I'll prove it."

The two conversed again before Mr. Mann eyed Caleb through one of his eyes that was starting to swell shut. "Mr. Tammedge will arrange a boxing match for you in Victoria. If it goes well, then I'll allow you to repay me for the loss of the key through the fighting."

"How much do you want?"

"One thousand pounds." Mr. Mann delivered the exorbitant amount without hesitation.

Several of the other laborers whistled.

The key must have been worth a lot. Whatever the case, Caleb had no choice but to go along with the gentleman. "Fine. But once you have one thousand, I'm done. I won't fight for you again after that."

Willow's shoulders sagged with disappointment. He was breaking his promise to her again. And wasn't that one of the reasons why he'd never be worthy of her love? Because he couldn't be trusted.

Without waiting for further details, Willow pivoted and began to stalk back to the house. He wanted to call after her and tell her he was doing this for her, to prevent her from getting into trouble, to help her protect Isaac, to keep himself from being sent to prison or worse—because there was no telling what kind of justice system existed in the colonies and whether it was fair or not.

But he forced himself not to look at her. Instead, he shook off Mr. Pidwell's hold and walked away in the opposite direction.

"You better not make a fool of me, boy," Mr. Mann called after him. "If you do, you'll regret the day you stepped foot on my farm."

Caleb didn't stop to respond.

Instead, he ducked into the open door of the cow barn. When he was hidden in the dark shadows, he leaned against a stall railing and bowed his head. He'd hoped to escape from his past here in the colony. But maybe the past was something he could never outrun, no matter how far he went or how hard he tried.

Sixteen

W illow tucked the key into the wooden box where she kept all the mementos from Caleb. Mr. Mann had already dumped out the box onto her bed and riffled through the contents when he'd stomped up and ransacked every inch of every item in her dormer room.

She was just glad she hadn't placed the key in the box to begin with as she'd been tempted. She'd done the right thing in hiding it under a rock in the tall grass behind the privy, since at the time she hadn't been able to sneak up to her room.

But the key would be safe in her room now. Mr. Mann wouldn't look in her box again—not when he believed Caleb had been the one to take it.

She fingered the unbroken clam shell Caleb had given her earlier in the week—his last gift before he'd stopped coming to see her. Of course he'd found one for her. He always gave her everything she wanted, and he always looked out for her—whether she wanted him to or not.

Like today . . . when he'd stepped in and shouldered the blame for taking Isaac's key.

With a huff, she snapped the lid of the box closed. Then she wrapped the twine around it to keep the top in place and slipped the box back under her bed. She hadn't ever told anyone about her box, not even Caleb. In fact, she'd be embarrassed if he found out about it and realized she'd saved every small item he'd ever given her. He'd think she was obsessed with him.

As she sat back up, she scrutinized the white-washed room again, making sure everything was back in order. The room didn't contain much, only the single metal-framed bed, bedside table, a narrow writing desk and chair, and a rug at the center of the floor.

Mr. Mann had clearly been surprised to see her sparse furnishings and her meager possessions in the one bag. But that hadn't changed his tempestuous mood as he'd been searching for Isaac's key.

With a sigh, she blew out the candle on the bedside table. Darkness descended over the room, a darkness that was beginning to match the despondency in her heart.

Caleb had noticed her earlier when they'd all been in the farmyard facing Mr. Mann's wrath. And he'd obviously still cared enough about her to intervene, probably to prevent Mr. Mann from investigating her further.

But he was still keeping his distance and neglecting their friendship.

She flopped backward onto the bed. The sight of him today had been like rain for her parched soul . . . except she hadn't gotten enough.

"Why?" she whispered into the quiet of the night broken only by Lum's heavy snores in the room beside hers.

Why did she have to care about Caleb so much? Why couldn't his friendship be more like Juliet's and Daisy's? She was content to see the two women during her trip into Victoria on Sundays and wasn't pining after them the rest of the week.

"Why?" she asked again.

A scrape sounded against her window, drawing her gaze. Through the soft gleam of moonlight, she could see the window inching up and Caleb's outline on the other side.

With hope fluttering inside her stomach, she hopped up from the bed and made her way to the window. As much as she wanted to be mad at Caleb and tell him to go away, she never had been able to stay angry at him for long.

She helped slide the window the rest of the distance until it was wide enough for him to fit through. As he climbed inside, the chill of the night breeze along with the dampness of the sea wafted inside with him.

He didn't say a word, not even a greeting. But his presence in the chamber was overwhelming, especially with the slanted ceiling forcing him to hunch so that he was hovering above her.

She shivered and took a step back. Should she wait for him to talk? Or should she break the awkward tension between them by speaking first?

He pivoted and quietly slid the window down.

She plopped back onto the bed and drew her cover around her nightgown mostly for warmth, but also because she felt strangely self-conscious tonight. Even though Caleb didn't pay attention to her body or what she was wearing, she supposed on one level she'd always been aware that he was a man and she was a woman in spite of her insistence that men and women could remain just friends.

That difference was there whether she liked it or not and whether she ignored it or not.

As soon as the window was closed, Caleb turned back to the room. He cocked an ear toward Lum's wall. At the undisturbed snoring, Caleb crept to the bed. He started to sit, then hesitated, obviously feeling the new tension between them too.

Finally he lowered himself until he was perched on the edge.

She had to say something to him. Whatever had happened to separate them this past week, he was trying to make an effort at reconciliation. The least she could do was show him she was glad he'd come.

She reached over and grasped his arm. But the moment she did so, her mind filled with the memory of the last time she'd held his arm in the hay pile when he'd caressed her fingers.

Rolling her eyes at herself for even thinking about the incident, she released his arm. She had to prove to herself— and to him—that there was no physical attraction between them. The best way to do that was give him a friendly hug.

Before she could overthink the situation, she threw both arms around him.

For a moment he didn't react, almost as if she'd taken him by surprise.

"I missed you," she whispered, squeezing him tightly and pressing her cheek against his chest in the process. Her world seemed to tip right side up now that she was with Caleb, almost as if she'd been living upside down without him.

"I missed you too." His arms came around her slowly, awkwardly, and his heartbeat echoed loudly against her ear.

"I'm sorry for pulling away. I needed time to think, and I should have just told you that."

"Yes, you should have." She breathed him in, his cotton shirt filled with the lingering scent of pine and hay. "But I forgive you."

"I don't deserve it." He held her loosely but gently. Unlike the other day, the intensity radiating from him seemed to be gone and only friendship remained.

She exhaled her relief. She'd never do anything ever again to disturb the balance of their friendship. And she certainly wouldn't let him shoulder the blame for the key.

Pulling back, she shoved at his chest. "You're terrible. Do you know that?"

"Me?" His whisper held a note of disbelief as he dropped his arms away.

"You shouldn't have told Mr. Mann you took Isaac's key."

"I wouldn't have needed to if you hadn't taken it in the first place."

So he had guessed her role in the missing key. "Mr. Mann tricked poor, sweet Isaac into playing cards and betting his key and map to a treasure of gold that his brother buried."

"Gold." Caleb scooted back on the bed so that he was leaning against the wall, his legs stretched out in front of him. "Now I understand why Mr. Mann is so desperate to get the key back."

"He wanted Isaac to bring him the map today too, but I told Isaac he can't give Mr. Mann anything else and to go away for a while."

"That accounts for why Jonas was piloting the boat today for the deliveries."

She'd been watching from Mrs. Mann's upstairs sitting

room window and had been relieved when only Jonas had hopped onto the pier from Isaac's steamboat. She hadn't had the chance to speak with Jonas to discover how much Isaac had explained about all that had transpired during the night of gambling at the White Swan. But Jonas had seemed to carry on with business as usual.

She leaned back against the wall beside Caleb, and for a short while, she explained all that had taken place yesterday when Isaac had come to the house to deliver the new hat for Mrs. Mann, his offer to give her the key, and how that had led to Mr. Mann inviting Isaac to dinner and then to a night of gambling that had culminated with all that Willow had heard in the hallway.

"I wasn't planning to take the key out of Mr. Mann's billiard room," she said as she finished her tale. "But it was just there, and I couldn't stop myself."

Caleb was silent for several beats. "What are you going to do with it?"

"I'll give it back to Isaac next time I see him."

"And how are you going to keep Mr. Mann from finding it before then?"

"He's already searched my room—"

"He'll search again. Now that he knows the rumors of the gold treasure are true, he won't let anything stop him from going after it. Not with the financial trouble he's in."

"I didn't know he was in financial trouble." Her eyes had adjusted to the darkness, and she could see Caleb's profile beside her—the hard lines of his jaw, the rough edges of his features, the tough way he held himself. She never got tired of staring at him, and after going without any sight of him over the past days, she was hungrier than ever to just take him in.

She could only half listen to him talking about everything

he'd learned from the other laborers about the Manns' financial situation, including the gambling debt Mr. Mann had accumulated since moving to the colony. Apparently he'd squandered his share of his family's fortune, and now the farm's income was the only thing keeping him from utter ruin. He had plans to expand the farm's operations and start brewing his own beer, which would be profitable in the long term. But currently, Mr. Mann was scrambling to find enough capital to invest in the endeavor.

"So once I give the key back to Isaac," she said, "Mr. Mann will probably just try to take it away again?"

"With the possibility of getting a treasure of gold? Yes, he'll go after Isaac again. My fighting will only delay him."

"About the fighting." She swatted at Caleb's arm. "At the train station, that day we were leaving, you promised me you wouldn't fight again."

He sighed. "I'm a liar."

"You don't have to be." She laid her hand on his arm and squeezed him.

His muscle flexed against her hand, but otherwise he didn't move. "You know about my past and my family. Sometimes I think there's no hope of becoming a better man." His admission was barely audible and held a despair that she hadn't heard in his voice in a long time.

"Caleb." She scooted closer, needing to be nearer, needing him to know she wasn't intimidated by his faults. "You're a strong man. Look at all you've already overcome to be where you're at."

"But the influences, the mistakes, the problems—they're all still there chasing after me." His head was down, his unruly dark hair falling over his forehead.

She had the urge to comb the strands off his forehead,

only to comfort him, but she pushed aside the need. "The past influences might be there in the distance when you look back, but they won't catch up to you unless you let them."

He was silent for several moments, Lum's snoring assuring them that they hadn't woken him, that Caleb's late-night visits were still undetected.

Her shoulder brushed against Caleb, and she couldn't keep from tucking her hand more securely around his arm, her earnestness driving her. He had to see that his future didn't have to be charted out by his past. He could set his own course for his life—one that was different than his father's.

"Don't box again, Caleb." Her whisper was a plea.

He expelled a tight breath. "If I don't, Mr. Pidwell said Mr. Mann will send me to back to England in chains."

"Oh my." She squeezed her eyes shut against the possibility. Caleb had confessed to taking the key to keep her safe. He was in this trouble because of her. And now she had to be the one to get them out of this mess.

Caleb's body tensed against hers. "If I land in prison, I really will end up just like my father, won't I?" Caleb never talked about why his father had gone to prison. But Willow had learned from her dad that it was because he'd murdered a man in a rage.

"You won't end up in prison." She opened her eyes, her whisper turning firm. "And we'll figure out another way out of this problem with Mr. Mann."

"After all that's already happened, I don't need you figuring anything else out." His words were spoken gently, without any malice.

Even so, they stabbed at Willow, her own inadequacies rising to taunt her. Why couldn't she prove that she was capable of handling the problems? She didn't want Caleb to have to step in and save her once again.

She shifted and started to climb off the bed.

"Wait." He reached out and caught her waist, drawing her to a halt.

At the feel of his fingers spanning her mid-section, she could do nothing but freeze. And of course, her mind went back to their time in the hay pile when his fingers had caressed hers so intimately.

Now those fingers were on her waist. And even though a blanket and her nightgown separated her skin from his, the heat spread through her nonetheless.

He tugged at her, as though he wanted her to return to her spot beside him. "I'm sorry. I shouldn't have said that. You were only trying to help Isaac."

She relaxed and sat back on her heels.

He didn't remove his hands from her waist. In fact, his fingers seemed to tighten. "I love that you're compassionate." His whisper dropped low.

"Then you're not mad at me anymore?"

He lifted one of his hands from her waist, and she almost made a small noise of protest, but in the next instant he grazed her hair hanging loosely down her back.

Her breath got lost somewhere inside her chest. What was he doing? He'd never touched her hair before either.

"I was never mad at you, Willow." Again his whisper was low, and this time he brushed aside her hair, sweeping it over her shoulder so that the back of her neck was bare.

The cool night air tickled her skin.

"I could never be mad at you."

"Are you sure?"

"Um-hm." He let go of her waist and pushed away from the wall, so that he was sitting next to her.

She was all too keenly aware of his chest and arms so close. And she tilted her head just slightly, so that the long stretch of her neck was more accessible . . .

More accessible for what? What was she doing? What was happening?

The same sparks from last time were spreading throughout her body, so that she was heating more with every passing moment—heating with that same unholy desire to lean back, pull him down, and kiss him.

But look what had happened the last time she'd felt that way. She'd alienated Caleb. She had to get off the bed and away from him before she pushed him away again.

His breathing caressed her neck.

Was he going to kiss her?

At the prospect, her insides trembled. From fear? Or desire? She wasn't sure. But one thing was certain. She was most certainly battling attraction toward him. As much as she'd tried to squelch it, diminish it, and even deny it, all it took was one tiny moment like this, and she was feeling everything for him.

The question was whether he was feeling the attraction too.

"Caleb?" Her whisper was wobbly.

He stiffened and the hand in her hair tightened.

Internal warnings started to ring. She couldn't ask him, couldn't bring it up, couldn't risk him walking away from her again. She'd already endured enough time apart and couldn't endure more.

With a huff of clear frustration, Caleb dropped his hand from her hair. Before she could say anything, he was releasing her altogether and was scrambling off the bed. In two steps he was at the window, and he was straining to open it.

"You *are* mad at me."

He paused, the window already up several inches.

Cold night air crept into the room and made her shiver. "Just admit it."

He held himself stiffly a moment longer, then his shoulders slumped, and he leaned his head against the window.

She drew her blanket around her more securely. For so long their relationship had been simple and easy. They'd both been content with friendship. They'd never even considered more. But tonight, as with when they were in the barn, this was *more*. She didn't exactly know what that meant, but it was different and scary.

"Caleb?" she whispered again, needing him to talk to her instead of running away and avoiding her.

"I'm sorry." His whisper was almost harsh, his head still against the window. "I thought I could make myself go back to the way things were . . . but I'm a weaker man than I realized."

"The way things were?"

"You asked me not to let anything change between us, and over the past week I tried—really tried—to make myself see you as just a friend the way you want . . . "

"I thought that's what you wanted too."

"Yes!" His voice rose, then he quickly lowered it. "No."

"I'm confused."

He dragged in a breath. "Yes. We're friends. Just friends. I'll make sure of it."

She tried to ease the tension from her body, tried to let the relief slip inside. But her nerves were tied in knots she couldn't untangle.

His broad back strained against his coat, his muscles taut, his frustration palpable.

She was going to lose him one way or another.

The certainty slapped her in the face so that she sat forward.

Something had changed between them, was continuing to change, and if she didn't stop the change, one of these times he'd leave her and wouldn't come back.

Desperation began to steal through her. She had to find a way to fix everything.

He tugged at the window, moving it higher.

"Wait," she whispered, refraining from crossing to him and touching his back.

He paused.

Her mind raced with a dozen scenarios and a dozen more solutions. Anything that would keep him from pushing her away. And anything that would keep him from getting into more trouble with Mr. Mann.

A plan started to take form. "I have an idea." Her whisper trembled with sudden excitement.

Seventeen

aleb closed his eyes but couldn't block out the span of Willow's neck that he'd almost kissed a moment ago.

He needed to get out of her room, needed to put space between his raging desires and her beautiful body. But at her earnest voice behind him, he couldn't make himself inch the window higher.

And the hurt in her expression. He couldn't—wouldn't—hurt her again. If it was the last thing he did, he was going to get himself under control and do what was best for her.

If only he'd lasted more than just a few minutes in her presence without turning into a lovesick fool. What had happened to the careful control that he'd cultivated for years?

He'd thought he'd had it back when he'd climbed up onto the roof and made his way to her bedroom. But clearly every ounce was gone.

"Please listen to my idea, Caleb." Her soft voice remained near the bed, which was good. Because if she came up behind him, he would probably turn around and draw her into his arms.

"I'm listening." Although he tried to sound calm, his voice came out clipped.

She hesitated.

He hated that he was confusing. Biting back curses at himself, he made himself turn around. Then he leaned against the window and gave her his fullest attention.

She stood at the center of the room wrapped in a blanket. And even in the dark, she was absolutely exquisite, with her hair unbound and hanging in disarray. "Let's leave the Manns'. We don't need to stay here."

"I owe him the fights."

"We don't owe them anything. And you know I hate when you box."

"If I box, at least he won't hold me—or you—responsible for the key."

"He shouldn't hold anyone responsible but himself."

"It doesn't matter. He's a powerful man in the colony."

She clutched the blanket closer, a determination emanating from her, one that was difficult to resist.

He knew the work at the Manns' hadn't been what she'd expected. Even after weeks, it was still demanding and endless, with Mrs. Mann and Lum both taking advantage of her and working her like a slave. She was hardly able to save anything since Mrs. Mann was still constantly docking her wages for mistakes.

If he could take her away from it all and give her a better life, maybe he should consider it.

She met his gaze levelly. "You said you wanted a place of your own on Salt Spring Island."

"Someday."

"Why not now?"

He shrugged. Did he really have an excuse? The land was available through pre-emption. He'd checked into the law the last time he was in Victoria, and sure enough Governor Douglas was allowing settlers to claim land for free on Salt Spring Island with the condition that the land be purchased later. In fact, if he went now, maybe he'd even be able to clear a portion of acreage before it was time for the spring planting.

He had four weeks of wages saved up, which would be enough for a few basics. Hopefully.

"We'll go now," she persisted. "We can build a cabin and farm the land. And once we start growing our own produce, Jonas can sell it for us like he does for the Manns."

Jonas had told him again just this week that the land on the island was largely unclaimed, that there was a nice parcel right beside his that was close to the waterfront and yet was level enough for farming. Jonas had also said every week more Blacks were coming up from America to escape the conflict there and because Governor Douglas wasn't denying pre-emption based on skin color. If Caleb waited too long, he might lose out on that particular piece of property.

"Just think about it." Willow's whisper was growing more excited by the second. "Maybe we'll have enough saved by mid-summer, most certainly by autumn, to send for my whole family."

"We'll have to invest some of the profits back into the farm." His mind began to spin with all that would be required. They would need seeds and tools and maybe even livestock.

"Then you'll do it?" She was smiling, likely knowing full well that she was convincing him to go along with her plan.

He crossed his arms, trying to look stern, but the truth

was, every passing day that he cleared more land for Mr. Mann, he'd been wishing he was clearing his own farm instead.

With all that had happened with Isaac and the key and the accusations of stealing, was it finally time for Willow and him to leave and forge their own way?

The prospect was daunting, especially because he'd be responsible for providing everything for Willow—food, shelter, clothing, and all the necessities of life. He'd have no room to fail or make mistakes, because if he did, she'd suffer.

He might be willing to take that chance for himself, but he wasn't sure he could put her at risk.

"I don't know, Willow. Starting our place won't be easy."

"But we've both learned a lot over the past month, haven't we?"

He had watched and learned carefully everything he could. And even though he still had a great deal more to learn about farming, especially the planting of crops, at least he knew the basics.

"We'll do fine," Willow continued as if reading his mind. "Even though it won't be easy starting out, as long as we're together, we'll be able to do it."

He wanted to nod and tell her yes. But deep inside he suspected that running away from Mr. Mann might make the situation worse. "Mr. Mann won't be happy if I disappear." That was an understatement. "What if he comes looking for me?"

She cocked her head, as if contemplating the possibility. "With so many places we could go, how will he know where to search?"

"If he suspects I've gotten to know Jonas, it might lead him to Salt Spring."

"Maybe you can drop a hint with one of the other workers or Mr. Pidwell that you're leaving for the mountains to look for gold."

"Maybe." Would that work to keep Mr. Mann off their trail? Maybe the gentleman would be desperate enough to find the treasure that he'd search for Isaac instead of them? Not that Caleb wanted Mr. Mann going after Isaac. But Mr. Mann didn't know that Willow had the key still. And Caleb wanted to keep it that way.

"Please, Caleb." She took a step toward him but then stopped, as if suddenly remembering all that had transpired between them a few moments ago.

He remembered it all too well, the way his hands had fit so perfectly at her waist, the silk of her hair, the warmth of her neck beckoning to him. If they started a farm of their own, how would he be able to resist her when he was with her day in and day out?

Or maybe he'd have to convince her that he cared about her as more than a friend.

He took her in again, this time letting himself admire her openly in a way he'd never done previously. She was so beautiful, even in the dark, that the sight of her made his chest ache.

He'd never had trouble winning women, and he could win Willow if he put his mind to it. He'd find ways to show her how much he adored her.

He'd make that his goal.

And he'd prove to her that they didn't have to lose their friendship if they let their relationship develop into more.

He'd have to start off slowly, or he'd scare her. But he'd relish the chance to show his affection without anything holding him back.

"Well?" She was watching him expectantly.

"Okay."

"Okay? As in you won't box for Mr. Mann, and you'll leave?"

"Yes."

She gave a small hop and clapped her hands softly.

He allowed himself a rare grin. Maybe everything would work out after all.

Eighteen

W illow waited in the shadow of the boulders and trees along the coast north of the farm. She scanned the waterway, glossy with the reflection of the morning sun, but there was no sight of the steamer.

"Where are you, Jonas?" she whispered again as she had over the past couple of hours of hiding.

The sparse woodland wasn't far from the main house, less than a quarter of a mile. But it was far enough away that hopefully no one would be wandering her way and spot her.

At the squawk of a seagull, she startled and glared at the bird circling overhead. "Go away," she whisper-called. "You'll give away my location."

Not that anyone was out looking for her the same way they had been for Caleb.

Of course, yesterday, once Mr. Mann learned that Caleb had run off without the boxing matches, he'd sent out a search party to hunt Caleb down as well as reported him to the Victoria police department with charges of stealing and attempted murder.

From the news Willow had gleaned once Mr. Pidwell and the others returned empty-handed, Caleb had been nowhere to be found. But he'd left hints that he'd taken off to search for gold, possibly heading to Yale where men wintered until spring thawed the mountain passes.

Mr. Mann had been livid for a short while, then had seemed to resign himself to the fact that Caleb's boxing wouldn't be the source of income that he'd hoped for. Perhaps Mr. Mann had also resigned himself to losing Isaac's treasure. Neither source of income had rightfully belonged to Mr. Mann anyway. He was not only a swindler with Isaac, but he'd proven himself to be unfair with Caleb too.

Willow had wanted to leave the same night as Caleb. But he'd asked her to wait so that he'd have the chance to speak with Jonas first and explain all that had happened, not wanting to involve the fellow into potential trouble without a fair warning.

So Willow had tarried a whole day and another night. And then when she'd crept out of her room earlier this morning by the first light of dawn, she'd left the house and hadn't looked back.

The trouble was, the longer she waited, the less certain she was that Caleb had been successful in gaining Jonas's cooperation. She wouldn't blame the man if he didn't want to take them on the steamer to Salt Spring Island and show them the land that he'd been talking about.

Caleb had assured her that if Jonas wasn't willing to help, he'd find her in the northern field, and they'd hike to the tip of the Saanichton Peninsula together. Once there, the distance to Salt Spring was within rowing distance, and Caleb was certain they'd find someone willing to transport them over to the island.

Either way, he'd told her to stay in the rocky forested area, and she intended to remain there as long as it took.

Except for the past hour, she'd been able to do little more than worry about Caleb. For all she knew, he'd been caught last night in Victoria and thrown into jail. And if he was in jail, then she'd have to find a way to get him out.

The fact was, she'd move mountains for Caleb. And he'd do the same for her. That's what best friends did for each other. Best friends also could plan to settle a farm together, couldn't they?

She rested her head against the stone and stared past the spindly branches of the Douglas fir that towered above her. Was she doing the right thing? She would, after all, technically be living with Caleb.

And even though he was just her friend, he was male. Of course, she would do the best she could to remain modest, but in such close quarters, seeing each other in a state of undress was sometimes inevitable.

What would her mum think when she arrived in the colony to find her living with Caleb completely unchaperoned? And her dad?

A flush spread through Willow. And her mind flashed back to the way Caleb had looked at her in her room as he'd stood before the window, how he'd scanned her the way he used to with other women, as if he was enjoying what he saw.

She shook her head. He hadn't been enjoying what he saw with her. She was probably making more out of everything than necessary.

At the distant bellow of a steamboat whistle, she peeked past the rock to find a small, rusty steamboat chugging around the bend in the bay, black smoke curling from the single smokestack. As the paddlewheel at the back pushed the boat closer, the bold red letters on the side that spelled *Boat* came into view.

She released a pent-up breath. Jonas had probably just finished his pickup at the White Swan Farm and was now coming for her. At least she hoped he was.

Would Caleb be on the steamer too? She squinted as she scanned the two decks, already loaded with crates and barrels and bags. But she didn't see Caleb among them. In the pilothouse, a thin, wiry man wearing a bowler over curly hair stood at the wheel—Jonas.

She glanced behind her to the field and then in the direction of the farmhouse. No one was in sight. Even if the Manns didn't care that she was leaving, she didn't want anyone witnessing her getting on the *Boat*. She needed them to assume she'd return to the Marine Barracks in Victoria.

She waited behind the boulder until the steamboat drew even with where she was. It was still out a distance in the channel. But it had slowed, and Jonas was likely trying to discover her whereabouts.

With her scarf pulled up and covering her hair, she stepped out into the open and began to climb down the rocky bank to the water's edge. She waved at the boat, and at the sight of her, Jonas began to veer the steamboat her way.

She wasn't sure what to expect, but he stopped, dropped anchor, and then lowered a small tender into the water. He easily climbed down into it and then rowed toward her.

When he reached the shore, he helped her into the boat and then began the short ride back. All the whilst, she peppered him with questions about Caleb, and Jonas just laughed and told her Caleb was already at Salt Spring Island and she'd get answers soon enough.

That didn't stop her from asking Jonas a dozen other

questions, mostly about Isaac. Jonas reassured her that Isaac had taken her advice and left right away, afraid of Mr. Mann coming after him. When Jonas mentioned the key and the map, Willow guessed Isaac had told his partner all about the treasure too.

Even though Jonas seemed loyal to Isaac and not the sort of person who would use him to get gold, she was still worried for Isaac because he'd clearly been telling more people about the treasure than he should have.

Jonas made short work of helping her up into the steamboat and raising the tender. He situated her in a hidden spot among the crates so that no one would see her at any of the rest of his stops up the coast.

She stayed tucked away as Jonas finished the route up the Saanichton Peninsula, stopping at two more farms. At last, the rumbling of the steam engine came to a halt.

"We're here," Jonas called.

She climbed out from the maze of cargo until she reached the railing. She blinked past the bright sunshine to find that the steamboat was anchored in a narrow harbor. It bobbed in waves beside a dock that led to a pebbly beach. Beyond the beach, grassy banks rose into a wooded shoreline filled with alder, hemlock, and cedar—just a few of the trees she was learning to recognize.

"Where is your farm?" She'd expected to see cleared fields like at White Swan. But here, the land was rugged and hilly without any sign of fields suitable for farming.

Jonas hopped over the railing onto the dock. "It's only a short hike back along the river." He nodded toward an inlet then bent and began to tie up the steamer. There weren't any other boats at the dock, but a canoe was tipped over and propped along the bank nearby.

She searched the shoreline for Caleb, eager to see him step out of the shadows. But the only other life visible were the herons in the eelgrass. They were easy to distinguish with their narrow, pointed bills, long slender necks, and spindly stilted legs.

A haze hovered over the forest to their north, and she breathed in the air, now heavily laden with the scent of woodsmoke. "Why so much smoke?" she asked.

"We're clearing more farmland." Jonas finished securing the steamer then held a hand out to her.

"By burning the forest?"

He laughed, something he seemed to do a lot, a deep, rich sound that showed his bright white teeth in contrast to his dark skin. "We're burning the trees we've cut."

As she steadied herself on the dock, she surveyed the smoke again. "That seems so wasteful, especially when I think of how cold my family might be this winter and how they'd gladly use the wood for fuel."

Jonas's expression quickly sobered, and his ebony eyes filled with compassion. "Sorry to hear that, miss. I sure do know what it's like to have a family suffering."

From the little Caleb had told her, she knew that Jonas had once been a slave but had escaped to California from wherever he'd lived in the southern part of America. She was curious to know more about him, but she didn't want to pry into areas that might be difficult to discuss.

"Where is Caleb?" she couldn't keep from asking again.

Jonas's wide smile slipped back into place as he hefted a crate onto his shoulder. "He's anxious to see you too. Ain't that for sure? But he's waiting at the cabin and keeping well out of sight. We reckoned that's best for a while."

She followed Jonas as he led her off the dock and along

the shore. As they reached the inlet, a wide, cleared path bordered a rushing stream, one so clear and clean, Jonas claimed it tasted better than anything else. Though the stream wasn't deep, Jonas explained that it was navigable and that they used the waterway to transport much of the farm produce to the steamer.

Farther upstream were waterfalls, that whilst beautiful, made the stream more difficult to traverse. "Our farm is on the eastern side of the stream," he said, as they broke into a clearing, with a large field spreading out among stumps. "Caleb's is on the western side."

A log home stood on a rise above the stream. It was just as small as the cabins the farmhands had stayed in at White Swan—if not smaller. A stove pipe projected from the roughly hewn shingles, and a curl of smoke circled above it.

A single log barn sat low to the ground beyond the house, its corral containing a pair of oxen, an old cow, and a sow. A few chickens roamed about the long grass that separated the house from the barn where clothes and towels on a line flapped in the cool February breeze.

She expected to see Caleb duck out of the barn or the house. But a Black woman stepped out of the front door of the cabin, her distended abdomen showing her to be well along with child. Willow assumed the woman was Jonas's wife and was surprised when he introduced her as his sister-in-law Frannie and explained that his brother lived on the farm and did most of the day-to-day work which freed Jonas to deliver the farm goods.

Frannie rested her hands on the swell of her stomach, her frayed apron pulled taut. Her hair was clipped short beneath a dull gray headscarf, and she wore a threadbare shawl over her shoulders. Though the woman was obviously poor, happiness seemed to fill her eyes and face, and she regarded Willow kindly.

"Elijah is over helping your man today." Frannie nodded toward the west.

"Oh, Caleb isn't my man," Willow offered with a light laugh. "We're just friends."

Jonas, in the process of prying open the crate he'd carried with him from the steamer, paused and slanted a serious look at Willow. "You're not married?"

She scoffed this time. "Of course we're not."

Frannie's smile faded, and Jonas shook his head as he straightened to his full height. "Nope, this ain't gonna work."

"What won't work?" Willow glanced between the two.

Jonas's eyes were wide, almost as if he was mortified. "You and Caleb . . . well, we're God-fearing people, you know what I'm saying?"

"So are we." At least they tried to be. Even if Caleb still struggled with the sins of his past, at least he was making progress.

Rubbing at the back of his neck, Jonas dropped his gaze to the half-open crate at his feet. "Begging your pardon, miss. But two unmarried folk living together? That's just asking for a heap of trouble."

The same flush from earlier came rushing back. She'd already questioned the wisdom of such an arrangement herself. She shouldn't be surprised that Jonas and Frannie were now doing the same.

"My family is coming soon." She offered the only explanation she could think of. "By the time we finish building our cabin, they'll be here." At least she hoped so.

Jonas's brows arched. "Didn't Caleb tell you? The land already has a cabin."

177

"No. I didn't know." What had she assumed? That she and Caleb would live with Jonas and impose on him for months?

Now that she was here, it was obvious Jonas didn't have room for them, not with his brother and Frannie living there and a baby due any day.

Willow wanted to roll her eyes at her stupidity. Why hadn't she thought to ask more questions? To plan better? To think of the details of all that she and Caleb would need?

"It's an old trapper cabin." Jonas peered at a bridge of logs that spanned the stream and a worn trail on the other side that cut through the woods. "We lived there until we got our cabin built. It's drafty, but it works."

Maybe Caleb could stay there by himself, and she could live in the cabin here . . . just until her family arrived in the colony. Frannie seemed kind enough to let her do so. But with the new baby on the way, Willow knew she'd only be a nuisance in the already crowded home, and they didn't need a stranger invading their privacy.

No, she'd have to stay in the trapper cabin with Caleb, and she'd reassure everyone that it would all work out and that there was nothing to worry about because nothing would ever happen between her and Caleb.

As the thudding of hammers filled the lengthening silence, she guessed the sound was coming from Caleb and Elijah. What had Caleb told everyone about the nature of their relationship? She wished he were present and could help her clear up the confusion.

"I realize our situation may seem unusual, but we aren't attracted to each other—"

Jonas whistled and shook his head in an exaggerated back

and forth. "Oh, Caleb's a goner for you. Never did see a man so in love with a woman as he is with you."

Goner? In love? When had Jonas seen Caleb interacting with her anyway? They'd never been together around him when he'd come to White Swan. "No. You're mistaken. Our bond is deep because we've been friends for over ten years. If there's any love, it's as friends."

Jonas opened his mouth as though to remark again, but Frannie spoke first. "Don't matter, honey. Elijah ain't gonna let the two of you live together unless you're married."

A strange panic rolled through Willow. Caleb would never agree to it. In fact, just the mention of it would send him running as fast and far away as he could get. "We can't rightly get married."

"Don't see why not." Jonas scrutinized her, as though searching for a blemish or flaw or some problem that would keep her from marrying.

Maybe he wouldn't be able to see her flaws, but they were still there. She was a weak and needy woman who couldn't stand on her own two feet.

Her thoughts flew back to the day when she'd first started at the mill, when her skirt had become tangled in a bobbin, and she had come close to crushing her fingers. Somehow Caleb had seen her distress and come to her rescue. Sage had rushed over too. And afterward, Sage had scolded her, like she usually did, and had said, "You're so helpless. You always need my help or Caleb's."

And it was true. She'd needed Caleb to come with her to the colony. She'd needed him at her job with the Manns. Now, she needed him in order to start this new life on a farm.

"It won't work, Jonas."

Jonas was done with his perusal and was studying her

face. "If you give the poor fellow a chance, he'll marry you today."

"He's opposed to marriage. He'll never agree to it."

"And if he does? You'll marry him?"

A month ago she would have staked everything on Caleb adamantly opposing marriage since he'd made his stance so clear over the years. But now . . . after he'd indicated that he was changing, could she really be so sure anymore?

Jonas grinned. "See, you're thinking about it."

"No, I'm not. He'll say no."

Jonas adjusted his bowler then cocked his head in the direction of the ringing hammers. "Let's go find out."

She started to protest again, but Jonas was already striding away, giving her no choice but to follow him.

She hefted her bag to her shoulder, only to have Frannie grab on and hold her back. "If you really can't marry that man, honey, we'll figure something else out."

Willow wanted to throw herself on Frannie and hug her. Or maybe cry. But she made herself smile instead. "Thank you. I'm sure Caleb has this all planned out. He usually does."

At least she hoped so.

Nineteen

"She's here." Elijah nodded through the barren trees in the direction of the river.

Caleb paused in hammering a new shingle in the roof and glanced up to the sight of Jonas's lanky form heading toward the cabin. Willow followed behind. Was she walking hesitantly? Was she afraid?

His body tensed. Had something happened to her?

He set his hammer down. Then he scooted to the edge of the roof, maneuvered around, and let himself drop to the ground, not bothering to use the ladder.

"You got it bad for your woman." Above him, Elijah chuckled. Like his brother, Elijah was thin and tall, with a ready smile and deep laughter. He wore his hair almost shaven to his head, covered with a neckerchief tied like a hat.

He'd been helping Caleb since dawn to make the home livable. After the past months of neglect, the place had not only needed cleaning but plenty of patching. But Caleb couldn't complain. The cabin had been better than Jonas had described. It had a few pieces of furniture that hadn't been chewed up by wild critters, and it even had an old stove that still worked.

He started toward Willow, unable to hold himself back a second longer.

"Real bad," Elijah muttered through a low laugh.

Yes, Caleb already knew he had it *real bad*—if that meant he was absolutely crazy about Willow.

His heart was pounding hard with the need to make sure she was okay, and he wanted to run to her, grab her in his arms, and pull her close. But he'd already warned himself dozens of times over the past few days that he needed to go slow if he hoped to win her over.

She was here, though. Now he could stop worrying every single second about whether she'd made it away from the Manns and whether Jonas had found her along the shore where she was supposed to hide.

Jonas shifted, and Willow caught sight of him. Her face lit up, and her lips curved into a smile, one that was unreserved and filled with her own relief at seeing him.

"Caleb!" She jogged toward him. "You're safe."

"I'm fine."

"I was worried." She was nearing him and wasn't slowing. He didn't mind. As she hurtled herself against him, he caught her, her body so light and lithe.

She wrapped her arms around his waist and hugged him tightly. She'd rarely hugged him over the years. It was his fault that she hadn't. He'd been the one to keep her at arm's length because contact with her womanliness only made his resisting her all the harder.

But at this moment, he didn't care. He needed to feel her and know that she was alive, here, and his.

He let his arms circle her. Her warmth, her softness, her

happiness at seeing him—all of it shot into his blood, giving him a renewed burst of energy, as if he hadn't been able to really live during the time they'd been apart, and now his heart was finally beating again.

Rather than holding her loosely as he usually did, he gave in to the need to draw her close. She didn't resist and buried her face against his chest.

He bent down and pressed his nose against her head and hair where her scarf had slipped away. He breathed her in. She was home to him. Wherever she was, that's where he wanted to be.

As if finally realizing that he wasn't opposing her hug, she wiggled to free herself, pulling back enough that she could look into his face. "What's wrong?"

"I'm relieved that you made it. I was worried about you too."

She smiled again, the blue of her eyes lighting into the color of the bright cloudless sky overhead. As she tilted her head up, her beauty was all right there in front of him, her lips so close, his for the taking.

His lungs seized. Saints have mercy on his poor soul. He couldn't kiss her. Not yet. He had a lot of work to do first to get her ready for a kiss. She'd never want one—never want him—as much as he did her. But he could try. He had to.

He loosened his hold and started to step back from her. But instead of cutting her off and hiding his feelings from her, he knew he had to do something different, something to show her he cared. As she backed up, he did the first thing that came to his mind—he lifted his hand and caressed her cheek.

She startled then froze, her eyes widening.

"Go on." Jonas stepped beside Willow, a broad smile filling his face. "Ask him."

She dropped her gaze, a rosy hue moving into her cheeks.

"Ask *him*, what?" Caleb arched a brow at Jonas.

Jonas's smile disappeared in a blink and accusation filled his face. "I thought you was married to your woman."

Elijah paused in his descent of the ladder, his eyes narrowing on Caleb. "You're not married?"

At the scrutiny from the two men, Caleb stiffened. "I never said I was."

Willow reached out a hand and touched his arm. "I've been trying to explain to Jonas that we've been best friends and that we're perfectly happy that way. People who aren't friends like we are just don't understand our relationship."

Elijah hopped the rest of the way down the ladder then spread his legs and folded his arms, his clothes hanging on him like a sack on a scarecrow. "You ain't living in this here cabin together if you ain't married. Simple as that."

"Um-hum." Jonas nodded. "That's what I told the miss."

The muscle in Caleb's jaw hardened. "It's none of your blasted business what Willow and me do."

"It sure enough is," Jonas growled.

Were these two planning to battle him? Caleb's hands curled into fists. He'd counted them as allies, but maybe he'd trusted them too soon. Maybe the only one he could really count on was Willow.

As though sensing the growing storm inside Caleb, Jonas pulled back his shoulders and leveled a severe look at him. "I ain't gonna let you ruin Willow's reputation."

Ruin her reputation?

Her forehead was creased. "I told Jonas you'd have a solution."

Did he, though?

He glanced behind him at the cabin. Even if it needed

new chinking in places, it'd been constructed of sturdy logs, had a window with shutters, and the floor inside was made of planks, not dirt. Yes, it was only one room. But that wasn't anything unusual for either Willow or him. The flats in Manchester had been one room for entire families. They were used to sharing space and crowded conditions.

But with a wooden framed bed built into the logs and the stove against the other wall, they would be living in tighter quarters than usual.

Willow watched him, waiting expectantly for him to present a plan that would allow them to live on the farm together, the farm they'd both been dreaming about having.

The truth was, he hadn't stopped to consider their living arrangements on the island. After all, he'd been visiting with her at all hours of the day and night for years, even sitting with her on her bed. He supposed he hadn't thought it would matter if they actually stayed in the same cabin together.

But were Jonas and Elijah right? Would living with her ruin her reputation? When the other residents on the island learned that they were staying in the same cabin together outside the bounds of marriage, people would gossip, might even shun them, might consider Willow a loose woman.

He didn't want that to happen.

He could feel his muscles tensing with the need to put an end to the conversation.

Jonas met his gaze levelly. "You love her, man. Just marry her."

Marry Willow.

After years of rejecting that possibility, he'd allowed himself to consider the prospect over recent weeks but always as a distant possibility, not something he would do any time soon, not when he still had a lot of work in the weeks and months ahead to convince her to love him in return.

Willow squeezed his arm, her eyes radiating with apology. "I told Jonas we love each other as friends. But he can't accept that a man and woman could care about each other without having ulterior motives."

Jonas didn't release Caleb's gaze. "She told me that if you're willing, she'll marry you."

With a shaky laugh, Willow took a step back. "That's not exactly how the conversation went. I told Jonas you'd never agree to it."

Something in Jonas's eyes seemed to be encouraging him to accept the bargain.

Caleb's pulse spurted with a strange nervousness. Was marrying her really an option?

"You get down on your knee and ask her proper-like," Jonas said with all seriousness. "And when you're done, I'll head right over and get the preacher. He lives on the north end of the island on Vesuvius Bay."

Was Jonas serious? Marry Willow today?

Would Willow really marry him if he asked her to? Or had she agreed to it because she didn't think he ever would propose?

"You don't need to listen to him, Caleb." Willow's voice stretched thin with worry. But worry about what? That he'd be upset by the suggestion?

"Better listen to me and not yourself." Jonas's tone held a twist of sass. "All you've been doing is talking yourself out of having the woman you love. Eventually all that talking is gonna leave you with no one when she finally gets tired of waiting for you."

"Hold on." Willow held up a hand toward Jonas. "I'm not waiting for Caleb. Let's be clear about that."

"You're waiting for him to stop being a big old coward." Jonas might have been speaking the words to Willow, but he looked directly at Caleb, the words hitting him directly in the chest.

Willow started to argue with Jonas again, telling him something about their friendship and how she was content with that. But Caleb couldn't focus on what she was saying. All he could think about was that Jonas was right. He was being a coward.

He might be tough in the boxing ring, but in life, he'd been a coward, letting his fear of becoming like his father control him.

Was it time to show as much courage with his fear of marriage as he always had with his boxing opponents? Surely if he could fight hard to win and become a champion in the ring, he could fight just as hard to make marriage work and be the kind of husband Willow deserved.

Jonas was nodding at something Willow was saying, but his eyes remained on Caleb. Near the cabin, Elijah was still glaring at Caleb, probably wondering why he wasn't already married to a woman as beautiful as Willow.

They were both right. He couldn't stay alone in the tiny cabin with Willow through the spring and summer until her family came. But where else could they go?

Now that Mr. Mann had reported him to the Victoria police for being a thief and attempting murder, Caleb didn't have the freedom to move around. He had to stay in hiding, maybe for a long while, until Mr. Mann forgot about him. Salt Spring Island was the perfect hideaway and the perfect spot to make a new life for himself.

But if Willow didn't live with him, where else could she go on the island? He couldn't ask Jonas and Elijah to house her. Even if they suggested someone else, he'd never trust a complete stranger. And he refused to send her away. He wanted to be near her, wanted to take care of her, wanted to make sure that she was safe and happy.

Why not just marry her? As Jonas said, the only thing holding him back was his own cowardice.

With his heart trembling against his chest, he took a step toward Willow as she continued her rant about how women and men could be friends and people just needed to accept it.

Swallowing hard and pushing away any more excuses that might try to rear up and stop him, he lowered himself to his knee in front of Willow.

Twenty

Willow's voice trailed off as Caleb's knee touched the ground. He wasn't doing what she thought he was, was he?

With all the talk of marriage and the pressure from Jonas and Elijah, why wasn't Caleb taking a swing at one of them? Or at the very least, stalking away?

He bent his head for a moment, his back rose and fell as he took in a breath, then he straightened his shoulders and looked up at her. His eyes were as dark as the thick woodland beyond the cabin. The muscles in his jaw and in his cheeks flexed. And his forehead was grooved with deep, serious lines beneath the brim of his cap.

Her heart picked up its pace, fluttering against her ribs. And her lungs tightened, squeezing the air in them. She started to lift her hands and press them against her chest, but Caleb reached up and caught them.

"Caleb, what are you doing?" She managed to get the words out. But the question wasn't necessary. She already knew he was about to propose that they get married. It really

JODY HEDLUND

was the only option available to them, and he'd obviously come to the same conclusion. Even so, he didn't have to get down on his knee to propose. Doing so made the moment seem too real, as if it meant more than it did.

Because if they did get married, it would be out of convenience, and it wouldn't be a real marriage. Would it?

The thick muscles in Caleb's arm flexed against his coat, and his chest again rose and fell, as though he were bracing himself—maybe even forcing himself—to ask her the question.

But she didn't want him forcing himself. Even if they'd have a marriage in name only, she wanted him to want to be with her, wanted him to be willing to take this step, wanted him to truly be ready.

"Willow? Marry me." His voice was taut, but he drew her hands deeper into the folds of his. The warmth and solidity of his hold enveloped her and made her want to forget about all the reasons why she needed to protest this proposal.

But how could she forget? Not when he'd been so adamant over the years about avoiding marriage. And what about those times when he'd gotten scared of being close to her and pulled away?

Maybe he'd agree to the marriage today. But what would happen when the reality of what he'd done sank in? What would he do then? Would he run away from the island and their marriage?

It was one thing to have him stay away from her for a few days. But if he left her after they were married? She wouldn't be able to survive that.

"No, Caleb." She shook her head and started to back up.

He clasped her hands tighter. "Don't say no." His tone held a note of desperation that she hadn't expected.

She halted.

His eyes searched her face almost frantically before locking with hers. The brown had lightened, as if he'd opened the windows of his soul and was letting her get a glimpse deep inside.

But what was she seeing? She couldn't tell. Was it more of the same attraction that had flared between them recently?

"Please give this a chance." His eyes seemed to plead with her.

Jonas and Elijah were silent, as if hardly daring to breathe. All around, the forest seemed to be holding its breath too. The air was quiet, with only the faint ripple of the stream nearby and the call of a bird. A slight breeze tugged at her scarf and tousled the yellowed grass growing in between the stumps in the clearing near the cabin.

Caleb rubbed his thumb across her knuckles, the gentle caress reminding her of the last time he'd held her hand in the hay pile.

She wouldn't deny that she'd liked his touch then or now. But it was the aftermath that frightened her. "I don't want marriage to ruin our friendship."

"It doesn't have to."

"What if it does?"

"We won't let it."

She wanted to believe him, wanted to have the same confidence. But she couldn't muster any enthusiasm.

From beside the cabin, Elijah cleared his throat. "Frannie and me, we were friends before getting married. And now we're better friends than before."

As nice as it was for Elijah to try to encourage them, he didn't know Caleb well enough to understand the complexity of their relationship. He didn't realize how volatile Caleb could be at times.

Before Willow could think of a response to Elijah and a kind way to turn down Caleb's offer, Caleb pushed up to his feet. He didn't release her hands. Instead, he glared at both Elijah and Jonas before pulling her along toward the cabin.

She stumbled after him, knowing she had to steel herself to resist him.

He pushed open the door and drew her into the interior. A musty scent greeted them along with plenty of dust, highlighted by the slants of sunshine coming through a crack in the shutter.

Her nose tickled with the need to sneeze. Her airways were still tight from moments ago, and she could feel them closing up even more. She had to speak now before her lungs refused to work altogether. "I know you think marriage is our only option," she whispered, guessing that it would be all too easy for Jonas and Elijah to hear their conversation even inside the cabin. "But we don't need to do this. I don't care about my reputation—"

"I care." His whisper turned ragged. "I don't want people talking bad about you." He was still holding her hands tightly, his handsome features dark in the shadows of the cabin.

"Eventually they'll forget."

"Blast it, Willow." He tugged at her, as though to draw her nearer, maybe even against him.

She pulled back. Someone had to oppose this crazy plan. And if he wasn't going to, he left her no choice but to put an end to the madness. "We can't—"

"You know I don't give a farthing what people think about me." He stood rigidly. "But I do care what they say about you. And I care what your mum and dad will say."

Her parents had already encouraged her marriage to Caleb. They certainly would do so now too if they'd had a say in the matter.

"It won't work." She was running out of reasons to protest. Even so, she had to stay strong.

"I'll make it work."

"But I don't want our friendship to change."

"What if it changes for the better?"

"It's already good enough."

"You heard Elijah. He's better friends with Frannie now."

"But what if marriage makes our friendship worse? What if you end up hating me?" She knew her own inadequacies all too well. A husband, no matter how well-meaning, would get tired of a stupid, needy woman like her eventually. At the very least he'd regret marrying her. Maybe he'd even decide he'd had enough and leave her once and for all.

The very thought closed up her throat. She tried to draw in a breath but couldn't get in air.

Caleb's brows furrowed as he took in her gasping. "Hey now." His voice gentled.

She bent over, fighting against the panic that assaulted her whenever she had trouble breathing.

"Calm down." He rubbed her back the way he always did. "Everything will be all right."

But would it? She didn't want to lose Caleb.

"I'll never, ever hate you." His tone was soothing. "That would be impossible with how much I . . ."

She lifted her head, needing to see his face, the solidness of his features, the tenderness of his expression.

He was hunched next to her and continued to rub in a circle.

"With how much you . . . what?"

193

"How much . . . how much I . . . value you and our friendship."

She nodded and managed to wheeze in a small amount of air. If Caleb was willing to try this, shouldn't she be willing to as well?

She struggled for another breath then closed her eyes and let herself focus on his hand on her back comforting her and his strong presence reassuring her.

She could do this.

With a fresh burst of determination, she drew in a large lungful of air and then straightened. "Okay."

"You're doing okay?"

"No. I mean, yes, I'm doing *okay*. But also, *okay*, I'll marry you."

He studied her face intently for several heartbeats, as though searching for the truth. After a moment, he took a step back from her. "I refuse to coerce you into this, Willow."

"And I refuse to coerce you. That's why I'm so hesitant."

He scrubbed a hand down his mouth and jaw. Then he stuffed both hands in his trouser pockets and shifted away. He seemed to be warring an inner battle before turning back to her. "If I told you I want to marry you, that I was thinking about that possibility eventually anyways, what would you say?"

"You were thinking about it already? Before today?"

"I told you I've been thinking about having more than just friendship."

"I didn't know you were talking about us."

"Well, I was."

Something about his tone was different, made her unsteady, almost dizzy. And something seemed to spark in the air. She wasn't sure what it was, but it was a strong force, one she'd felt with him on occasion recently, one she liked too much.

Whatever it was, she had to be careful. "So you're not upset?"

"As long as you're not upset."

Maybe she was nervous, worried, uncertain. But she wasn't upset. If this was what they needed to do in order to get by in the new colony, then she'd resign herself to it.

"Marriage is permanent, Caleb."

"As far as I'm concerned, so is our friendship."

"True." A smile finally worked its way up her lips. "So does that mean marriage won't have to change anything between us?"

He started to nod, then hesitated.

If she kept everything the same between them, then maybe she wouldn't have to worry—as much—about eventually pushing him away. "Aren't you happy with the way things are?"

"I'm always happy with you." He didn't meet her gaze. "But I'd be lying if I said I won't ever want to sleep with my wife."

Embarrassment swept through her, sending heat to her cheeks. She reached over and swatted him on the arm. "You're terrible."

A grin tugged at his lips. "It's the truth. I am just a man, and you're a beautiful woman."

"Eww!" She pushed him this time, even as the heat seemed to move from her cheeks to pool in her stomach. "I don't want to think about that. Please."

"Fine." He shrugged. "But someday you'll want babies, and you do know that you can't have a baby without—"

"Caleb!" She clamped her hands over her ears, but that

didn't stop her from hearing his laughter . . . along with the echo of his words from a moment ago. *You're a beautiful woman.*

Caleb thought she was beautiful.

She smiled. She couldn't help it. And as she lowered her hands and met Caleb's gaze, she realized his eyes were happy. *He* was happy.

She hadn't seen him genuinely happy too often over the years she'd known him. If she could make him happy—if this new arrangement would make him happy—then she wanted to do it. She just hoped the happiness would last, and that someday he wouldn't come to regret this hasty decision to marry her.

Twenty-One

Caleb wanted someone to punch him just to make sure he wasn't dreaming. Was he really standing in front of the preacher, getting married to Willow on the beach with the sunset coloring the sky?

He'd hardly been able to take his eyes off her from the moment she'd walked down the path that led to the beach, dressed in the gown she saved for church and special occasions, a pretty blue one that made her eyes a brighter shade.

Elijah's wife, Frannie, had helped Willow get ready and had styled her hair in loose waves pulled away from her face by two small braids that were intertwined with a white ribbon, the ends fluttering in her long hair.

His knees had nearly buckled when she started across the pebbly span of beach toward him, a shy smile upon her lips. The low rays of the sun had cast a warm glow on her skin and turned her hair into a golden fire.

The lines for a new poem had easily surfaced:

I've been chasing after empty dreams,
Trying to ease the ache with all I do.
But I'm finally wide awake,
And the only one I'm chasing is you.

Standing beside him, Jonas had seen his reaction and had clamped him on the shoulders and laughed. "Told you so." Jonas had chuckled. "Yessir, you gonna be thanking me for a long time to come."

Caleb *was* thanking Jonas for pushing him into the marriage. There was no telling if he ever would have gathered the courage on his own or if he would have let things continue on as they'd been.

Jonas had also been the one to track down Reverend Wallace—Wally as he liked to be called. The middle-aged Black man hadn't been home when Jonas had arrived in the northern settlement of the island, so Jonas had spent a good portion of the afternoon looking for him.

Caleb could admit he'd been hesitant to reveal his presence on the island to Wally. But Jonas had insisted that the reverend—and all the other refugees on the island—had experienced injustices for themselves and would be sympathetic to him.

By the time Jonas had returned with the preacher, Frannie had already prepared a wedding dinner of roasted eels, potatoes, and bread with raspberry preserves.

When they'd finished the fine meal, Willow had asked if they could hold the ceremony on the beach. Somehow that simple request had soothed the guilt Caleb had been battling for convincing her to marry him when she'd been hesitant.

Now, with Frannie and Elijah and Jonas watching, Caleb held Willow's hands and she finished reciting her vow promising to have and to hold him. Her voice contained a sincerity that was also working to soothe his guilt. Maybe she wasn't so opposed to marrying him after all.

He understood her reservations and that she was worried about losing their friendship. He wouldn't deny he had reservations too. He'd been battling his ghosts ever since she'd agreed to marry him.

Regardless of everything, he intended to take things slow with Willow and show her how much he adored her without scaring her. He only had to think about his proposal earlier to know how easily spooked she got. And even though they were getting married, she'd made it clear that she didn't want anything to change.

At least he'd been brave enough to let her know that eventually he wanted to have more than just a friendship. Maybe he hadn't exactly been tactful about it. He should have told her that he loved her as more than a friend and that someday, hopefully, she'd love him as more than a friend too. But he'd never been particularly smooth at sharing his feelings aloud. He was better at putting them on paper.

Now that she knew he was planning on more between them, maybe she wouldn't feel deceived or frustrated when he began to show his feelings for her more often.

"Your turn, Caleb." Wally stood with his back facing the setting sun in a dark evening suit, his coattails long like Mr. Mann's and a tall top hat upon his head. With dark sideburns and a trimmed beard surrounding his ebony face, he had the air of a gentleman—refined, educated, and proper. Perhaps he'd even been wealthy at one time. Why was he now living on Salt Spring Island among poor farmers?

As Wally recited from the book in his hand, Caleb

repeated after him. "I, Caleb, take thee, Willow, to be my wedded wife."

Willow peered up at him, her eyes wide. The questions danced around the beautiful blue. Even though she wasn't asking them aloud, he guessed she was wondering what his vow meant. After all, he hadn't been all that great about keeping his vows in the past. But this was different, wasn't it?

"To have and to hold," he continued, "from this day forward, for better, for worse, for richer, for poorer, in sickness, and in health. To love and to cherish, till death us do part—"

He paused, his throat going suddenly dry. What made him think he could actually be a good husband to her?

His mind flashed to the image of his father gripping his mother by her throat, squeezing it so that she couldn't breathe. Her eyes had rounded with panic. She'd clawed at his hands, trying to break his hold. Caleb couldn't remember how old he'd been, but he'd grabbed the only weapon he could find, the iron skillet on the stove, and he'd whacked it against his father's back. His father had probably hardly felt the hit. But at least he'd released her and turned and grabbed Caleb instead.

Wally cleared his throat, his warm brown eyes encouraging Caleb to continue.

Could he, though? What if he was making a huge mistake? He wanted to be the kind of man who would love and cherish Willow all the days of her life. But what if he failed?

As Willow's fingers trembled against his, he dropped his gaze to their hands. His tanned skin contrasted against her pale flesh. And his large fingers engulfed her delicate ones.

She'd agreed to this, agreed to marry him, agreed to be his. He couldn't walk away from that now.

He shoved aside the doubts and forced himself to finish the vow. "According to God's holy ordinance, and thereto I give thee my troth."

Willow seemed to swallow hard, as if his hesitancy was unleashing hers.

They needed to hurry up before either one of them changed their minds. "Are we done?" He directed his question to Wally.

"Almost." Wally flipped the page in his prayer book.

They'd already established that they would have to skip the ring part of the ceremony since Caleb didn't have anything to give Willow. Someday he would, but they'd both agreed that right now saving for her family to come to the colony was more important than a ring.

"For as much as Caleb and Willow have consented together in holy wedlock, and have witnessed the same before God, and this company, and thereto have given and pledged their troth to each other, I pronounce that they be man and wife together. In the name of the Father, of the Son, and of the Holy Ghost. Amen."

"Amen!" Jonas called out.

"Hallelujah!" Frannie came up from behind and gave Willow a side hug, her face wreathed with a smile.

Willow started to pull her hand from Caleb's, but Frannie stopped her by folding a hand over hers. "Now hold on. We ain't gonna make you jump the broom like me and Elijah did when we got married. But I have a tradition from my family that I'd like you to do."

Caleb opened his mouth to protest, but Willow was already nodding at Frannie, giving her permission to proceed.

The sky was still streaked with a hue of beautiful colors unlike anything he'd ever seen in Manchester. With every passing day living in the colony with the open skies and the unending forests, the gray bleakness of life in the city grew more distant, like a bad dream that was fading in the light of the new day.

This evening, this wedding, his life with Willow—it was just one more step in the new life he was making for himself as he left the past behind. He couldn't forget that.

Frannie began to unwrap a bundle that she'd pulled from her pocket. She tugged it open to reveal four small brown bottles. "This is what we call the taste of the four elements."

Even though Caleb wanted to be done with the ceremony, Jonas and Elijah and even Wally were watching Frannie with solemn expressions that said they took the tradition seriously.

She handed a bottle to Willow. "Take a tiny sip."

Willow didn't hesitate. She uncorked the bottle, lifted it to her lips, and tasted the liquid. Her lips puckered. "Oh my. That's sour."

Frannie smiled. "Caleb, your turn."

As Willow held out the bottle to him, Caleb was tempted to push it away. But at the curiosity brimming from Willow's eyes, he took it and made himself drink a sip. The sourness hit him too, but he forced himself not to react, especially since everyone was staring at him.

"It's lemon juice." Frannie retrieved the bottle and began to cork it. "The sourness of the lemon represents the sour times you will face in your marriage—the disappointments, the frustrations, and the less than perfect moments. After all, we can't have successes without also having failures. If you'll remember and accept that, then say 'we will.'"

It was almost as if Frannie had heard his thoughts and his fear of failure from moments ago.

"We will." Willow spoke first.

"We will," he echoed, even though he wasn't planning to have any failures if at all possible.

Frannie did the same ritual for the next three bottles. One was filled with vinegar to represent the bitter times in life—the adversity, suffering, and grief. Another contained honey which symbolized the sweetness of marriage in all stages of life. And the final one held an ale with cayenne pepper.

After Caleb handed Frannie back the fourth bottle, she shared the meaning. "The cayenne pepper represents the heat, spice, and passion that you'll feel for each other. God created marriage to be that place where the deepest longings and desires can be expressed without any hindrances, holding back, or hiding. If you'll remember and accept that, then say 'we will.'"

Willow's cheeks had grown decidedly pinker with the revelation of the meaning of the cayenne pepper. Even so, she responded with "we will" at the same time that he did.

As soon as the words were out of his mouth, Jonas bumped Caleb in the arm. "Might as well start expressing that spice right here and now." He was grinning widely, a gleam in his eyes.

Caleb's stomach tumbled. He knew exactly what Jonas was referring to.

"What do you say, Wally?" Jonas turned an expectant gaze upon the preacher. "Don't you usually have the newly wedded couple seal their vows with a kiss?"

Wally nodded. "I agree. Caleb, you may now kiss your bride."

Willow took a rapid step back, bumping into Frannie and the swell of her unborn child.

Frannie—even with her hands full with the bottles—forcefully thrust Willow toward Caleb.

She stumbled and landed against him, but she braced herself with both hands against his chest as if she had every intention of shoving him away if he made any move to kiss her.

Caleb wouldn't force himself on her, not in a million years. But saints have mercy on his soul. He'd been thinking about kissing her for years, and the desire had been simmering for so long that now, with everyone giving him permission and practically demanding it of him, he no longer had a reason to restrain himself.

He had been wanting to show her that he cared about her beyond mere friendship. He'd even warned her that he wanted to be more than friends. How could he turn down the opportunity being handed to him?

He couldn't.

He settled his hands on her hips, the curves there beckoning to him. He spread his fingers, relishing the feel of her, while at the same time drawing her closer.

At his movement, Willow ceased struggling and studied his face, as if attempting to read his intentions. If he hadn't made himself clear yet that he was going to kiss her, then he needed to do a better job of it.

He slid one of his hands to the dip of her lower back, that spot where he could lose himself if he lingered too long. Then he glided his hand up her spine, skating his fingers along gently until he reached her hair.

All the while, he watched her reaction, her eyes widening with each move he made. In fact, the blue was so wide and deep and clear that he wanted to sink in and let himself drown there. But as his fingers reached her hair, he paused. He'd briefly touched her hair that night on her bed earlier in the week. It had been nothing more than a light sweep. But now . . . ?

He plunged his fingers in, letting himself get the full feel of her silky tresses in a way he'd only dreamed about. In fact, she felt better than he'd imagined, like the richest of velvets. A groan pressed at his throat, but he swallowed it.

Her lashes fanned out, long and thick. And her lips parted just slightly, as if he'd taken her by surprise by touching her hair.

He was going to kiss those lips finally, and just the thought of doing so made him dizzy with how much he wanted her.

He dug deeper into her hair and used the pressure to guide her head closer to his.

She didn't resist. In fact, those lashes fell, brushing against her cheeks, as if she was giving him the freedom to do whatever he wanted to her. What would he do if he really could do whatever he wanted?

Heat speared his body at the prospect. He'd wrap his arms around her and pull her flush until he could feel her heart beating against his. Then he'd taste her, starting with her hair, her forehead, nose, lips, chin, then her neck, and her shoulder blade.

But he couldn't do any of that now. He had an audience. A waiting audience.

With his fingers still stuck deep in her hair, he positioned her head until her lips were almost touching his. He could feel the whisper of an exhale, as if she'd stopped breathing and was waiting in anticipation of what he'd do.

Was she wanting the kiss too? Was she wondering what it would be like?

He lightly grazed her mouth, his own lashes falling at the exquisiteness of the connection, so light and yet sizzling with a humming energy of possibility.

She started to pull back, as though she believed the two seconds of their lips brushing amounted to a kiss.

It wasn't even a prelude, not even close.

Using the hand still on her hip, he brought her body flush against his. Her softness, curves, and warmth ignited him into a thousand fires. Unable to hold back any longer, he captured her mouth.

The stirring of her lips against his was light, tentative. And somewhere in the back of his mind he registered the fact that this was her first kiss, that he was her first, that he would be the only man she ever kissed.

Even though he wanted to hungrily devour her mouth like a man who'd been waiting for this moment, this taste for years—because he had been—he shifted against her lightly, restraining himself. Even so, he deepened the kiss, his lips moving against hers like they'd been made to fit.

The problem was, now that he'd started kissing her, how could he ever stop?

Twenty-Two

Caleb's kiss was so earth-shattering, Willow felt like the ground beneath her was crumbling with nothing to hold her steady.

She grabbed onto his shirt and clutched the fabric, as if that could somehow keep her from toppling. But nothing could keep her from slipping farther into an abyss where it was just the two of them floating together, the beating of their hearts the only sound.

His lips were firm and yet tender, their rhythm against hers demanding and yet careful. His muscles surrounding her flexed as though he would crush her to himself and kiss her much harder if he allowed himself. But from the way his hand at her hip fisted and the hand in her hair tightened, she sensed that he wouldn't allow himself anything more.

But as the world spun around her, her stomach was spinning too, in an endless twirl.

This closeness to him, the length of his body, the scrape of his chin, the heat of his mouth—all of it only made her want to stay right where she was with him and never return to earth. Sensations she couldn't explain were pulsing through her with greater intensity, sensations that were pleasurable and filling her with a tight wanting.

She longed to keep kissing him, didn't want his lips to move away, and she couldn't explain the need, except that this was Caleb, and maybe she'd always wanted to kiss him and had just been lying to herself about it.

"Now that's what I'm talking about," came a man's voice from beside them.

Caleb broke the kiss and ducked his head so that his cheek brushed hers and his mouth grazed her ear. His breathing was choppy and warm, and it sent her into another spin, one that made her grasp his shirt harder, although she wasn't sure why.

"I'm thinking that cayenne pepper is working its magic." The teasing voice belonged to Frannie.

Willow buried her face against Caleb's chest. What had she done? How had she dared to kiss Caleb that way, especially in front of everyone?

The laughter of the others around them seemed happy, as if she and Caleb had done something good that they should be proud of. But what would Caleb think? Even if in the moment he'd done what everyone had pressured him to do, the kiss was bound to scare him.

Willow pushed against Caleb's chest, needing to put some distance between them.

His hold only loosened a little.

Beside her, Frannie gave her a smile and a wink. "It's clear to see that you're gonna need a bigger cabin soon, just like we did."

"Oh my." Willow scrambled backward, almost desperate

to escape Caleb's arms. And thankfully, this time he released her. She was in such a hurry to get away from him, that she stumbled into Wally and knocked off his top hat. She hastily bent to retrieve it, feeling Caleb watching her every move, his gaze somehow searing into her and leaving her breathless.

She did her best to focus on Wally as she returned his hat, but she was all too conscious of Jonas and Elijah slapping Caleb's back and congratulating him. And he was accepting their teasing with a grin.

Caleb was grinning after kissing her?

How was that possible?

Even though she didn't want to look at him—or have him catch her looking—the grin made him irresistibly handsome, so much so that her heart squeezed painfully at the sight of him carefree and happy as he talked with Jonas and Elijah.

How could any one man have so many muscles and such darkly chiseled features? And why did that one man have to be her best friend? The man who'd been off limits for so many years? The man who'd now become her husband?

As his gaze slid to her, almost as if he'd sensed her ogling, she forced her attention back on Frannie and the preacher. But just that one tiny sideways glance made her stomach start bobbing like a boat in waves.

What was wrong with her? Why was she reacting to Caleb this way?

With the last rays of the sun sinking behind the western horizon, the coolness of the February night seemed to settle around them. Willow gathered her cloak tighter to ward off the chill, but a new kind of heat was pumping through her veins.

She could feel Caleb watching her again, and immediately

her mind returned to the kiss, the way he'd taken control and pulled her close. The moment his hands had touched her hips and back and hair, she'd grown breathless. Had his grip been possessive? As if he'd wanted to hold her and never let her go?

She gave a quick shake of her head to throw off such thoughts. She had to pull herself together or things would grow increasingly awkward until she lost him and what they had together.

As Jonas finally directed the steamboat away from the dock to return Wally home, they watched it in the growing darkness for a few moments before turning and starting up the path back to the cabins. Willow fell into step with Frannie, and Caleb and Elijah followed behind them, conversing about all that still needed to be fixed on the cabin.

Even without the repairs, the place was livable. She and Frannie had spent part of the afternoon cleaning the inside. Frannie had offered Willow as much as she could spare—a couple of blankets and towels, a few cooking items, a worn rug, a rusty lantern, and even an old broom.

In addition to the help with the cleaning, Frannie had shared tips on how to be resourceful with the little they had, including showing Willow how to stuff the mattress with dried grass, how to make a pillow out of a grain sack, where to fetch clean water, how to find edible root vegetables, and how to fish for eels and dig for clams.

Willow hadn't wanted to admit just how overwhelmed she was by the prospect of having to learn so much again. She'd finally adjusted to her chores at the White Swan, and now her work would be even harder, and she would have to survive on so much less.

Even so, the thought of the months ahead filled her with a

thrill that she and Caleb could own land and have a farm—something that would have been impossible back in England.

They both had their earnings saved from their work at the White Swan, and if they were careful, they could make their money go a long way. They would have to wait longer to send money back to her family, but in the end, they'd earn more from their farm than from working for the Manns.

As they said goodnight to Frannie and Elijah and continued on their way across the stream, Caleb was quiet.

She didn't quite know what to say either. The day had certainly taken a turn she hadn't expected. Never would she have believed when she'd woken at dawn that by the day's end she'd be married to Caleb, that she'd be his wife.

Wife.

The very word sent a strange shiver through her.

Their footsteps crunched on the pebbles that lined the path. It was the only sound except for a raspy call of a gull or hawk. She wanted to talk about their day, but the silence seemed somehow charged, and she wasn't sure what to say about everything.

Though the darkness of night had settled, enough faint light remained for them to see where they were going and to view the cabin across the clearing against the backdrop of the forest.

The woodpile Caleb had chopped was stacked beside the cabin, and a few tools were propped nearby.

Soon enough they'd have a garden and cleared field. Eventually they'd build a barn and add on to the cabin to make it bigger. Someday, they'd have livestock, and the place would be everything they'd hoped for.

She didn't realize her steps had slowed to a stop until

Caleb spoke from beside her. "What are you thinking?" His voice was low, tentative.

He wasn't having doubts about what they'd done, was he? About moving to the island or getting married or both?

She had to reassure him that everything would be fine, that they would be fine, that their friendship was strong enough to survive all the changes. "This is more than we could have hoped for, Caleb. I know we're going to be happy here."

He exhaled slowly, as if he'd been holding his breath. "Then you're not upset at . . . anything?"

By *anything* did he mean the kiss? "No, I'm not upset at . . . anything."

"Good."

"Yes, good." She waited for him to say more.

But he shifted, rubbed at the back of his neck.

"Are you upset at . . . anything?" she finally asked.

"No." The one word came out rushed. "Not at all."

"Okay, good."

"Good."

She rolled her eyes. They were starting to sound like toddlers who weren't able to speak in full sentences. But she couldn't make herself bring up the kiss directly. It was too astonishing to think that Caleb had held her and kissed her as if she were a desirable woman and not just a friend.

In fact, just remembering how his mouth had plied at hers made her insides quaver. . . a quavering she didn't want to feel.

Shaking off the memory, she started forward again, hurrying ahead of Caleb. When she reached the cabin, she let herself in. She stopped short at the darkness that greeted her.

As she blinked and tried to remember where she'd placed

the lantern, Caleb bumped into her from behind. His chest thudded against her back, knocking her off balance. Before she could stumble, his hands landed on her hips, steadying her.

At the same time, his hold unsteadied her, and all she could think about was his hard chest against her back, his fingers pressed firmly into her sides, his face just behind her head, so close that she could hear him breathing.

Her entire body was suddenly in tune with him, as if he'd caressed her again. But he hadn't done anything except bump her.

Was this how it would be every time they touched, even accidentally? How would she survive such attraction to him every day?

She stepped farther into the cabin, pretending not to notice the way they'd just touched and the feelings it stirred. That's what she needed to do, keep pretending that nothing was changing between them, and maybe eventually the sparks would settle down and go away. After all, fire without more fuel always had a way of dying.

She fumbled with an outstretched hand until she found the shelf on the wall near the stove. It wasn't long before she had the lantern lit and placed it on the planks laid across barrels that would serve as a table until they could afford a real one. Within minutes, Caleb had a small fire burning in the stove, and the room turned cozy.

As she started to tug her nightgown out of the crate underneath the bed, Caleb made up an excuse about needing to get more kindling and stepped outside, closing the door firmly behind him.

With her heart pounding an unusually fast tempo, she changed and then dove under the blankets on the bed. Caleb had seen her wearing her nightgown plenty of times in the past, so why did she care if he saw her tonight?

She was being a prude, that's why. And she needed to relax, stop acting so silly, and just be herself.

She sat up, but before she could make up her mind on whether to sit on the edge or stand up, a soft knock came against the door. "I'm coming in." Caleb's voice held a warning of sorts.

Her heart took off into a gallop even though she tried to rein it in.

Several seconds passed before the door began to slowly open.

She curled her feet up and tugged the blanket up to her chin, although she still didn't know why she felt so awkward.

As he stepped inside, he cast a glance her way before closing the door, a visible tension easing from his shoulders.

He crossed to the stove where he emptied the kindling piled in his arms. He fiddled with the fire for another moment before standing, stuffing his hands in his pockets, and glancing everywhere but her.

"Are you warm?" he asked.

"How are you?" she asked at the same time.

She released a small huff, already growing weary of their arrangement after only having been married for less than an hour. "Please, Caleb. Can we please act normal around each other?"

His jaw ticced, and his dark eyes seemed stormy. "What's normal?"

"You know. The way it's always been."

"Don't you think we need to change . . . at least a little?"

"No." The word came out passionately. "Not at all."

He kneaded the back of his neck, hesitated, then fished in

his pocket before pulling out something. "I found this for you today." He crossed to the bed and held out a small stone.

She took it, knowing that this was his way of trying to respect her request to act normal with each other. "Thank you, Caleb . . ." Her words drifted off as she fingered the stone. It was in the shape of a heart.

Under any other circumstances and any other day, she would have exclaimed over it, called it beautiful, and bubbled with gratitude. But today, on her wedding day, his giving her a heart-shaped rock seemed to send a message, whether he was really sending one or not.

Of course she'd heard the others teasing Caleb about loving her. And there was still Juliet's declarations of Caleb being madly in love with her and having eyes for no one else but her. What if Caleb did love her as more than a friend? He'd certainly kissed her as more than one.

"I found it along the riverbank yesterday." He offered the explanation as if that cleared up his feelings and made everything all right.

Nothing was actually cleared up or all right.

Caleb began to shrug out of his coat, his muscles straining against his seams as they usually did. She'd watched him take off his coat a thousand times, watched his muscles flex even more.

But this time, her stomach did a strange flop, sending a splash of heat into her face, and she turned her focus to the rock, twisting it around in her hand.

Where did he plan to sleep tonight? The bed was big enough for two people, and it didn't seem fair that she should take up the entire luxury whilst he was relegated to the floor.

Before she could figure out how to bring up the subject,

he swiped the extra blanket on the end of the bed and tossed it onto the floor beside her.

She breathed a sigh of relief.

He paused.

She stopped breathing altogether. Had he heard her?

He hesitated only a moment longer before spreading out the blanket. Then he lowered himself and sprawled out on it. He crossed his arms behind his head and stared up at the log ceiling beams, his biceps rounded and his strong chest visible through his shirt.

She leaned back too, the tension in her body only growing tighter with each passing second. Already things were changing between them for the worse. They shouldn't have gotten married. "Caleb, I wish we wouldn't have—"

"Do you want to hear my latest poem?" He rolled over and dug in his bag beside the bed.

"Of course." She expelled another breath, trying to do so softly this time.

"I wrote it last night."

She shifted to her side and settled her head against the makeshift pillow. "Read them all to me."

She loved when Caleb read to her. She'd never learned to read well, had always mixed up the letters of the alphabet. Even though her mum and her Ragged School teacher had tried to help her learn the differences between b's and d's and p's and q's, she'd never caught on. Eventually, after struggling and only growing more frustrated, she'd stopped going to school.

Of course, it hadn't helped that Sage had always excelled at everything she did. She'd been the best student, the best mill worker, the best daughter. She'd even found the best man to marry—a man who had steady employment and who wasn't afraid to show her that he loved her.

Willow had always been happy for Sage, or at least she'd tried to be. But she could admit that sometimes it seemed as though Sage had gotten all the good gifts, and Willow had received the leftovers.

Caleb was pulling out his journal, one of many he'd had over the past couple of years for his poetry writing. Much of his early poetry had been about the poverty and sadness that he saw in Manchester. Some of his poems had been about the mills, the working conditions and the people he worked with. Sometimes he'd written silly verses about her and her sisters. Other times, he'd penned more serious poems that gave her glimpses into the hurt and heartache of his family and past.

Caleb had only brought a couple of his older journals with him to the colony, had apparently burned the rest before leaving. Whilst she'd been disappointed at their destruction, he'd kept her entertained with his new prose, which had been filled with his impressions of the voyage to the colony and of Vancouver Island.

More than his impressions, his poetry gave voice to all that was going on inside him—maybe not *all*. But hearing his poems was like getting a glimpse into emotions that he so carefully locked away most of the time. And she liked seeing the side of him that no one else knew about.

Caleb paged through the journal until he reached the spot where he'd left his pencil. As he stuck the short stub behind his ear and scanned the page, she smiled.

He glanced up, catching her watching him. "What?"

"Nothing. I just love your poems. That's all."

He focused back on the journal, then a moment later, he

began to read in his usual quiet tone, as if he was afraid of someone else overhearing him.

> *"Broken pieces, crushed down, smashed into*
>   *dust.*
> *I'm shattered and can't go on, but I must.*
> *The water and waves beckon to me*
> *Sweeping all the fragments into the sea.*
> *Some of the shards sink down deep*
> *But there are others that the water wants to*
>   *keep.*
> *Floating and tossing in the ebb and flow*
> *The current takes me to a place I don't know.*
> *As I finally reach the edge of the shore*
> *Those broken parts inside me grasp for more.*
> *The land spreads out before me new*
> *It's a place I want to share with you."*

He fell silent and grew pensive as he always did whenever he finished reading one of his poems. It was something she liked about him immensely, that he thought so deeply about life.

She didn't respond. Instead, she waited for him to look up at her with his beautiful, questioning eyes when he was seeking her reaction.

And sure enough, a moment later, his gaze lifted to her with arched brows.

"It's full of both hurt and hope." She gave her candid thoughts, the way he liked. "The imagery makes me feel like no matter how much adversity I might face, that through it all, God will carry me, letting the old slip away and the new take its place."

He nodded. "The brokenness might never go away, but that doesn't mean we can't find hope again." His eyes were filled with hope—hope of starting over in this new place, hope of a future, hope to share it with the people they loved.

Willow smiled and let his hope settle inside her. Maybe everything would work out fine between her and Caleb after all. Maybe she was worried for nothing.

But even as she rested her head against her pillow, the sliver of worry taunted her that she'd never be enough for him.

Twenty-Three

W hat was wrong with him?

With a sigh of frustration, Caleb tugged on the reins and halted the team of oxen pulling the plow. The ornery creatures didn't need much encouragement to stop. They flicked their ears and tails as though to tell Caleb to go throw himself into the sea.

Maybe he should. To cool himself off. And not just from the late afternoon sunshine on the mid-March day. The heat burning him up had more to do with the image of Willow from early in the day when she'd been lying in bed, tangled in the covers, her hair spread all around her pillow, and her sleepy eyes peering at him in the low lantern light as he'd started the coffee.

He'd been married to Willow for over three weeks, and he wasn't making any progress in winning her. Not a single step.

If anything, he was regressing.

Every time he made an effort to show her his feelings, she seemed to ignore it. If he touched her hand, she slipped it in her pocket. If he gave her a compliment, she merely gave him one in return. If he fingered her hair, she tucked it away. If he let his gaze linger on her too long, she grew quiet.

A breeze filled with the smoke from smoldering windfall tickled his nostrils, drawing his gaze skyward to the hazy clouds and the darkness of evening settling in. Though the days were growing longer, night fell earlier than he preferred.

He had too much to do to let darkness stop him. So most evenings, he continued doing other tasks by lantern light. He'd built a chicken coop. When he'd finished with that, he'd started planing off the bark from the logs he'd saved to use for building a barn.

He wiped his perspiring brow with his sleeve then leaned against the wooden plow handle, his back and arms burning from the effort of turning up another acre of hard earth among the stumps. The black soil he'd just plowed spread out around him, still in large clumps and littered with stones and roots and brush.

But he'd been doing well. He'd already cleared a couple of acres of land with the fewest trees and brush. Willow had helped him for hours every day, chopping off branches and dragging what they couldn't use into piles that he'd already started burning.

With the past week of warmer spring weather, though, he'd stopped the clearing in order to start getting the land ready for planting. Jonas said potatoes grew well on the island and did better among the stumps than other crops. And potatoes were hardy enough to sell.

So Caleb had purchased seed potatoes from several other farmers on the island, including Jonas, and he'd spent the earlier part of the week plowing the potato patch and planting the spuds. Now he was plowing more of the cleared land to plant peas, which also grew well among the bracken.

Jonas and Elijah had let him borrow the oxen and the plow, since they'd already completed their plowing the previous week. And they'd been generous with him and Willow in countless other ways too, giving them advice and teaching them all they knew.

Frannie had helped Willow dig up and plant a vegetable garden near the cabin, showing her how to arrange the plot to get the most from it. She'd given Willow several baby chicks that were growing fast. And she'd even offered to give Willow a piglet once it was ready to leave the sow.

Frannie had given birth to a boy two days ago, and Willow had been caring for Frannie and the baby. He couldn't begrudge Willow taking the time away from their farm to help Frannie, not after how much Frannie had done for them.

Even so, he missed having Willow around as he worked. She was good company, and even when they were both too exhausted from the work to talk, at least she was there with him.

He loved being with her just as much as he always did, and he was actually relieved that he finally could stay with her every night instead of having to sneak around trying to spend time with her the way he always had.

Although it was still awkward at times, he tried to give her the privacy she needed for dressing. And so that he didn't embarrass her too much, he took off his clothes in the dark when the lantern was extinguished.

The only trouble with sleeping beside her on the floor was when her breathing or shifting or soft sighs made him think thoughts that he shouldn't about her—or at least thoughts he shouldn't be thinking yet.

When he saw her like he had this morning looking so

beautiful . . . he'd wanted to pull out his journal and create another poem about her. He already had dozens and dozens of them penned between all the others. Of course he never read those to her, never mentioned them, never showed them to her. And he'd never worried about her trying to read his journal and discovering them, not only because she couldn't read well, but also because she'd never been meddlesome.

The truth was, he loved her more with every passing day. But with every passing day, she seemed more determined than ever not to allow anything to change between them.

A whistling of a merry tune wafted toward Caleb, a whistling he'd come to recognize as belonging to Elijah. Sure enough, a moment later Elijah came hiking through the sparse woodland that separated the cleared fields from the cabin.

At the sight of Caleb, Elijah stopped and grinned. "You ever stop working?" Elijah had proven himself to be as hard a worker as Caleb, and even though he was much thinner and lankier, he was strong and could lift heavy loads, often surprising Caleb with his abilities.

"Do *you* ever stop?" Caleb called back.

"Nope." Elijah kicked a large rock from the soil, as if to make his point. "A fellow I know on the north end of the island is looking to hire help over the next week with butchering if you're interested."

Caleb didn't know the first thing about slaughtering livestock. But he was learning now why Jonas had the job on the steamboat while Elijah manned the farm. It provided them with a steady income that helped them through the leaner times.

A few days ago, Caleb had confided in Elijah the need for extra work, especially now that he'd used up the last of his earnings from the White Swan to purchase the potato seedlings and pea seeds. Not only did he need money to buy more seeds—this time for barley and oats—but he needed more nails, coal oil, and some staple foods like flour and coffee beans so that Willow wouldn't go hungry.

Of course, Caleb couldn't go into Victoria for employment or even assist Jonas on the steamboat for fear of being recognized. Jonas kept him regularly apprised of the news, and Jonas didn't think Mr. Mann was actively searching for Caleb and was more interested in locating Isaac.

Regardless, Caleb knew Mr. Mann wouldn't be quick to forgive him for all that had happened or be willing to drop the charges.

"His name's Stark, a real nice man," Elijah continued. "He's got a herd of longhorns he brought up from Oregon and has been supplying beef to Victoria and Nanaimo—"

"I'll do it." Caleb didn't need to know any more about the job. He'd do anything, just like he had in Manchester after the mills closed.

"That's what I told Wally." Elijah wound through the potato hills, drawing nearer. "You can take the canoe first thing tomorrow morning."

Gratefulness welled up within Caleb. Elijah and Jonas had no reason to help him and had enough hardship of their own to deal with. But they'd offered him one kindness after another since the moment he'd arrived.

Elijah helped him unhitch the oxen from the plow, and together they walked the creatures back to the barn. Caleb took care of the barn chores so that Elijah could be with his wife and new baby, Malachi.

By the time Caleb ducked outside the barn, the darkness of night had fallen. As he made his way over the stream and the short distance home, his pulse began to race with the anticipation of seeing Willow. She'd probably have a simple fare simmering on the stove like she did most nights, having learned from Frannie several easy meals that stretched the little food they had a long way.

When the cabin came into view, he stopped short at the sight of darkness in the shutter and door cracks where usually there was light. For a moment, he wavered. Was Willow still with Frannie and the baby? Maybe he ought to go back and see.

But no, she would have left—like she had the previous evenings—when Elijah and Jonas came home. If she wasn't with Frannie, where could she be?

Had she encountered problems with the natives? Even though no natives lived permanently on Salt Spring Island, the island had been part of the hunting, fishing, and clamming grounds for several tribes. The island was also on the annual migration route of the Haidas and other northern tribes. So the natives hadn't been pleased to have the settlers here.

According to Jonas and Elijah, the natives had been aggressive last year. But this year, after a smallpox outbreak among the tribes, they hadn't seen quite as many on the island until the past week or so when several groups had been spotted in the area fishing and hunting.

Even though Caleb wasn't afraid for himself, he was always worried about Willow. And now, at the darkness of the cabin, he picked up his pace until he was moving at a jog. As he reached the cabin, he threw open the door.

"Willow?" He didn't care that his voice contained a note of panic.

At the sound of sniffling coming from the bed, his

muscles tensed, and he strained to see in the dark. Had someone broken in and hurt her?

He couldn't see much, but from what he could tell, nothing was out of place. Everything looked normal except that Willow was lying on the bed.

"Willow, what's wrong?" He closed the door and crossed to her. Was she having trouble breathing?

A soft sob slipped from between her lips. Willow didn't cry often, but the anguish in that sound was clear enough.

His chest seized. Something had happened. He lowered himself to the wooden box frame. Now that he was beside her, he could see that she was curled up under her blankets, her face buried against her pillow.

He fumbled to reach for her, and as he clasped her arm, he could feel his hand tremble. "What happened?"

She sniffled again and thrust something at him.

He took hold of it, a crumpled and damp sheet of paper.

"It's a letter from home, from Sage," she whispered. "Jonas brought it from Victoria." She'd had him pen a short note to her friends Daisy and Juliet a couple weeks ago so her friends wouldn't worry about her, and she'd told them where she was living, although swearing them to secrecy for Caleb's sake.

Apparently, the two friends had gotten the letter from Sage to Jonas somehow. And clearly, it didn't contain good news.

"Wally was still here and read it to me." She offered the simple explanation with another sob.

Caleb started to rise to light the lantern and read the letter for himself, a new urgency rushing through him. Before he could stand, her fingers grasped his hand and held on to him as though he was the only thing keeping her from falling overboard.

He lowered himself and waited for the bad news.

"Mum caught pneumonia over the winter." Her whisper rushed out on a shaky breath. "Oh, Caleb. She's gone." Another sob slipped from her lips.

He closed his eyes briefly, a sharp pain slicing into his heart. The pain was less for himself and more for Willow. Without giving her a chance to protest or push him away, he scooted onto the bed more fully, lay down beside her, and gathered her against him.

The moment his arms surrounded her, she pressed her face into his chest and the sobs came fast and deep and full of regret.

He held her tightly, smoothing his hand over her hair still tied into the usual knot at the back of her neck. Then he pressed a kiss against the top of her head.

He wished he could make the situation better, that he could take away her pain, that he could shoulder it himself. But the only thing he could do was hold her, feeling her agony like it was his own.

His eyes remained dry, as they always had, but with each of her heart-wrenching sobs, he felt more torn apart than ever before. When finally the crying turned quieter and then changed to sniffling, he could feel her tremble again.

He ran his hand up and down her back to soothe her.

"She would have loved our farm, Caleb." Willow's comment was calmer.

He just kissed the top of her head again, knowing that she wouldn't expect him to answer, that all she needed was for him to listen.

"Of everyone, she would have been the most excited to be here."

For what seemed like hours, they talked and shared memories of her mum. At some point, she grew quiet. When her breathing evened, he knew she'd fallen asleep. He waited long minutes to be sure she was okay, and then he began to scoot away.

Her hand at his chest dug into his shirt. "Don't leave me, Caleb," came her soft whisper.

He froze, hands stalled above her back.

She snuggled into him, as if getting more comfortable. "Please." Her plea was so soft he could hardly hear it. "Stay."

He waited another moment for her to shove him away, sit up, and tell him in a sassy voice to get out of her bed, that friends could never spend the night lying together like this. But she didn't say anything.

Slowly he returned his hands to her back. As he did so, her body seemed to relax even more, and she released a long, almost relieved, breath.

Eventually, he could sense that she'd fallen into a deep slumber. Even then, she clung to him as though she needed him there.

The rational part of his mind clamored a warning, that he should move to the pallet, that in the morning she'd be embarrassed to be in bed with him.

But he couldn't make himself get up, told himself he was only offering her comfort the way any other friend would. The trouble was, he knew he was lying to himself.

Twenty-Four

W illow's chest and throat ached. But as wakefulness wafted through her, the sorrow didn't weigh on her quite as heavily as it had when she'd first heard the news of Mum's death. Yes, the grief was still deep. But it wasn't so crushing.

She started to stretch, but at the tightening of arms around her, she halted. Her eyes flew open to the darkness of the cabin. The slight lightening told her it was yet before dawn.

A hand absently rubbed her back for a few seconds, then warm lips pressed her forehead.

At the gentle contact, the events of the past night came rushing back. She'd been crying in bed, and Caleb had climbed right in. He hadn't hesitated. He'd held her. And he'd comforted her.

He hadn't tried to make her feel better, hadn't offered her platitudes, hadn't promised her anything. Instead, he'd just been there for her during her deepest moments of pain. And he hadn't left. He was still with her.

His hand on her back slowed and finally stopped, and his breathing evened out as though he was still sleeping.

This man. What would her life be like without him?

An emotion she couldn't name swelled within her, one that made her want to lie right there in the bed in his arms all day.

He was so good and kind. She couldn't imagine any other man who would care about her feelings so much that he'd comfort her like this. Not only was he good and kind, but he was always there for her in so many big and small ways. He didn't think about himself or his needs. He always put her first.

She didn't deserve a friend like him. But for some reason God had seen fit to bless her anyway. Even if her mum was gone and even if her family was so far away, she had to hang on to the good that she still had in her life.

And Caleb was the best thing that had ever happened to her.

Her hands rested on his chest, and she slid them up, letting them explore the hills and valleys of his muscles—terrain that had always taunted her.

"How are you?" came a sleepy whisper in her hair.

"Better," she whispered, unable to stop her hands from gliding higher until she reached his shoulders. Somehow in traveling that short distance, she'd become addicted to the feel of his body against her fingers. And she couldn't stop—didn't want to stop—as her fingers slid higher, up his neck, then behind his head, and finally into his hair.

She could feel him tensing, as though he was planning to break free and climb out of the bed, likely not wanting her to think he was taking advantage of her or the situation. But he hadn't used her. And he wouldn't. He'd always treated her honorably and always would.

Yet, for a reason she didn't understand, she wasn't ready for him to leave her. She wanted him to stay and hold her longer. "Don't go," she whispered, and then she did the unthinkable—she dug her fingers into his hair and angled his head down toward hers. Before she could even make sense of what she was doing, she lifted up and pressed her lips against his.

All she knew was that she wanted to be close to him, closer than ever before.

As she let her lips mesh with his, he held himself still—as though he wasn't sure what exactly she was doing or what she wanted.

She didn't know how to kiss, had only ever kissed a man once and that had been Caleb on their wedding day back in February. As much as she'd tried not to think about the kiss, it had lingered in her memory and in her dreams. Even so, she didn't know how to meld her lips to his, didn't know how to move, didn't know how to make him want to kiss her in return.

With a wanting deep inside, all she could do was press in.

Thankfully he took the cue and pressed back. But the return pressure wasn't what she'd expected. It was like the aligning of two parts that fit together, smooth, perfect, and made for each other.

His lips revered hers softly and gently, tasting and testing.

As he tugged against her bottom lip, the sensation awoke her fully, so that her nerves began to plead for more, and she couldn't hold back a soft sound of pleasure. She surprised herself even more by tugging back at his lip, needing him, wanting him in a way she'd never experienced before.

He gave a tiny growl at the back of his throat and then plunged in for more, letting her know that he'd been holding himself back but wasn't anymore. He was diving into the deep, and he was dragging her down with him into a warm current that was carrying them away from reality.

As his kiss enveloped her, she became conscious of his hands now moving over her body, one on her back and the other pulling out the pins in her hair. It was such an intimate thing. And he was proficient at it.

The very idea that he was taking her hair down made warmth slide through her middle.

He shifted, and she found herself rolling to her back with the weight of his body following her. He wasn't exactly lying on top of her. It was more like halfway on, halfway off. But she couldn't deny that it was heavenly.

One of his hands still worked at her pins and the other slid to her ribs. And she couldn't deny again that she loved the feel of his hands on her. Lying in bed and kissing him was filling her with sensations that she didn't want just once, but that she wanted over and over for the rest of her life. But what did that mean?

She paused.

He immediately broke the kiss, and his ragged breathing bathed her lips. "What's wrong?" he asked, skimming his thumb across her ribs and sending shivers of more pleasure through her.

"Caleb, I . . . " She wanted to tell him that nothing was wrong except that he'd stopped kissing her and nothing would be all right until he started kissing her again.

But what was she doing? She couldn't say anything like that.

A flush worked its way into her cheeks, and she turned

her head away from him, wanting him but also needing to remain sane. And if she kept kissing him, she most certainly wouldn't stay sane.

His warm breaths caressed her cheek. "I love you."

At his quiet declaration, her breathing snagged in her chest. Even though there had been other times when she'd talked about loving Caleb and him loving her, it had always been in the realm of friendship. But this time was different. She could sense it.

But what did he mean by it?

She tried to draw in a breath, but her lungs were already closing up. She pushed against Caleb, and for a second he didn't move off her, seemed to want to say more. But she shoved again, this time harder.

He rolled away.

She scrambled off the end of the bed, stood to her feet, and then bent over, struggling to breathe.

Behind her, she could hear him stand. He approached hesitantly, but a moment later he rubbed her back as he normally did, which always calmed her and helped her breathe better.

After a few moments, she straightened and took a step away from him.

"Do you have anything to say?" he finally asked quietly.

Things had been mostly normal between them over the past weeks since their wedding. She'd tried hard to keep it that way. Why had she gone and kissed him now? And why had he said he loved her? Surely he'd meant as friends. That's all. "Of course we love each other. That's what friends—"

"No!" His whisper came out harsh. "Don't say it."

She wheezed in a breath. "We've always loved each other."

"Blast it, Willow!"

"Don't get mad at me. I'm just stating the truth."

He blew out an exasperated breath. "Do you want to know the truth?"

"I already do—"

"No, you have no idea." His voice was no longer a whisper. It was hard and even . . . and filled with hurt. "I have loved you for years. And not just as a friend. As a man loves a woman."

He'd loved her as more than a friend? For years? That couldn't be possible. Could it?

Clutching her tight chest, she pivoted. Even though the room was still dark, she could see his outline where he stood a couple feet away beside the bed. "No." It was the only word she could think of to answer him.

"Yes. I've always loved you."

If he'd loved her all those years in that way, then why had he pushed her away anytime she'd hinted at the least amount of attraction? "You've only ever treated me like a friend."

"That's because you were always so against anything more."

"And you were always against more too. You never wanted marriage."

"We're married now."

She shook her head, all her dormant fears rising up. "Because we had no other choice." He was changing everything too fast.

But now that they'd kissed again, how could it not change? And where would those changes lead? Would she be able to be what he needed?

"If you'd had another way out of our situation" —his voice was low and angry— "you would have taken it?"

She hesitated. Would she have? "Probably," she

whispered. Maybe even for this very reason, to avoid having him upset and disappointed with her.

His body had turned rigid, and even through the dark, she could see that his hands had fisted, as though he wanted to punch something, the tension radiating from him like it did whenever he was angry and ready to fight.

He'd never hit her. She knew that deep inside. Even so, she hugged her arms to her chest and took a step backward.

For long seconds he stared at her and didn't move, held himself absolutely still, as though he was waging an inner battle. Then with stiff movements, he grabbed his coat and hat from the bed where he must have shed them at one point during the night. He didn't bother putting either on and instead stalked toward the door, threw it open, and then exited, slamming it behind him.

The echo of the slam reverberated deep inside. Tears sprang to her eyes, unwanted tears, tears she thought she'd shed thoroughly the night before as she'd grieved over her mum. She blinked them back, but her chest was still burning from the shortage of air, and now her lungs ached with the need to throw herself on the bed and sob again.

With tears brimming over, she groped for the edge of the bed and lowered herself. He'd said he loved her, that he'd loved her as more than a friend for years. How was that possible?

She shook her head. Even if he'd kept his true feelings hidden from her in the past, he'd been hinting at more over recent weeks. She'd just been too afraid to acknowledge his gestures—the small ways he'd tried to show her his attraction. It had been easier to ignore his hints and pretend everything was the same as it had always been.

A part of her hadn't been able to accept—and maybe still

couldn't—that he'd ever really want her as more than a friend. Why her? What could he possibly see in her that would make him love her?

And, besides, if they changed the nature of their relationship, what if it ruined them and their friendship? The changes were already adding strain. They'd never fought before. And Caleb had never gotten visibly angry at her before. Was this just the beginning of the end? The first step of him pulling away?

The truth was, if she insisted on only friendship, she was bound to lose him, especially after what he'd just revealed. But if they pursued falling in love with each other, what if she wasn't enough for him?

Either way, her friendship and love with Caleb was doomed, and that thought was simply too much to bear.

Twenty-Five

H e hated himself.

Sitting at the center of the canoe, Caleb savagely plunged the paddle into the water, directing the vessel along the shallow waters of the island. The first rays of dawn had broken, but he couldn't see anything except Willow standing in the cabin, holding herself away from him in fear.

"I've become my father." The whispered words were laced with disgust.

He wouldn't have hit her. Never. But he'd been angry enough to hit something. And that thought scared him just as much.

He blinked against the sunshine glinting on the glassy surface, unbroken except for the ripple of his canoe slicing through the water. The narrow channel between Salt Spring Island and the other small islands to the east was deserted except for a red-necked grebe nesting on a pile of twigs he'd just passed.

The unsettled wilderness all around him would have been inspiring any other morning. The thick evergreens hung over the water in places and jutted out from boulders in others. The pine-covered hills beyond rose high toward the center of the island. Not the high mountains like those on the mainland, but they still towered majestically.

None of that mattered, though. Not after all that had happened a short while ago with Willow.

How had he gone from being on the brink of heaven, holding and kissing her one moment, to plunging into the dark depths of a nightmare the next? After all, he hadn't even been the one to initiate the kiss. He'd woken up to her stirring and touching him. And then the next thing he knew, she'd drawn him closer and pressed her lips to his.

At just the thought of the kiss, a groan escaped into the quiet morning. The kiss had been even better than the one on their wedding day because no one had coerced her into giving it. She'd kissed him freely and willingly.

She'd seemed to relish every moment, had risen into the kiss, had responded fervently. He'd half expected that the kiss wouldn't end for a while, that he'd be able to show her how much he adored her body.

But he'd sensed her pulling away even before she'd hesitated, and he'd panicked, hadn't wanted the moment to end, hadn't wanted her to revert back to friendship only. Instead, he'd wanted to push them forward into the uncharted territory that they could learn to navigate together.

He'd put his whole heart out there for her to take. But she'd thrown it back at him. Hadn't been able to tell him she loved him in return.

"I pushed her too fast." The anguished words settled around him, weighing him down.

He shouldn't have blurted his declaration of love, should

have waited, should have continued to move slowly in winning her heart.

But by finally admitting his love, maybe he'd hoped she'd reciprocate, especially after her willingness to kiss him. He hadn't imagined her desire or the way she'd pressed into him as if she couldn't get enough. He hadn't imagined the moan or her tight grasp or her eagerness.

She'd wanted him. She couldn't deny that.

But clearly, she didn't want to allow her love for him to develop.

And now he could see why.

She was afraid of him. Even if she'd always seen the best of him, always accepted him, always believed he could forge a new life different from his past, reality had finally manifested itself. He was a brute. There was no denying it any longer.

He switched the paddle to the opposite side of the canoe and thrust it in with more hard strokes. He'd thought he could make a new life for himself, especially here in the colony so far away from all that had shaped him. Willow had even told him that the past was far behind him and wouldn't catch up to him unless he let it.

But here he was, only a step or two ahead. In fact, his past already seemed to have grabbed hold of him, intending to drag him down no matter what he did to cut himself loose.

He'd always told himself that he didn't deserve Willow, that she needed a better man than him. Why hadn't he listened? Why had he pushed forward with changing their relationship?

Because he'd been selfish, that's why. He'd wanted to experience everything with her—life, love, happiness, and passion. And he hadn't wanted to give her up to some other man. He'd wanted her all for himself forever.

He used his paddle to steer himself the way Elijah had shown him during the few times they'd gone out fishing. It was much easier to canoe with two people than by himself. But the distance to the Stark ranch on the northern part of the island wasn't far from what Elijah had explained.

Although originally Caleb had planned on coming home each night after his day of helping with the butchering, maybe he'd be better off staying and giving himself time to calm down. And while he was away, he could decide what to do about his relationship with Willow.

Of course he'd never leave her. He couldn't. But maybe it was time to admit he shouldn't have let himself dream of having more with her. Maybe it was time to put aside all aspirations to win her. And maybe it was time to accept that all he'd ever have with her was friendship.

The trouble was, he wasn't certain he could only be satisfied with just friendship—especially now that he'd had a taste of what more could be like.

He'd told himself all these years that he'd rather take just friendship with her than nothing at all. And he'd always believed it.

But a part of him no longer did.

Twenty-Six

Willow knelt beside the stream and tried to wipe the tears from her cheeks. Even if the cold water in the early morning could wash away the streaks from another night of crying after Caleb's departure, it couldn't take away the pain.

He'd left her again. Without telling her where he was going. Without telling her when he'd be back. Without even a goodbye.

And after two full days and two full nights since he'd slammed the door on her in the cabin, she couldn't bear his absence any longer. It was tearing her up inside, so much that she'd hardly slept last night. She'd cried off and on, silently railing at Caleb one moment and the next pleading with him to come home.

Yesterday, she'd hardly been able to climb out of bed and had lain there for several hours of the morning, until Elijah had finally knocked on her door, asking her if she was alright.

She'd insisted that she was just fine. But he'd told her she had to open the door in thirty minutes, or he was breaking it open. So she'd been forced to get up and had eventually made her way over to Frannie and the baby and had distracted herself there most of the day. Of course Frannie had noticed something was bothering her, but Willow had been too embarrassed to admit that Caleb had run away.

How long would he be gone this time? Three days? Four? More?

The ache inside pulsed upward, and more tears slipped down her cheeks.

Quickly she bent her face closer to the stream again and splashed the water up, letting it drench her flushed and swollen skin.

This morning, she'd been tempted to lie in bed again. But she didn't want Elijah checking on her like he had yesterday. So she'd forced herself up and wandered over to the stream. In the process, she'd hoped to wash away some of her heartache.

But it wasn't working.

At the sound of Elijah's whistling across the stream as he exited the barn, she stood and waved at him, letting him know that she was indeed awake and alive—even though she didn't feel that way. He gave her a nod and started to veer her direction. Thankfully at a call from Jonas by the house, he turned his attention away, and she escaped down the path toward her cabin.

She didn't want to see anyone today, didn't want to have to worry about explaining where Caleb was. But the longer he was gone, the more obvious his absence would be, until eventually she'd have to tell everyone that Caleb had left.

Because of her. She hadn't handled their conversation well, had reacted poorly. She should have said something to ease his mind. She could have at least let him know that she cared about him.

Instead, she'd done the very thing she feared. She'd pushed him away again.

As she passed by the chickens, she grabbed a handful of their feed from the pail where she kept it tacked to the wall of the henhouse. She tossed them their breakfast before returning to the cabin and closing the door behind her.

Leaning against the planks, she pressed her hand against her chest and tried to breathe, tried to make her heart beat. But every part of her body protested his being gone.

The cabin was still shrouded in darkness, but enough daylight peeked through the cracks in the shutter to reveal the untidiness from the past two days. Dirty dishes were scattered on the makeshift table of planks over barrels. The bed was unmade. Her nightclothes were strewn on the floor.

Her gaze snagged upon the small wooden box under the bed that contained all the gifts that Caleb had given her over the years. She crossed over to it, knelt, and pulled it out.

She untied the twine and placed the lid on the floor beside her. Isaac's key still lay on the top right where she'd left it. She removed it and set it on the floor too. Then she began to finger the other items—the heart-shaped rock Caleb had given her on her wedding night, the long white swan feather he'd found at White Swan Farm, and all the other items he'd ever given her.

She'd hung on to everything for years because she'd thought it would keep her connected to him. But none of it truly could. None of it could keep him from leaving. Not even his love. Because he said he'd loved her, but he'd walked away anyway.

The truth was, he wouldn't have walked away—this time or any of the times—if she'd been enough for him.

She sat up straighter and pushed the box off her lap. It toppled over, and the contents clattered to the floor.

Was that her solution to the problem? Was it time to do what she should have done long ago? Grow stronger? Stand on her own?

All along she'd wanted to be stronger and smarter and more capable like her sister Sage, and now maybe this was her chance. Maybe if she learned to be stronger, smarter, and more capable, she'd eventually be the kind of wife Caleb deserved and needed.

But until then . . .

She stood, paced to the door and stopped. What could she do? The only option that was available was for her to return to Victoria, approach the Immigration Committee—maybe Mrs. Moresby—and ask for another domestic position.

She turned and took in the cabin again. All the memories of the past weeks of marriage came rushing back—the late nights with Caleb reading his poetry as they each lay on their beds, the mornings drinking coffee together, the meals they'd eaten by the warmth of the stove, the long conversations sharing their dreams and hopes.

She swallowed the sudden lump in her throat and crossed to the bed. She packed her few personal items in her bag. As she started to pick up the items from the box, she halted.

No, it was time to stop clinging to him so tightly and find her own footing.

She swiped up the key and turned it over in her hand. What should she do with it? Should she take it with her and try to deliver a message to Isaac that she had it? When he returned to Nanaimo over the next month or so, maybe she could find a way to take it to him. Or would it be safer here in the cabin, hidden until Isaac came back from wherever he was staying?

She hesitated a moment then tucked it under the mattress. As long as Mr. Mann didn't find Caleb, the key would probably be safest on the island. Even if Caleb decided never to come back, no one would suspect she'd left the key in the cabin. Eventually, she'd tell Isaac where it was, and he'd be able to come with Jonas on the steamboat and get it.

She swept her gaze over the cabin one last time, her chest tightening. She didn't want to go. But she had to leave now, before she changed her mind and before Jonas disembarked for the day.

He probably wouldn't approve of her leaving the island, but he was too kind to deny her transportation to Victoria. She'd have to admit the truth to him, that she'd pushed Caleb away, and even if he came back to her, things wouldn't be the same between them ever again.

Twenty-Seven

T hree days was all he could stay away from Willow.

Caleb dragged the canoe up the bank, the stones crunching and the dirt crumbling. As he flipped the vessel over, he peered in the direction of his cabin, hoping to spot it through the trees. But the new spring growth was too thick and the cabin too far back from the shore.

He straightened and then combed his fingers through his damp hair. He'd stopped in a secluded nook during the passage home to rinse off the grime and grit and sweat from the slaughterhouse.

The butchering had been hard and bloody. But Mr. Stark had paid him a fair wage each night for a full day's work and had provided two meals a day. He'd even let Caleb bed down in the hayloft at night.

But tonight . . . Caleb expelled a taut breath. Tonight he had to be with Willow, even if it was on the floor beside the bed. He'd have to leave at dawn tomorrow, had told Mr. Stark he'd be back to finish the week of work. But he'd needed to come home, needed to see Willow, needed her more than he ever had.

He'd tried hard not to care. He'd wanted to stay angry at her for rejecting his love. He'd hoped he could make himself give up on her and his dream of winning her.

But he'd utterly failed. His heart hadn't permitted him a moment of rest, had instead pumped hard with the need to be with her.

Finally, tonight after work, his chest had ached so much and his muscles had been so tense, that he'd given in, tossed his canoe in the harbor, and started back to the farm.

Now here he was . . .

Jonas's steamboat was docked, which meant he was already back for the evening. With the sun having dipped low behind the western hills and peaks, the shadows were long, and the air was losing the warmth of the spring day.

Caleb pressed a hand against his trouser pocket and the shillings there, hopefully enough to send with Jonas tomorrow for the purchase of more seeds. Soon enough he'd be back working his own land and planting more crops.

His own land.

The satisfaction he normally felt when thinking about the farm didn't waft through him. He'd immigrated to the colony to be with Willow. His plans had always included Willow. And this dream to have the farm had belonged to both him and Willow.

Could he really live with her on the farm without her ever being willing to reciprocate his love? Would he ever truly be able to resign himself to friendship if that's all she was capable of giving him?

That was the question he'd been wrestling with since he'd

paddled away. The question still gnawed at him. And he didn't know the answer.

With a final comb of his fingers through his hair, he situated his cap and started up the trail along the stream in the dark shadows of thick growth. The rushing water seemed to chastise him severely, and the tall fir trees along the banks looked down on him as if frowning their rebuke.

"I know," he muttered, hiking the slight incline without slowing. "I should have at least told her goodbye and where I was going."

Hadn't he vowed to himself the last time he'd stayed away from her that he wouldn't do it again, that he'd talk with her instead? But he'd been so angry and hurt, he hadn't known what else to do. And he'd been afraid that he was turning into his father.

Was it just a matter of time before that finally happened?

He wanted to be godly like Willow's dad, had prayed for God to help him become a new man. But somehow he always seemed to fall short of truly changing.

As the thick trees gave way to cleared land, two men came into view—Jonas and Elijah standing in the grassy yard between the house and barn talking. From their raised voices and the stiffness of their bodies, he guessed they were arguing.

He didn't want to interrupt them. But they must have sensed his presence or perhaps seen him from the corner of their eyes because they halted their conversation and turned to face him.

"It's about time," Elijah called, his voice less than welcoming.

Jonas crossed his arms and glared at Caleb.

Clearly, they both knew he'd had an argument with

Willow. And they were taking her side. He supposed that was only fair since he'd run off without a word to her.

He wanted to head directly to his own cabin. Now that he was so close, the need to see Willow was stronger than ever. But he forced himself to cross toward the men.

As he stopped in front of them, an undercurrent of tension charged the air.

They didn't say anything, just watched him, as if waiting for him to speak first. Caleb guessed they wouldn't be satisfied with anything less than a full apology.

"I'm sorry," he offered. "I should have come home each night."

"Yessir, you should have." Jonas's tone was even more menacing than Elijah's had been.

"I was trying to calm down."

"Willow told Jonas that you two had a fight." Elijah's dark eyes pinned Caleb into place.

How much of the argument had Willow shared? "It's none of your business."

"It is our business now," Jonas growled and exchanged a look with Elijah that made Caleb's blood pump erratically.

"What?" He could only manage the one-word question.

"She left you and made me take her to Victoria this morning."

Caleb staggered backward a step, almost as if Jonas had punched him in the gut.

Willow had left him? "No." He spun and started toward the stream, panic propelling him to find her. She couldn't have left. She'd never done so before, had always been there for him.

"She told me she had to learn to be stronger," Jonas called

after him, "and make it on her own without relying on you so much."

Caleb only made it half a dozen strides before his steps slowed to a halt. His insides were already bottoming out, and his heart was dropping out of his chest. He faced the two men, his hands forming into fists. "You took her away? Even though you knew I wouldn't want you to?"

Jonas squared his wiry shoulders, as if preparing for a fight.

Heat sliced through Caleb, making him want to charge at Jonas and pummel him.

"You can blame me all you want," Jonas called. "But you're the one who drove her away. I was just her ride."

Elijah was still glaring. "If you'd been here, maybe she wouldn't have wanted to leave."

"I had to go so that I could calm down." The words came out before he could censor them. But they were the bare truth, an ugly truth, a truth that he'd hated about himself.

"You been hitting her?" Elijah's hands fisted now too.

"No." Caleb wanted to curse under his breath but held back the oath. "I've never hit her, not once in all the years I've known her."

The tension seemed to ease from Elijah's shoulders. "If you haven't yet, what makes you think you will?"

The question was probing, one Caleb couldn't answer.

"Listen, man." Elijah cast a glance toward the cabin on the rise, the windows bright with light in the dusk. His gaze softened as though he was picturing his wife and baby inside. "I get angry at Frannie once in a while."

"You do?"

"Oh yeah."

Jonas snorted as if to confirm the marital discord.

Caleb had only ever seen Elijah interact with his wife with kindness and tenderness, and he couldn't imagine the fellow ever feeling anger.

"Conflict in marriage happens." Elijah spoke matter-of-factly. "And if I'm getting too angry, then sometimes I do walk away to cool down."

"That's what I was doing—"

"Yep, I walk away." Elijah's voice rose above Caleb's. "The difference between me and you is that I don't *stay away* like a coward. Instead, I go back, humble myself, and serve her the way the Good Book says that I should."

Caleb unclenched his hands. Jonas had already accused him of being a coward right before the marriage ceremony on the beach.

But even after he'd given himself permission to marry her, he was still being a coward. He thought he was just protecting her from his brutish behavior. But in trying to shelter her—by running away—he was only hurting her anyway.

He let his muscles go slack, his shoulders drooping and his body sagging.

The two brothers stood side by side, their dark faces finally reflecting some compassion.

The same desperation that had been swirling through Caleb the past few days rose inside him. What would it hurt to share more with these fellows? Already things were bad enough with Willow and couldn't get any worse, could they? "I love her, but she doesn't love me in return."

Jonas broke into one of his easy grins. "Oh, she loves you."

Caleb had thought he'd felt her love that morning when they'd kissed in bed. She'd responded with such passion, tenderness, and desire, what else could it have been except love? Even so, she hadn't been ready to admit her feelings. Maybe she never would be. "She did warn me on our wedding day that she didn't want anything to change."

Elijah's forehead creased with a frown. "That's impossible. Marriage changes us. It's supposed to make us better."

"She said she was afraid marriage would ruin our friendship, that I'd end up hating her."

"You leaving like that made her more fearful her prediction is coming true."

Caleb's runaway thoughts came to a standstill. Elijah was right. He'd contributed to Willow's fears. In fact, he'd been the one for years who'd insisted he would never get married. He'd withheld his love, had given her no hope of a future together, and had pulled away whenever he'd gotten too close.

No wonder she was scared to take the next step.

He pressed a hand to his throbbing temples.

"Listen man," Elijah said earnestly. "Instead of running away, you've got to show her you'll love her no matter what. Wally calls it unconditional love—love given freely without the other person having to do anything to earn it."

Caleb desperately wanted to give her that kind of love. "But how do I show her?"

Elijah was peering at his cabin again. His gaze softened. "Every single day, you wake up and you love her and sacrifice for her in a dozen ways."

Caleb nodded. But how could he keep from hurting Willow?

"When you have conflict," Elijah continued as if reading his mind, "you prove to her that you'll stay and work it out. Those are the times you show her you love her in *two* dozen different ways." The man radiated sincerity, so much so that Caleb knew he was speaking from his own experience.

Could he follow Elijah's advice? Even if he did, he suspected he and Willow would still have many long days ahead where they'd have more conflict, or he'd feel like running away from her to protect her. But he'd have to remember that staying and working out the issues would hurt her less.

Caleb shifted his gaze to the dark path that led back to the harbor. Overhead, the moon had already made an appearance, hanging low and bright, casting a silvery glow over the evergreens. "Jonas, I need you to take me to Victoria. Now. Tonight."

The fellow chuckled. "Not at all anxious to get your woman back, are you?"

Elijah was shaking his head. "Wait till morning. Give her a night to prove to herself that she is strong enough, and then go show her how much you love her tomorrow. Show her so that she'll never doubt it again."

Caleb wanted to protest. He didn't want to spend one more night away from Willow. He'd already been apart from her for too long. But if he hoped to win her once and for all, he had to do things right this time.

Twenty-Eight

What was she doing here? Away from Caleb?

Willow huddled outside the service entrance behind the Firth Mansion on Fort Street. The chill of the night seeped through her cloak and made her shudder.

The scullery maid who'd answered Willow's knock had promised to let Juliet know she was there. But that had been long minutes ago, and Willow was only growing colder and more miserable by the moment, especially at the thought that soon enough she'd be back in domestic service in a house like this.

The Firth Mansion was bigger than most of the other homes in Victoria. From everything Juliet had already told her when they'd still been meeting on Sundays on their half day off, Willow knew that the Firth Mansion had eleven bedrooms, two drawing rooms, an enormous dining room, two pantries, seven fireplaces, and more.

From the outside, the three-story brick home had the castle-like look of an English country estate. Its large surrounding grounds with formal gardens took up most of the block.

The glow coming from the windows on the rear side of the house provided enough light for Willow to see the outbuildings a short distance away—the carriage house, a second kitchen, paddocks and a stable, along with other structures that likely provided storage of some kind.

At the late hour, Willow had hoped Juliet would be done with her duties and that she'd have the chance to talk. But Willow should have known after working for Mrs. Mann that the demands were never ending.

Willow peered up into the dark sky, to the moon that had slowly risen and was also providing her enough light to sneak around. Of course, she wasn't supposed to be wandering around Victoria this late at night by herself. But the Marine Barracks was nearly empty of the rest of the mill women who'd come on the *Robert Lowe*. Only a handful remained, and several were like her, in between positions, their first employment having come to an end for one reason or another.

Mrs. Moresby had stopped by the Marine Barracks after learning of Willow's return, and she'd inquired into all that had happened since Willow's disappearance several weeks ago from the White Swan Farm. Willow had wanted to tell the dear woman about her marriage to Caleb, but she didn't want to risk anyone learning that Caleb was on Salt Spring Island and chance Mr. Mann finding him. Instead, she'd twisted the truth a little and told Mrs. Moresby that she'd taken a job on a different farm but that it hadn't worked out the way she'd hoped.

Besides, even if she was married to Caleb, it had only been

a practical arrangement, hadn't been a real marriage. And she shouldn't have kissed him, especially that last time.

Even though she knew she shouldn't think about it again, her mind traveled back to that kiss anyway—as it had dozens of times already—to all the feelings and sensations she'd experienced with him, feelings and sensations that were so new and even slightly forbidden.

Warmth pooled inside, and desire stirred all too easily again. Before she could chastise herself again, the back door opened, and Juliet stepped out, wearing the typical maid's black uniform with the white apron and collar. A lacy hat attempted to tame Juliet's blond hair, but wayward strands slipped out anyway.

"Willow?" Juliet's pretty eyes rounded. "What are you doing here at this day and hour?" Before Willow could answer, the young woman drew her into a hug.

Willow had told herself that she wouldn't cry, that she'd already shed enough tears over Caleb, but before she knew it, she was sobbing against Juliet's starched collar.

Juliet squeezed her tighter and didn't speak.

But a moment later, at the slap of approaching footsteps, Juliet latched onto Willow's arm and tugged her away from the house toward what appeared to be one of the formal gardens with carefully trimmed shrubs. Juliet led her through a maze of pathways until they reached a stone bench positioned near a water fountain that was quiet and glassy in the moonlight.

As they sat, Willow relayed the news about her mother's passing away along with everything else that had happened over the past few weeks since marrying Caleb—sharing the cabin, kissing him, then his declaration of love.

Juliet's smile was saucy, and her eyes glimmered with mirth. "Can I say I told you so?"

"No." Willow's cheeks flushed, even with the cool breeze brushing her skin.

"I told you so." Juliet laughed lightly. "That man is crazy about you."

At a shout from the servants' entrance, Juliet stood and peeked through the hedges and sighed with exasperation. "Holy Moses. A woman can't even use the privy in peace here."

"I hate to point out the obvious," Willow teased, already feeling better, as if she wasn't bearing the full weight of her burden any longer. "But you're not using the privy."

"They don't know that."

Willow rose and drew her cloak tighter. "Go, before you get in trouble."

Juliet waved a dismissive hand. "I deserve a few more minutes to do my business, don't I? Sometimes the body can't be rushed."

"Eww."

Juliet laughed again, and Willow joined in.

A moment later, though, Juliet's expression turned serious. "Why are you back in Victoria, Willow? If I had a man who loved me the way Caleb loves you, I'd never leave him."

"He left me."

"He's hurt that you didn't tell him you loved him in return."

She had hurt him. She should have let him know how much he meant to her. But she couldn't tell him she loved him, could she?

"No." Juliet placed a finger on Willow's lips, cutting her

off. "Don't tell me that you don't love him. It's been obvious all along that you do. You might as well just admit it."

The objection rose swiftly inside Willow again.

But this time Juliet cocked her head and leveled a stern no-nonsense look at her, one that said she wouldn't tolerate anything but the truth. Was that why she'd sought Juliet out and not Daisy tonight, because she desperately wanted to know the truth?

But what was the truth? Did she really love Caleb?

"It doesn't matter how I feel," she finally whispered. "I came to Victoria so that I could learn to be a stronger and more capable woman."

Juliet squeezed her hand. "You're already one of the strongest women I know, Willow Rhodes. You sailed halfway around the world, came to a new colony, started a new job, and then ran away and got married to your best friend. All of that took courage and strength."

"But Caleb helped me—"

"He was there with you, but he didn't do any of it for you. You did it all yourself."

Willow's spiraling thoughts halted. Yes, Caleb had been there to encourage her and listen to her and support her. But she'd worked hard. She'd persevered. She hadn't wavered.

"The way I see it," Juliet continued, "you and Caleb are both strong, two parts of a whole that balance each other out."

Maybe that was true too, but that didn't diminish her ineptness that came out all too often. "But I am so slow at figuring out how to do things, make messes, can't follow instructions well, and need help with so much."

"You might need a little more help with things, but you're not as inadequate as you make yourself to be."

"But what if Caleb gets fed up with me? What if that's why he walked away before and ran off now?" Ultimately, that was her greatest fear, losing him. And maybe it was easier to hold him at arm's length than to risk the chance that she'd eventually lose him.

"I've had people abandon me," Juliet said somberly. "It happens. And it hurts."

Yes, it hurt every time Caleb cut her off. Her heart hadn't stopped aching since he'd walked out the door of the cabin.

"But, even if we are strong women" —Juliet's smile was tender— "we don't have to handle it all in our strength. God gives us His strength too, especially when we reach the end of ours."

At another shout from the service entrance, this one louder and more frustrated, Juliet gave her a final quick hug before scurrying away.

When Juliet was gone, Willow lowered herself back to the bench. *You're already one of the strongest women I know.*

In the next second, Sage's voice battled for a place in Willow's thoughts again as it always had. *You're so helpless. You always need my help or Caleb's.*

Was Juliet right? Or was Sage?

Willow had compared herself to Sage for so long and had always come up short. But what if she'd never fallen short in the first place because it had never been a competition? It was true that Sage would always be better at some things, maybe smarter and quicker to catch on.

But over the past weeks, Willow had done more than she'd ever believed possible. Juliet was right. She was stronger than she'd realized. And during those times when she didn't feel strong enough to handle the situation, maybe God was there ready to lend her His strength.

And if Juliet was right about all that, what if she was right about Caleb?

Willow hugged her arms over her chest to ward off a chill. She'd tried to stamp out her attraction. She'd convinced herself that she had none. But what if she really had loved him all along and had just been too afraid to admit it? Was it possible that she was deeply and desperately in love with Caleb but had hidden it behind friendship?

Yes. It was not only possible. It was reality.

She loved Caleb. She loved him not only as her friend, but as her husband.

He'd had the courage to face his fears of marriage by offering to wed her. He'd had the courage to try to change the nature of their relationship since their wedding. He'd even had the courage to declare his love.

In return, she'd been so callous and careless with his feelings. She'd rejected and hurt him. And now, what if he decided he didn't want to love her after all?

Willow's breath snagged painfully. She stood and tried to draw in air. She'd thought the worst thing was not having his friendship anymore. But there was something worse . . . not having his love.

Whatever his decision, she knew she had to find out. Maybe it would be the hardest thing she'd done yet and would require the greatest strength. But first thing tomorrow, she had to find a ride back to the island and back to him.

Twenty-Nine

"I'm married." Willow paced the front hallway of the Marine Barracks.

Mrs. Moresby would arrive at any moment to inform her of a new employment opportunity. The matron had a couple of possibilities in mind yesterday when they'd talked, but she'd needed to speak directly with the families to learn if the positions were still available. This morning the kindly woman was planning to come by to give Willow the details.

"I'm married," Willow said again into the quiet of the hallway. "And I neglected to tell you yesterday."

She halted and rolled her eyes. How could she explain her situation to Mrs. Moresby without bringing Caleb up?

Willow paced again to the end of the hallway, passing the parlor and dining room and the stairway that led to the bedrooms on the second floor. She stopped at the closed kitchen door and drew in a breath, the scent of coffee lingering in the air.

The voices of the women in the kitchen wafted into the hallway in happy, pleasant conversation. From the footsteps and creaking of floorboards overhead, Willow could tell that the rest of the remaining women were finally awake and beginning their day.

Everyone had welcomed Willow back kindly enough. They'd been full of questions about her disappearance from White Swan Farm—questions she hadn't known how to answer. She'd learned that Mrs. Mann had already hired another bride-ship woman to fill the empty position, which was for the best since Willow couldn't imagine going back and working there.

She was hoping she wouldn't need to take another domestic position anywhere, that she could remain with Caleb.

As soon as she finished speaking with Mrs. Moresby, she needed to hurry to the waterfront where Jonas normally docked the *Boat* for the pickups and deliveries in Victoria. She wasn't sure if this morning he'd be in Nanaimo first or Victoria. But he'd take her back to the island without any hesitation, especially since he'd been vocal that he thought she was making a mistake in leaving.

After getting away from Salt Spring Island, after thinking about her future, and especially after talking with Juliet, she was certain going back was the right thing. The hard part would be waiting for Caleb to return from wherever he'd run off to. Jonas had insisted that Caleb had taken work on the north side of Salt Spring Island for a few days or maybe a week. Even if he had, that didn't mean he'd come back when he finished. And if he did return, he'd probably be angry with her.

Would he be able to forgive her? Would he be willing to try again?

She wasn't sure what a relationship with him would look

like that wasn't friendship. But she wanted to be open to something new.

She stalked again to the front door. Right now, her biggest problem was what she was going to tell Mrs. Moresby.

"I'm sorry, Mrs. Moresby," she whispered. "I already have my situation worked out and no longer need employment." Would that work?

Before she could think of another way to phrase her revelation, a firm knock resounded on the door in front of her.

She hopped back a little. Was that Mrs. Moresby? Yesterday she'd come through the back kitchen entrance.

What if it was Jonas coming to check on her? Surely it couldn't be Caleb. Could it? Maybe he'd returned and found her missing and had come to Victoria to talk to her.

Her pulse spurted forward in large, leaping strides, and she threw open the door with a ready smile.

"Mr. Mann." He stood just outside on the front stoop. Attired in an immaculate dark suit, he doffed his top hat to reveal his blond hair and sideburns.

She took a step backward.

He offered her a polite smile, one that didn't reach his eyes. "Willow. I'd heard you returned to Victoria to the Marine Barracks and thought I would visit you to see for myself."

She'd been back for less than twenty-four hours. How had the news reached him already? Did he have informants around town?

Mr. Pidwell and another farmhand stood well away from the door on the stone pathway that led up to the house. Mr. Pidwell tipped the brim of his hat at Willow in greeting, his eyes seeming to hold an apology.

Unease pricked her. Why was Mr. Pidwell apologizing? And why did Mr. Mann care about seeing her?

"I learned that you're looking for work." He spoke as if sensing her unasked question. "And I came to offer you your former position."

"I was told Mrs. Mann hired a replacement."

"No one can compare to you, and my wife would much rather have you back."

That was an outright lie. Mrs. Mann had been frustrated with her most of the time for never getting anything exactly the way she wanted. No doubt she was much happier with her new maid. "I see."

"If you'll be so kind as to gather your bag and all your belongings, we'll escort you to the farm." He looked pointedly at her small sack sitting on the floor beside the coat tree.

She didn't move. Was he serious?

"Come on with you now." Mr. Mann cocked his head toward the walkway outside. "Mr. Pidwell has informed me that he and his workers have a busy day ahead of them and that this trip is an inconvenience."

Willow could only imagine the inconvenience if the farmhands were half as busy as she and Caleb had been. They were probably plowing and planting many of the early crops. So why had Mr. Mann brought the workers along?

She glanced over her shoulder to the kitchen door. Where was Mrs. Moresby when she needed help? Or Caleb?

No, she was a strong enough woman to handle this situation on her own. Hadn't she just resolved that last night?

She squared her shoulders and then spoke the words she'd practiced for Mrs. Moresby. "I'm sorry, Mr. Mann. I already have my situation worked out and no longer need employment." She began to close the door.

"Situation?" Mr. Mann stepped over the threshold and wedged his foot against the door. "And what exactly is your *situation*? Do you find it as odd as I do that you ran off about the same time as my farmhand Caleb Edwards?"

No doubt her guilt was all too easy to spot. Even so, she had to protect Caleb. "I don't know what you're talking about."

"After inquiring around and speaking with some of the other bride-ship women, I also learned Caleb arrived on the same ship as you and that he was your friend."

Although she and Caleb had tried to keep their friendship private, it was inevitable others had noticed them talking at the train station in Manchester and even on the ship during the long journey.

But she couldn't admit that to Mr. Mann, not when he was obviously still trying to track down Caleb.

She took another step backward. "I don't think it's any of your concern whether or not I know Caleb—"

"It is most definitely my concern." Mr. Mann stepped after her and clasped her arm. "He's a wanted criminal, and I suspect you know where he's hiding."

She jerked against him to wrest her arm free.

His fingers clasped her more firmly, and his eyes darkened with determination.

"Please release me, Mr. Mann." She tried to keep her voice even but couldn't prevent the chill that raced up her spine.

His expression was still polite. "Perhaps you may even know where Isaac is. Or the key? After all, he did offer you his key first."

Yes, she did have the key, had hidden it away back on the

island, and she was glad now that she'd had the foresight to leave it behind.

Without releasing his hold on her arm, Mr. Mann bent and picked up her bag. "Maybe after having time to think about the treasure, you decided to take the key for yourself after all."

"I don't want the treasure, Mr. Mann. It belongs to Isaac."

Mr. Mann tossed the bag to Mr. Pidwell. "Search her belongings."

Mr. Pidwell caught the sack and at the same time released a sigh of exasperation. Nevertheless, he opened the drawstring and began to dig around inside. When his search didn't unearth the key, Mr. Mann demanded that he dump the contents. Mr. Pidwell did so with another apologetic glance at Willow. Of course, Mr. Mann also demanded that Willow turn her pockets outside of her skirt to prove the key wasn't hidden in her garments.

With each passing moment, Willow's resolve to remain strong began to wane, and she prayed that Mrs. Moresby would arrive and intercede.

But as Mr. Pidwell finished his search and was putting the items back in her bag, Mr. Mann was already guiding her down the stone path toward the gate, insisting that she return to White Swan Farm to resume her duties.

She protested with each step she took. But his grip on her arm didn't waver as he led her past the government building and down the embankment toward the harbor, using the same planks that she'd walked on during her first day in Victoria.

That cold January day, among the hundreds of men lining the shore and walkway, she'd found Caleb. It was true even then that he'd been the only man she'd ever had eyes for, the only one she'd ever wanted.

At the early morning hour, the fishermen with their sloops were already gone for the day. But the waterfront near the Marine Barracks was still busy with longshoremen at work unloading cargo from a schooner. As Mr. Mann forced her down the dock, some of the longshoremen stopped to watch.

Did she dare call out to them?

Mr. Mann didn't falter in his stride. "Don't think about trying to evade me. I have every right to bring you back to my farm and require you to finish out the terms of your employment."

She wasn't sure how true his statement was. She'd have to find out from Mrs. Moresby. In the meantime, she had to fend for herself and try to escape his clutches. "Even if I had the key, which you can see that I don't" —she tugged against him— "I wouldn't give it to you."

"You know more than you're letting on." He stopped in front of his rowboat and leveled a severe gaze at her. The wind coming from the strait tossed the boat and stirred the waves. The steady splash sent up a spray that threatened to drench them.

Mr. Pidwell and the lone farmhand, who'd been following behind, stepped down into the boat and began to make ready for their return voyage to the farm.

"One way or another," Mr. Mann said quietly, "I intend to get the information from you that I need."

"I have no information to give you."

"I think you do. It's possible you know where Isaac is. At the very least, you can lead me to Caleb."

"I would never tell you." She wouldn't reveal the position of either man, not even if Mr. Mann threatened to beat her.

Mr. Mann's lips pursed but lifted into a slight smile. "If my hunch is right, I might not need to wait long before Caleb comes looking for you."

A cold knot twisted around Willow's throat, silencing all her bravado. Mr. Mann was right. Caleb would come after her once he learned of her predicament. No matter how angry he might be with her and no matter how hurt, he'd never allow anyone to bring her harm or hold her against her will.

And once Caleb came, Mr. Mann would arrest him and would follow through with pressing charges. She had the feeling the only way to stop Mr. Mann from ruining Caleb's life would be to give him what he wanted—the treasure. At the very least, she could hand over the key.

Should she do it now? If she gave in, she could bring an end to all their problems. And yet, how could she? Doing so would be the cowardly way.

She scanned the other wharfs that lined the harbor. Yesterday when she'd arrived on the *Boat* with Jonas, he'd docked some place farther to the west in a different harbor. It was unlikely that she'd find him nearby, that he'd even be in Victoria this morning.

Regardless, she searched, hoping to see him. But his familiar face was nowhere in sight and neither was his boat.

As Mr. Mann stepped down into the rowboat and began to haul her inside, she stiffened with the need to escape his clutches before it was too late to save Caleb.

Thirty

Where was Willow?

Caleb paused on the street outside the Marine Barracks and dragged a breath into his burning lungs. From the moment the steamer had docked, he hadn't waited for Jonas to secure the boat, had instead hopped off and run all the way to the government complex.

But he'd been too late. She wasn't there, and the other women hadn't known where she'd gone.

"Find her?" Jonas called as he jogged toward the Marine Barracks.

Caleb surveyed the wide street lined with other businesses, none of them as big as the brick government building that rose several stories high and overlooked the harbor.

Had she already taken a job? And if so, how would he find out where? Maybe he should hunt down the matron from the Immigration Committee who'd initially helped her find the job at White Swan Farm.

His muscles tensed. They'd been tight since he'd arrived

back home last night to find her gone. He'd hardly been able to sleep and had been up well before dawn, helping Jonas with his morning farm chores so that they could get an early start.

Clearly he hadn't left early enough.

Jonas stopped beside him, breathing hard. "No luck?"

"Not yet."

Jonas's dark eyes darted around, taking stock of the few passersby, mostly laborers who were probably heading to their places of employment. His brow furrowed with worry. "You should stay on the boat and let me look for her."

Caleb didn't respond. He'd already said all he had to about that topic during the ride to Victoria. Jonas didn't think Caleb should show himself yet, claimed that Mr. Mann was a powerful fellow who could get away with lawlessness.

Caleb didn't disagree. But he needed to find Willow and assure her he'd do anything she wanted, as long as she didn't leave him. He'd even promise her that he'd never again push for anything beyond friendship if that's what she really wanted.

If he had to go back to that place in her life that he'd always occupied, he'd do it. Even if that place would never totally satisfy him, he'd resign himself to it if that's what it took. Whatever happened, he'd spend every day the rest of his life showing her unconditional love.

Jonas adjusted the brim of his bowler to shade his view as he scanned the waterfront. "You ain't gonna be any help to your woman if you—" He halted abruptly, his eyes widening.

Caleb tensed and followed Jonas's gaze.

"She's there." Jonas nodded toward the wharf straight ahead. "Mr. Mann's got her."

Caleb homed in on the dock that went several dozen feet

out from the shore, and sure enough, the gentleman was standing half in and half out of the White Swan rowboat, and he was attempting to pull a struggling Willow inside. He was speaking angrily to Mr. Pidwell, who was sitting at the back of the boat, oars already in hand. Was he asking Mr. Pidwell to help him lift Willow into the boat?

Caleb didn't wait to find out. He bolted forward, sprinting down the embankment, heedless of the mud and sand. He had to get to Willow. The need pumped hard and fast, filling him with the kind of rage he'd felt whenever his father had beaten him or whenever he was in the boxing ring.

The heat of his fury fueled his blood, making him want to lash out at anyone and anything that stood in his way. All he knew was that he had to reach Mr. Mann, and when he did, he'd beat him senseless for the way he was treating Willow.

He could hear Jonas calling out a warning, but Caleb couldn't stop himself.

Ahead, a group of longshoremen who'd been unloading crates from a vessel had stopped their work and were watching the interaction between Mr. Mann and Willow. Two of the men had begun to make their way down the dock toward the rowboat.

One part of Caleb knew that they intended to help Willow. But the other part was too angered to care about their effort.

Willow was saying something to Mr. Mann too. As Caleb reached the dock, he still couldn't hear what she was saying with the wind blowing her words the opposite way. But he was close enough to see the flash of fear cross her beautiful features.

A gust of wind swept off the harbor and threatened to slow Caleb, but he pushed against it. At the same moment, the wind loosened Mr. Mann's top hat. He released his grip on Willow and grabbed at his hat. But he was too late, and it flew back toward the dock and across the other side, landing in the water.

Willow didn't hesitate. She took advantage of being free from Mr. Mann and started running down the dock. She cast a frantic gaze over her shoulder to find Mr. Mann launching himself out of the boat.

He was hatless, revealing eyes narrowed upon Willow as if he had every intention of getting ahold of her.

She raced faster, wrestling against the wind, her face set with determination.

Caleb shouldered past the longshoremen. Even though he slowed his pace, his heartbeat kept sprinting.

Her eyes locked upon him. "Caleb!" Her voice held censure. "Go away before Mr. Mann gets you!"

An instant later, she reached him, her blue eyes frantic. More than anything he wanted to drag her into a hug and never let her go, but Mr. Mann was striding toward them, and Caleb refused to let the fellow get his hands on Willow ever again.

He maneuvered Willow behind him and out of the way, then he spread his feet and blocked the dock. Mr. Mann would have to kill him first to get to her.

From behind, Willow latched onto his coat. "No, Caleb. Don't fight."

Caleb hadn't realized he'd fisted his hands. But he had, and he'd lifted them in readiness to box, the way he did at the start of a match. The heat of his fury was pumping through his body, into his muscles, and nearly blinding him to anything else but Mr. Mann's face, to the spot he intended to hit first.

"Please, Caleb!" Willow pulled at him, trying to drag him backward.

But he could barely feel her tug. He needed to fight more than he needed to breathe.

Mr. Mann's steps slowed, and he began to shrug out of his coat, as if preparing for the battle.

"You promised me." Willow's voice was filled with a desperation that pierced through him, reminding him of the desperation he'd just felt at the thought of losing her. "And it's time to make your word stand for something."

Make his word stand for something. Yes, he'd told her he would stop fighting. And yes, he'd meant it. But this time was different, wasn't it? He'd also told her he wouldn't leave again, and then he'd done it anyway.

"Please!" She was wrenching at his coat. "I know you're a good man. It's time for you to start believing it too."

He could hardly comprehend her words, didn't want to think about them. But they penetrated through the haze like water dousing a fire.

She was right. He'd never believed he could be a changed man—even after he'd asked God to forgive him. Instead, he'd wallowed in his mistakes, letting himself keep one foot in his old life and one in his new. Maybe it was time to let himself finally believe he could live differently, could make different choices, and could forge a different life.

Mr. Mann finished shrugging out of his coat and tossed it onto the wharf. Not far behind him, Mr. Pidwell had climbed out of the boat and was standing on the dock, his weathered features creased with uncertainty, but his gaze seeming to urge Caleb to listen to Willow.

Caleb wanted to drop his fists, wanted to loosen his grip, but his muscles seemed to act on a reflexive instinct.

Mr. Mann braced himself, preparing for the first punch. As he met Caleb's gaze head-on, his eyes filled with taunting and his lips curled into a smirk, one that seemed to say that he'd already won.

Had Mr. Mann won? Was he expecting Caleb to lash out again and in so doing prove that Caleb was dangerous and violent and deserving of jail?

Yes, that's exactly what would happen if he took a swing. He'd be blamed for the whole incident again. And this time, he wouldn't be able to bargain his way out of the charges.

With Willow still pulling at him, Caleb let his arms drop.

He drew in a deep breath. If he wanted to prove to himself that he wasn't like his father and wouldn't end up in jail, then he had to start now in choosing to believe he was different and that he could live with honor.

"Don't ever touch Willow again." The words came out full of force, but he could feel the fury inside his blood beginning to fade.

"Or what?" Mr. Mann lifted his chin as though daring Caleb to hit him there. "Will you kill me?"

Caleb clenched his jaw against the temptation of answering.

Mr. Mann closed the distance between them so that he stood only a foot away. "I know you at least want to hurt me."

The fellow was instigating him. In his head, Caleb knew it. But the taunt stirred him anyway, and he had to fight hard to keep his fists from clenching again.

"You're not a champion fighter." Mr. Mann's voice dripped with derision. "You're a nothing, a nobody."

"Don't listen to him, Caleb." Willow's worried whisper came from right behind him.

Caleb took a step away from Mr. Mann. In doing so, he

had the feeling he was taking another step away from his past. A big step.

A sense of relief whispered through him as if encouraging him that day by day he'd be able to keep making steps. The changes would be slow, but he could be that man of honor Willow saw.

Mr. Mann shoved Caleb's chest.

Instinct prodded Caleb to raise his fists and defend himself, but he didn't move.

With a loud curse, Mr. Mann shook his head as if disgusted, then spun and stalked away toward his boat.

Caleb let out a breath. He'd done it. He'd stayed strong, he hadn't given in to the temptation to swing back, and he'd honored his vow not to fight again.

Slowly he turned to face Willow.

Her shawl hung off one shoulder, blowing in the wind. And strands of her golden-red hair fluttered around her face. Her features had softened, the tension from moments ago gone. Her eyes were wide and big and—

Were they full of love?

His stomach gave a strange flip.

She started to lift a hand to his face. "Caleb, I—"

"Watch out behind you!" The call came from Jonas standing on the bank near the end of the dock.

Something hard slammed into his back. The momentum threw him into Willow and in turn knocked her into the longshoremen who'd come out on the dock. They easily caught and steadied her.

Caleb staggered and started to turn, but a hit against the back of his head sent dark spots into his vision and pain through his skull. Another slam came in quick succession, first to his neck then again to his head. Was Mr. Mann hitting him with an oar?

His knees buckled, and he felt himself falling.

Shouts erupted around him. The last thing he heard as he landed on the dock was Willow screaming.

Thirty-One

H e could have died.

Willow sat on the dock, Caleb's head resting in her lap. He was motionless, still unconscious, his long lashes resting against his cheeks.

The doctor was standing several feet away in discussion with the constable and the judge. He'd already assessed Caleb, determined that there weren't any lacerations or broken bones. Most likely Caleb was suffering from a concussion. And the doctor wouldn't be able to determine how bad the head injury was until Caleb woke.

On the banks, a crowd of onlookers had gathered, men from nearby businesses as well as other dockworkers. They'd all come running the moment the assault had started and now had each given their testimony to the constable and judge.

Although Mr. Mann had denied any involvement, the stories from the witnesses had been the same—Mr. Mann had picked up an oar, rushed at Caleb, and started beating him with it. Even Mr. Pidwell had stepped forward and admitted that Mr. Mann had instigated the attack. Mr. Pidwell had gone as far as confessing that Mr. Mann had been trying to abduct Willow too.

As the constable, judge, and doctor deliberated on what ought to be done, Mr. Mann sat in his rowboat, a cigar in his mouth, as though he didn't have a single care in the world and hadn't just brutally attacked another man. He'd put back on his coat and had somehow retrieved his hat and looked every bit like a gentleman.

Thankfully, no one was being deceived by appearances, and the blame was falling squarely where it should, on Mr. Mann's shoulders. Of course, he hadn't brought up the real reason he'd turned against Caleb or attempted to abduct her—because he wanted to steal Isaac Sayles's treasure.

Willow hadn't mentioned it either because she didn't want the news spreading about Isaac's treasure, especially since too many people already knew about it.

She smoothed back Caleb's hair, her fingers lightly grazing the swollen bump at the top of his head.

Even though her breathing was ragged and her heart thudded hard against her chest, she was finally calming down. She was still anxious for Caleb to wake up, still anxious to make sure he was okay. But the doctor had assured her that Caleb was a strong man and would live.

The moment reminded her of the time he'd been knocked out during one of his final boxing matches, when one of his nephews had come after her and informed her that Caleb was dying. She'd rushed with the boy to the Flying Donkey where she'd found Caleb bleeding and broken and passed out on the floor.

She'd gone after her dad, just as she had the first time she'd rescued Caleb when he'd been a boy, and her dad had gathered some friends and they'd carried Caleb back to her family's tenement. And like previously, she'd helped her mum nurse him back to health.

"Oh Caleb," she whispered, her heart swelling with tenderness. "I'm proud of you for walking away from Mr. Mann and not fighting, even if you did get battered up in the process."

After how badly she'd hurt him with her rejection of his love, she hadn't deserved to have him to come to Victoria looking for her. But he'd done it anyway. He'd been faithful and true to her through everything, including those times when she hadn't loved him in return.

She trailed a finger over the ridge of his strong cheekbone, down along his hard jaw, then to his chin and the scar there. She'd always secretly wanted to graze his face like this. But she'd never had the courage to do so.

She glanced up to see if anyone was watching her, but many of the onlookers were beginning to disperse, no longer paying attention to what she was doing.

Even so, was she being too bold? She'd held herself back for so many years, and she simply couldn't do it any longer. Not even if she tried.

She caressed his other jaw and cheek and then finished by tracing the scar above his left eye, and then the one above his lip.

As she lifted her fingers away, Caleb's hand shot up and grasped hers. He was peering up at her, his eyes wide, the brown clear.

"Hi," she whispered. "How are you feeling?"

Had he been awake whilst she'd been grazing his face? And had he disliked it?

"I'm sorry." The apology slipped out, and it contained all of her regrets for pushing him away, for not accepting his love when he'd offered it to her, for running away from him. Even for touching his face.

He held her gaze and lowered her hand to his mouth.

Her pulse stuttered. What was he doing?

In the next instant, he brushed his lips against her fingers. The touch was feathery light, but it scorched through her skin into her blood, so that heat flooded her.

How could the faintest caress of his lips make her wish he was kissing her like he had that morning they'd lain in bed together?

His eyes were still holding hers and seemed to be reading her thoughts. Was he able to see that she was thinking of their kisses and wanting more?

A flush began to crawl its way up her neck.

"Caleb is awake," came the call from the constable, who was now hurrying down the dock toward them. He stood out from the rest of the crowd in a flat box-like cap and his dark blue uniform with its single row of silver buttons that were fastened all the way to his chin. At his side, a baton swung from a black belt.

He stopped above them and peered down at Caleb with a grave expression. "Young man, do you know what happened?"

Grimacing, Caleb shifted his head in the direction of Mr. Mann in the rowboat. "Mr. Mann tried to take my wife, and then when I came to free her, he attacked me."

The constable shifted his gaze to Willow briefly before focusing on Caleb again. "This young lady here is your wife?"

"Yes." Caleb said it without hesitation. But did he really still want to be married to her after all that had happened? She wouldn't blame him if he wanted to go back to the way things used to be.

"I have at least a dozen—if not more—witnesses who saw everything." The constable nodded toward Mr. Mann who was still puffing away at his cigar. "Do you want to press charges against the gentleman?"

Caleb was still watching Mr. Mann. "If he agrees to stop harassing me and my wife regarding a possession that belongs to Isaac Sayles, then I won't press charges."

"Now why would he be bothering you about something that belongs to poor Isaac?" The constable spoke loudly enough to reach Mr. Mann in his boat.

Mr. Mann released a disgruntled growl. "I won it in a card game."

"A card game? With Isaac?" The constable's brows rose. "I didn't realize Isaac knew how to play cards."

"Exactly right." Willow couldn't keep from chiming in. "Dear, sweet Isaac was swindled by Mr. Mann."

"I didn't make him play." Mr. Mann glared at her. "He said he wanted to."

"Now, Mr. Mann," the constable said sternly as he started toward the rowboat, "you know as well as any other person in the colony that Isaac Sayles isn't a smart fellow."

As the constable continued to chide Mr. Mann for playing cards with Isaac, Caleb shifted his head on her lap and winced again, but he gazed back up at her, his eyes turning murky and his expression growing unreadable as usual. "I don't want to lose you, Willow."

"And I don't want to lose you—"

"I'm sorry I wanted more than friendship." His handsome features hardened with his earnestness.

"No, it's okay." She had to tell him how she really felt, had to explain it all somehow. But how? After years of keeping all her feelings and all her love locked away, how could she simply let it out?

He lifted his hand as though to brush back a strand of her hair that was blowing across her face. "It'll take me some time," he continued softly, "but I'll be able to keep our friendship the way you want it."

"I don't want it to take you any time." She took a deep breath, trying to make herself say the words that needed to be said.

"I'll do it now, then," he rushed. He dropped his hand to his side. "We'll go back to the way things were—"

"No." The conversation wasn't going the way she wanted it to. Her mind whirled and came upon only one solution.

She bent and pressed her lips to his, silencing him in one swift move.

He didn't respond, and she didn't blame him. After all, the last time she'd initiated a kiss, she'd gotten scared and rejected his love.

She lifted away from him just slightly and met his gaze— which had turned even darker. She had to tell him, had to stay strong, had to be the woman she knew she was capable of being. "Caleb?"

He didn't answer, just waited, watching her eyes.

"I've always loved you too. I've just been too afraid of losing you to say it." She lifted a hand and this time boldly stroked his cheek.

His mouth was close enough that she could feel the warmth of his exhalations. What was he thinking? Was he willing to give her another chance?

"Tell me I'm not too late," she whispered. "Tell me that we can still have our friendship but also have so much more—"

This time he arched up and cut her off. His mouth captured hers with a powerful surge she felt all the way down into her soul.

Her lashes fell with the pure bliss of being with him, of tasting him again, of experiencing this passion of his . . . for her. His hands skimmed up her arms to her neck and then to the back of her head. And as he fused his mouth more fully to hers, she was ready for him and famished for his kisses.

But in the next moment, as he turned his head, he winced, clearly still in pain from being beaten with the oar.

She pulled back, breaking the kiss and releasing his hold on her neck.

His breath came in soft bursts. "I'm sorry for leaving and pushing you away."

"But I was afraid and pushed you away first."

"Maybe we both let our fears push each other away. But we don't have to do that anymore."

It would be difficult to let go of her fears of not being enough for him, but she had to move forward, remembering all of Juliet's encouragement from last night, that even when she was weak, she had God's strength to help her.

"Are you sure this is what you want?" He studied her face, as though seeing the battle she was waging and beginning to win.

"All I really need is you, whatever you're willing to give me."

A smile tugged at his lips. "I've been ready and willing to give you my heart for a while. It's already yours, if you'll have it."

"Only if you'll have mine in return."

His smile finally broke free, a slanted one that simply

begged her for a kiss. If he was begging, how could she not oblige him?

She bent again and touched his lips, letting hers ply his eagerly. Oh the bliss of it. She was kissing Caleb again. Was she living in a dream?

"What?" The word rumbled against her lips.

She tilted back. "Do I really just get to kiss you like this whenever I want?"

"As long as I get to kiss you whenever I want too."

"Okay." She brushed another kiss across his mouth and another, her body tightening with each stroke.

"Come on now, you two." The voice belonged to Jonas and was filled with humor. "Time to go."

After so many years of denial, it was hard to deny herself any longer, but she forced herself to sit back, overwhelmed by Caleb and what he was capable of doing to her.

He sat up slowly, then held out his hand to her.

She didn't hesitate. She placed her hand within his and intertwined their fingers.

He lifted her hand and pressed a kiss to the back. "Let's go home."

She nodded and smiled. "Yes, let's go home."

Thirty-Two

C aleb fingered the treasure in his pocket as he left the shore and started across the pebbly beach.

The evening sky was streaked with the last rays of the sun, and his thoughts returned to his wedding to Willow that cold night on the beach over two months ago when they'd tasted the four elements. They'd had to go through the sourness and bitterness before they'd been able to have the sweetness.

The sweetness had finally come that day he'd gone to Victoria and chased her down on the dock and saved her from Mr. Mann. The reunion had been sweet, her concern for him, her caresses on his face, her declaration of love. He couldn't think of anything sweeter.

Later that day, they'd gotten to taste the fourth element. Caleb's blood pumped extra hard just thinking about when he'd carried her back to their cabin, deposited her gently in their bed, then had lain down beside her and hadn't come back up for hours and hours.

Heaven help him, he couldn't get enough of the heat with

her. Thankfully, she never seemed to get enough of their heat either.

His gut tightened, and he hastened his pace up the pathway toward the farm. Two days away from her was too long.

With most of the crops planted, he'd been working odd jobs—hauling or chopping or building—anything that required strength. He'd gotten a reputation for being a strong, hard worker, and Jonas brought back requests for help from around the island and even from over in Victoria.

Unlike Manchester, the work in the colony was plentiful. He was never without opportunities. And when he wasn't away working, he was clearing more land for farming. The more he cleared, the more he could plant. The more he planted, the more profit he'd bring in at harvest. And then soon enough they'd be able to send the money to Willow's family.

Willow had gotten another letter from Sage describing their grief with their mum's passing, along with the desperate conditions and their continued reliance upon charity to stave off starvation. Willow was more anxious than ever to bring her family over and let them experience the beauty and plenty of the colony the same way the two of them had. But saving money was taking more time than they'd anticipated.

Thankfully, all of Mr. Mann's accusations had been dropped, and Caleb could travel about freely. Word of the beating on the dock had spread throughout the area, and Mr. Mann had returned to his farm and kept to himself, although Caleb suspected the gentleman was biding his time and waiting for Isaac to make an appearance.

No one had heard from Isaac in months, not even Jonas. Willow still had the key to the treasure hidden in their cabin and was waiting for Isaac to return so that she could give it back to him.

Caleb pushed past the new foliage that was growing thickly now that April had passed into May. As he climbed up the incline, the gurgling song of the stream along the path seemed to welcome him home. The canopy of the trees darkened the shadows around him. But the trail was becoming more familiar—and he was learning the way back to Willow—more with every passing day.

Even though there had been days—and nights—where his past still taunted him, he'd kept his vows, and he hadn't run away again. He was learning to say no to his bad habits and sins.

He knew he had a long way to go, probably a lifetime of growing. But he was staying and facing his ghosts—like he had that day when he'd refused to fight Mr. Mann. As a result, he could feel himself growing stronger and becoming a man of honor.

He broke through the woodland and into the clearing and paused as he usually did to take in the sight of the tamed land and fields and the thick wilderness of towering trees that surrounded them, a constant reminder that for all the taming God did in his life, there was always more work to do.

"Caleb!" At the shout of Willow's voice, his heart leapt in his chest. She stood on the rise with Frannie beside the cabin. Frannie held her infant in one arm and was carrying a pail in the other, likely water that had to be hauled from the stream.

With the warmer spring temperatures, Willow was without her shawl, and her head was bare, with her hair hanging in a simple, long braid down her back. After the months of fresh air and plenty of food, her body had lost the emaciated thinness that had plagued her in Manchester, and she was becoming healthier and more beautiful with every passing day.

She smiled at him and began to descend the path. "Jonas brought me a letter from Daisy. She's moving to Nanaimo and taking a seamstress job there."

Willow still stayed in touch with her two bride-ship friends and talked about wanting them both to find love the way she had.

"And guess what else Jonas said?" Her eyes were bright with excitement. "Isaac finally returned to Nanaimo."

It was about time. With the spring thaw having opened the mountain passes, the miners were heading back into the high country. Isaac would have no trouble now starting his treasure hunt. Hopefully, he'd have a trustworthy friend who could help him, maybe even go with him, and keep him safe from swindlers like Mr. Mann.

"Guess that means you'll be wanting to go to Nanaimo?" he asked.

She reached level ground and started toward him. "Jonas said he'd take me soon."

Oh how he'd missed being with her, even just for two days. His chest pulsed with an urgency to hold her, bury his nose in her hair, and breathe her in. The words from the first stanza of his newest poem, the one he'd been composing all day, filled his head.

> *Your friendship is the air that I breathe,*
> *And your love is the blood that my heart beats.*
> *Our bond goes beyond the deepest of measures,*
> *What we have together is the richest of*
> *   treasures,*
> *Don't you forget that you're all I'll ever need.*

He'd read it to her later in privacy. He'd been reading her all the poems that he'd written about her. Of course, it was easy to do now, because with every love poem that he read or wrote, she responded by wrapping her arms around him and kissing him until they were both breathless with wanting.

He touched his pocket again and the newest gift that he'd found for her.

He'd never realized that she'd saved every little item that he'd ever given her until he'd found her box dumped out on the cabin floor after she'd left him. He'd known in that moment that she cared about him more deeply than she'd ever revealed, although he hadn't known the true depths until he'd been reunited with her.

As she drew nearer, he jogged the last few steps toward her. With a happy laugh, she launched herself at him. In the same motion, he lifted her up against him. She wrapped her legs around his torso and her arms around his neck, just the way he loved.

Without a single word, she greedily brought her lips against his, tasting and drinking of him in the deep and consuming way that she always did. Of course, he tasted and drank of her in return. It never failed to surprise him at how his thirst for her was never quenched, how he always wanted more.

With Frannie's laughter echoing in the air, Willow was the first to pull back and wiggled to be put down on her feet.

He was loathe to release her, but he wanted to give her his gift.

"I missed you." She still held onto his arm, the same way she always had, even when they'd only been friends.

"Did you?" He dug into his pocket.

"Very much." She was taking in his face and then his body with narrowed eyes, eyes that fairly sizzled with heat.

His body easily sparked into flames. "I guess you'll have to show me how much you missed me."

This time when she smiled, it was slow, almost seductive. "I'm looking forward to it."

He almost groaned aloud, wanting to pick her up off her feet and carry her back to the cabin. But he pushed down the desire and instead held out the treasure to her. "For you."

Reverently she fingered the ridges. "You found one."

She'd been wanting a double clam shell that was still connected, but all he'd been able to find were the single shells. Until today.

"It's just like us," he whispered. "It's chipped and weathered and stained, but it's beautiful anyway, in spite of the imperfections. Perhaps it's even more beautiful because of them."

She took it and turned it over in her hands before finally lifting her gaze to his. "I love you, Caleb Edwards."

He couldn't keep his hands off her and drew her against him again. And as he settled his lips over hers, he let his kiss speak of his love for this best friend who had finally become his bride.

Return to Vancouver Island in our second Bride Ships: New Voyages historical romance, *His Treasured Bride* by Jody Hedlund and Patti Stockdale.

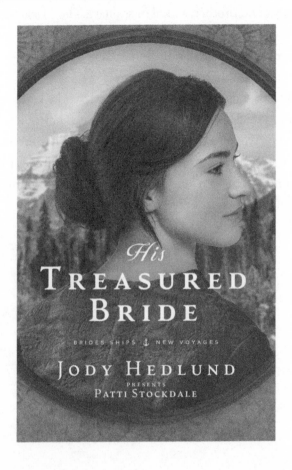

In twenty-four hours, marriage, mystery, and mayhem.

After recently arriving in Vancouver Island on a bride ship, aspiring seamstress Daisy Harper is determined not to rush into a hasty and quarrelsome marriage, a mistake her parents made. To avoid choosing the wrong man, she creates a rigorous list of ten requirements for a potential husband.

Mapmaker Seth Ryann moved to the colony to assist his partially blind brother, a local missionary. They'll soon return to Ireland, but first, Seth is tasked by a friend to find a treasure of gold hidden in the mountains. Seth has the map to the treasure, but he's missing the key.

When he discovers Daisy somehow has the key, the two agree to search for the treasure together. They're left with little choice but to quickly enter a marriage of convenience. As they venture into the wilderness and work together to overcome danger, an undeniable attraction grows. But will they find the treasure only to lose what matters most?

Turn the page for a sneak peek . . .

His Treasured Bride

BRIDE SHIPS: NEW VOYAGES ⚓ BOOK TWO

NANAIMO, VANCOUVER ISLAND
MAY 1863

"I've had nine or perhaps ten marriage proposals." Daisy Harper stuffed her dress in the bureau drawer of her new living quarters, bumped it shut with her hip, and spun to face Willow, her treasured friend. "Or maybe it was eleven."

"You've had so many you've lost count?" Willow was perched on the edge of the bed, her blue eyes growing wide. "And you've declined each one?"

"Yes." Daisy opened another drawer. All the bride-ship women had had their pick of suitors after arriving in Victoria four months ago. In fact, there had been so many eligible men, the choices had overwhelmed her.

"At least you're not putting on airs. Some girls might, with all those proposals."

Daisy wasn't proud of declining multiple offers. But she also wasn't willing to make a lifelong blunder by marrying the wrong man. "Believe it or not, one fellow called me Miss

Harpoon instead of Miss Harper, and another said I had beautiful blue eyes."

They matched the color of dingy brown corduroy.

Willow smiled. "It's possible they were so overcome with your beauty they couldn't speak or see correctly."

Daisy snorted. "I've missed your unbiased opinions." The truth was, with her dark brown hair and freckles and dimples, she sometimes felt like sturdy poplin fabric compared to Willow, a shiny-patterned brocade with her lush reddish-blonde hair, beautiful heart-shaped face, and flawless fair skin.

But it was neither the time nor place to feel sorry for herself. Not after just arriving in Nanaimo on a fresh Monday afternoon, where a new future spread out before her, along with a new home, new opportunities, and perhaps even a new start with new suitors.

Her life as a domestic in Victoria was behind her. Now, she'd finally do what she loved—work as a seamstress. Even though it wasn't a fancy position at the Butterwick's store, this was her opportunity to make something of herself, prove her skill, and gain a trusted reputation. With enough hard work, she and Mum would hopefully own a seamstress shop on the island one day.

They had heard women had more opportunities in the colony, and Daisy prayed it was true. But how long until they reached their dream? Some days, it felt like a century or two.

In the cozy room above the dry goods shop, wallpaper of pink and blue posies bloomed in every direction Daisy turned. The fanciness thrilled her, and she ran her finger along a seam. A fine rocker with a needlepoint seat waited in the corner near the window, and a plump bed with a goose-down pillow held court to the right of the doorway beside the bureau.

A double dose of evening sunshine streamed onto the wooden floorboards, and a faint ballad tinkled from the nearby saloon and filtered into the room. Fir trees and water from the Strait of Georgia scented the air, a sharp blend of sweet, salty, and refreshing for the lovely May day.

"I hope you'll be happy here." Willow removed a small pile of fabric from the valise on the four-poster bed—a treasured mix of silks, satins, wool twills, and linens—and passed the bundle to Daisy.

"I'm sure I will." Daisy ran her fingers over the edges, relishing the different textures before tucking the stack into one side of the drawer. "I'll earn more now as a seamstress. My wages are tied to the amount of sewing I complete and the number of new customers I attract to the shop."

"Sounds reasonable."

"I agree. I like the Butterwicks. They seem very fair." The terms didn't scare her, for she had faith in her skills and a strong desire to succeed.

And goodness, she needed the money. Between mailing home most of her pay packets for Mum's eventual passage to the island and helping a bride-ship friend fund her emergency medical care, Daisy barely had two coins to jingle in her fist.

She grabbed her valise and tipped it upside down on the bed. A stuffed pincushion, sewing scissors, a couple of loose buttons, and threads spilled higgledy-piggledy. A red ball of yarn rolled toward the floor. Willow lunged for the wayward string, then lobbed it to Daisy. "Catch."

Daisy tossed the empty valise on the bed before snagging the throw at the last second. Grinning, she reached for Willow's hand and squeezed it. "I'm so glad to see you today. I've missed you. And Juliet too."

The three of them had become fast friends as bunkmates

during their voyage from England on the bride ship, the *Robert Lowe*. Juliet was still in Victoria, toiling as a domestic. Willow had recently wed and now farmed on Salt Spring Island.

Over the past months, they hadn't seen each other often, too busy with their work. Willow's arrival today in Nanaimo had surprised Daisy, and she'd toppled a display of hats downstairs while rushing to hug her friend when they first spied each other.

Willow collected the bag, peeked inside as if double-checking Daisy hadn't missed anything, and then stuffed it under the bed before sitting on the coverlet. "Tell me more about your failed suitors. Why did you find fault with the last fellow who proposed? Dirt under his fingernails? Giant earlobes? He smelled like a barrel of rotten fish?"

"None of that. He simply didn't meet my requirements for a husband."

Willow's eyebrow arched. "How many requirements made your final list?"

"Just ten."

Willow's rich laughter pushed a smile to Daisy's lips.

During the three months on the ship, she'd confided in Willow and Juliet about Christopher, about their long friendship that had slowly blossomed into love, and about his beautiful proposal and their engagement. She'd cried on their shoulders, explaining that his rejection had broken her heart. And she'd told them her plan to make a list of the important characteristics her future husband must possess. That way, she'd never again fall for the wrong man.

She set the ball of yarn on the top of the bureau and retrieved a small piece of paper from the drawer before plopping on the bed. His rejection still stung with the sharpness of a needle prick. But now that she knew the attributes she desired in a husband, her list would help her to stay on course.

"So let's hear it." Willow bumped Daisy's shoulder.

Daisy unfolded the paper. All the deception and frustration with Christopher wasn't the only reason she'd made the list. She'd also needed help finding someone different than her papa. Her parents had bickered endlessly. Well, up until he left for good. The constant strife had soured her on marriage.

She cleared her throat and began to read it:

> Not prone to arguments.
> Kindhearted.
> Churchgoer.
> Never leaves me.
> Supports my dream to open a business
> one day.
> Has similar goals.
> Defends me.
> Never lies.
> Likes me for me.
> Romantic.

Willow sighed. "That's quite the list."

"I agree, although not every man wants a wife who labors beyond the home."

With brows knitted, Willow tucked a loose strand of hair behind Daisy's ear. "I can't imagine anyone refusing a wage earner."

"Perhaps you're right, though I'll leave the requirement in place for now."

Often, women married for practicality and little more. Was it wrong that Daisy longed for love? Everyone on the bride ship had the right to pick and choose—not accept the first, or even the tenth, proposal.

Granted, she dragged her feet more than most.

"I particularly like number ten—romantic," Willow said. "Maybe you'll eventually find someone as romantic as Caleb." Her eyes brimmed with love at the mention of her husband.

"I'll be very blessed if I do. But I doubt I will. Caleb is one in a million."

"I'll not argue with you there."

Daisy rose to sniff the wildflowers, mostly purples and yellows, Mrs. Butterwick had arranged in a vase on the bureau. Nobody had ever given her a bountiful bouquet. Earlier in the afternoon, when Daisy had stepped from the steamship to the shore, her landlady had been there waiting to greet her. A showering of kindness followed, with Daisy wishing for a bucket to catch all the sweetness.

She glanced around the cozy room again. She couldn't have imagined living in such splendor a year ago. She and Mum had squeezed into her brother's tiny apartment in Manchester with little to eat, little warmth in the winter, and little privacy. But they'd had a roof over their heads when many did not.

Daisy folded her sheet of husband requirements and tucked it in her pocket. She would be more than content here, and eventually the right man would come along, wouldn't he?

The bed creaked as Willow stood. "Can I ask a favor from you, Daisy?"

"Of course."

Willow hesitated, then dug in her pocket. "It's something important that needs to stay a secret."

"You can trust me." Daisy had a knack for keeping secrets. Plus, she had nobody to tell. She barely knew a soul in town.

A soft knock sounded against the door. "May I interrupt?" Mrs. Butterwick's voice came from the corridor.

"Hold tight to your thought," Daisy whispered.

Willow bent to straighten the messy pink coverlet as Daisy hurried to open the door to find Mrs. Butterwick, wearing a colorless straw hat that concealed her pinned-up graying hair. Her dress—a sad, brown, lifeless flour sack—hid her diminutive frame.

What a pity. The shop downstairs sold a slew of gorgeous fabrics. Only her gray eyes, matching the whale Daisy had spied from the steamer earlier in the day, added warmth to her ensemble.

Nothing about her landlady's physical appearance resembled her flamboyant sister, Mrs. Moresby, who lived in Victoria and had graciously been assisting the women from the bride ships. In fact, Mrs. Morseby had connected Daisy to the seamstress position in Nanaimo with her sister.

Even if the sisters were opposites, both women possessed kind and generous hearts.

"Sorry to interrupt you, dearie. I know you're still settling in and have company and all. But the mapmaker next door ripped a jacket seam. Might you repair it straightaway before he leaves town today for work?" Mrs. Butterwick rubbed her knuckles. According to Mrs. Morseby, her sister's rheumatism had slowed her fingers and ached her joints too much to continue the shop's sewing tasks.

What a shame, forced to stop a livelihood due to aging. Or was she ready for a change?

Daisy's fingers itched to start. "It would be my pleasure, and I'll hurry down real soon."

"Splendid." Mrs. Butterwick straightened her hat. "I'm off to a meeting with the Literary Institute. We've raised forty-four dollars to start a circulating library."

"How exciting." Daisy had never stepped inside a library. Maybe Mrs. Butterwick owned novels she'd share with her until the establishment opened.

"Otherwise, I'd try to fix the tear myself." Mrs. Butterwick curled her hand next to her mouth and hushed her tone. "My husband Kaine, bless his heart, cannot sew a stitch to save his soul."

Daisy had briefly met him downstairs before he rushed off to assist a customer desiring kerosene. Her first impression? Brusque. But in fairness, he operated a busy, prosperous business that needed his attention. "I'm happy to help you. That's what I'm here for."

"By the way, the mapmaker is also unattached. His charming blue eyes and blond curls have made more than one young lady swoon."

Daisy bit back a scoff at the matchmaking shenanigans. Well-meaning landladies couldn't snap their fingers and produce an ideal, marriageable man. Especially one who met her ten requirements. "I'm not prone to swooning, but he'll undoubtedly make some other young lady happy as a songbird."

"Most assuredly." Mrs. Butterwick poked her head farther into the room and gave Willow a bright smile. "I'm delighted the two of you could see each other today. It was a pleasure to meet you. You'll need to come again soon."

Willow paused from straightening the items Daisy had dumped on the bed. "Thank you. I look forward to it."

With a nod and a grin, the landlady descended the stairs, her hand on the banister.

A soft sigh whispered past Daisy's lips as she closed the door and leaned against the wood. "Despite her meddling, she's lovely."

"I agree."

"Now, what did you want to tell me?"

Willow's brows drew together. "Caleb and I hoped to visit a friend in Nanaimo today, give him something he left behind. But when we arrived, we learned he's in a coma."

"That's dreadful."

"His name is Isaac, and he recently returned to Nanaimo." Willow fidgeted with an item in her pocket.

"I remember you talking about him." Willow had mentioned him during one of their conversations on Sundays when she, Juliet, and Willow had taken advantage of their afternoons off to spend time together. A slow thinking but sweet man, Isaac had operated a steamboat that picked up produce from the farms between Victoria and Nanaimo. Willow had gotten to know him from his frequent stops at White Swan Farm, north of Victoria, where she'd worked as a maid after first arriving on Vancouver Island.

"I was never able to tell you everything that happened and why I left my maid position at the Manns' and went into hiding on Salt Spring Island."

Daisy nodded. "Juliet always insisted there was more to the story than you'd revealed in the note you sent us."

"She was right." Willow glanced at the door and then lowered her voice. "Mr. Mann swindled Isaac out of a key while gambling, a key for a treasure of gold. Of course, I couldn't stand by and let Mr. Mann cheat poor Isaac like that, so I stole the key when Mr. Mann was sleeping."

"Oh, goodness."

"Mr. Mann finally stopped harassing Caleb and me, but I have no doubt he's still after the key and the map to the treasure. We suspect he's who beat Isaac up and caused his coma."

Key? Map? Treasure of gold? Daisy blinked at the outlandish information. Was it true or a hoax of some sort? "How did your friend obtain a treasure?"

"His brother, a miner, buried gold and has since died."

Daisy's heart clacked to an erratic beat. When she'd walked up the street to the dry goods store earlier, she'd not missed the two empty coffins bumped up against the pretty storefront with a green awning and attractive window displays. Mrs. Butterwick had warned that Nanaimo was unfortunately more lawless than Victoria.

"If Mr. Mann hurt Isaac, then he should go to jail."

"Caleb has asked around about him," Willow continued quietly, "but no one saw Mr. Mann in town that night. We can't be certain he was behind the attack."

"If not him, then who?"

"Isaac was too open and trusting. And there's no telling how many people he told about the gold. Unfortunately, there could be others—perhaps even many others—who are after his treasure."

Daisy shuddered at the ugliness that came from greed, people who stooped to hurt, even kill, innocent people like Isaac to get rich.

Willow rose, moved to the window, and drew aside the drape to peek outside. "So about the favor I wanted to ask of you."

Daisy braced herself for what she knew was coming.

"Will you be the keeper of the key until Isaac recovers?"

She hesitated.

Willow continued with a hurried whisper. "Now that Mr. Mann knows where Caleb and I live, we're afraid he might come to search our place. But he'd never suspect you have it. No one would."

Daisy wanted to tell her friend no, that it was too dangerous, that if someone had already hurt Isaac to get the key, what would they do to her if they discovered she had it?

But if Willow was brave enough to help Isaac, shouldn't Daisy do her part too? After all, what had she ever done to correct an unjust situation? Nothing. Surely she could hold on to the object for a spell. "All right."

Willow raised a questioning brow. "I hesitate to tangle you in this mess, so are you sure?"

Of course, Willow was right. Nobody would suspect Daisy of having a connection to the gold. Besides, friends helped friends. "Yes, I am."

Willow crossed to her and held out the key. "Thank you, Daisy. You're the only one I trust."

Daisy took it gingerly and twisted it back and forth, catching the sunlight and admiring the bow's swirls and brassy lion's head framed by a heart. "Do you truly think it opens a treasure chest?"

"Caleb says that rumors float around regarding Isaac's brother and his gold. So it's possible."

Daisy swiped up the scissors from the bed along with the red ball of yarn from the bureau and snipped off an arm's length. "This way, I'll always keep it close to me." She quickly strung the key and tied off the ends of her temporary necklace.

It was Willow's turn to look hesitant. "What about

burying it among that stack of fabric you just put in the drawer?"

"Don't worry. It'll be fine right here." Daisy looped the yarn over her head and tucked the key into her bodice. Nobody would ever believe such a precious item hid in her cleavage. She barely believed it herself. "Now come on. I'd best mend that jacket, and you have a husband to meet."

Author's Note

Welcome back to the Pacific Northwest and the world of the bride ships! Thank you, dear reader, for joining me again in this new series that continues the saga of the women who sailed from England to Vancouver Island on the bride ships.

If you haven't read the previous books in my series (*A Reluctant Bride*, *The Runaway Bride*, *A Bride of Convenience*, and *Almost a Bride*), I invite you to read those as well. However, your enjoyment of this new series, Bride Ships: New Voyages, doesn't in any way hinge upon the previous books. Rest assured, this new series involves a brand-new cast of characters and explores their reasons for joining the bride ships.

You might be wondering, like me, why would women embark on a bride ship? What would drive someone to leave their home and everything familiar to sail halfway around the world and live in a strange land and find a husband there?

As I've mentioned in other Author's Notes, a valuable resource I used in writing this series was *Voyages of Hope: The Saga of the Bride-Ships* by Peter Johnson. He gives some background into the social climate of England at the time, including the fact that in the decades before the bride ships, thousands upon thousands of young men had left England because of a depression. By the early 1860s, the Columbia Mission Society stated that there were 600,000 more women than men living in England.

The opposite problem existed in English colonies where men outnumbered women. An 1861 census of Vancouver Island and British Columbia revealed that females comprised only 11 percent of the total population, which meant that men outnumbered women approximately 10 to 1. Thus to many, it seemed only reasonable to begin sending England's surplus of marriageable women to the colonies to provide wives for the many men who wanted them.

The *Robert Lowe* was a real ship that really did bring thirty-six mill women from Manchester to Vancouver Island. The women really were intended to be used as domestic servants in the households of the wealthier English people living there. And many of the mill women did really go into service upon arriving. Many of them eventually found husbands and married too.

In *Finally His Bride*, it was my hope to show how difficult life was in Manchester and what drove some of the women to leave their homes. I also hoped to show that life wasn't necessarily easier for the women after arriving in the colony. They faced many challenges adjusting to work as domestics and the long hours for such little pay.

I hope you enjoyed going on the journey with Willow and Caleb. And I hope you were encouraged by their growth through all the challenges they faced and overcame together. Be on the lookout for more installments in Bride Ships: New Voyages in the months to come.

Discover more sweet romance from Sunrise Publishing.

Fall in love with Tricia Goyer's cherished Big Sky Amish Collection.

Start reading the series now!

Faith. Forgiveness. A future they never imagined.
It's time for a fresh start for the Fox Family.

Return to Susan May Warren's beloved town of Deep Haven now.

FIND THEM ALL AT SUNRISE PUBLISHING!

Connect with Sunrise

Thank you again for reading *Finally His Bride*. We hope you enjoyed the story. If you did, would you be willing to do us a favor and leave a review? It doesn't have to be long—just a few words to help other readers know what they're getting. (But no spoilers! We don't want to wreck the fun!) Thank you again for reading!

We'd love to hear from you—not only about this story, but about any characters or stories you'd like to read in the future. Contact us at www.sunrisepublishing.com/contact.

We also have a monthly update that contains sneak peeks, reviews, upcoming releases, and fun stuff for our reader friends. Sign up at www.sunrisepublishing.com or scan our QR code.

CONNECT WITH SUNRISE

About Jody Hedlund

Jody Hedlund is the best-selling author of over fifty sweet historical romances and is the winner of numerous awards. She lives in central Michigan with her husband and is the mother of five wonderful children and five spoiled cats. When she's not penning another of her page-turning stories, she loves to spend her time reading, especially when it also involves consuming coffee and chocolate.

facebook.com/AuthorJodyHedlund

x.com/JodyHedlund

instagram.com/jodyhedlund

pinterest.com/jodyhedlund

bookbub.com/profile/jody-hedlund

goodreads.com/jodyhedlund

amazon.com/stores/Jody-Hedlund/author/B003JLXD6A

Books by Jody Hedlund

Bride Ships: New Voyages

Finally His Bride

His Treasured Bride (With Patti Stockdale)

Bride Ships Series

A Reluctant Bride

The Runaway Bride

A Bride of Convenience

Almost a Bride

A Shanahan Match Series

Calling on the Matchmaker

Saved by the Matchmaker

Colorado Cowgirls

Committing to the Cowgirl

Cherishing the Cowgirl

Convincing the Cowgirl

Captivated by the Cowgirl

Claiming the Cowgirl: A Novella

Colorado Cowboys

A Cowboy for Keeps

The Heart of a Cowboy

To Tame a Cowboy

Falling for the Cowgirl

The Last Chance Cowboy

Bride Ships Series

A Reluctant Bride

The Runaway Bride

A Bride of Convenience

Almost a Bride

Orphan Train Series

An Awakened Heart: A Novella

With You Always

Together Forever

Searching for You

Beacons of Hope Series

Out of the Storm: A Novella

Love Unexpected

Hearts Made Whole

Undaunted Hope

Forever Safe

Never Forget

Hearts of Faith Collection

The Preacher's Bride

The Doctor's Lady

Rebellious Heart

Michigan Brides Collection

Unending Devotion

A Noble Groom

Captured by Love

Historical

Luther and Katharina

Newton & Polly

Knights of Brethren Series

Enamored

Entwined

Ensnared

Enriched

Enflamed

Entrusted

Fairest Maidens Series

Beholden

Beguiled

Besotted

Lost Princesses Series

Always: Prequel Novella

Evermore

Foremost

Hereafter

Noble Knights Series

The Vow: Prequel Novella

An Uncertain Choice

A Daring Sacrifice

For Love & Honor

A Loyal Heart

A Worthy Rebel

Waters of Time Series

Come Back to Me

Never Leave Me

Stay With Me

Wait for Me

Made in United States
Orlando, FL
24 February 2024

44069293R00200